The Mummy King's Realm

ROY POND
THE MUMMY KING'S REALM

#1 IN THE *ARROWFLIGHT* SERIES

AN ALBATROSS BOOK

© Roy Pond 1994

Published in Australia and New Zealand by
Albatross Books Pty Ltd
PO Box 320, Sutherland
NSW 2232, Australia
in the United States of America by
Albatross Books
PO Box 131, Claremont
CA 91711, USA
and in the United Kingdom by
Lion Publishing plc
Peter's Way, Sandy Lane West
Oxford OX4 5HG, England

First edition 1994

This book is copyright. Apart from any fair dealing for the purposes of private study, research, criticism or review as permitted under the Copyright Act, no part of this book may be reproduced by any process without the written permission of the publisher.

National Library of Australia
Cataloguing-in-Publication data

Pond, Roy
The Mummy King's Realm

ISBN 0 7324 1037 1

I.Title

A823.3

Cover illustration: Michael Mucci
Printed and bound by Griffin Paperbacks, South Australia

Contents

1	Tomb machine	7
2	Corridor	20
3	The Opener of Ways	26
4	Primordial dawn	31
5	Horus and Seth	38
6	The radiance of the past	45
7	The backbone amulet	59
8	Janet	72
9	The demon charioteers of Seth	81
10	Stronghold of the lioness	90
11	The Heqet frog	99
12	Tombworld city	109
13	House of the Secluded	117
14	The sacred beetle of chalcedony	126
15	Renenutet, Lady of Serpents	135

16	The scorpion goddess	144
17	The hazards of Hathor	154
18	The pursuit of the elusive jackal	166
19	Snakeback	175
20	Death tomb	184
21	The swallower of secrets	193
22	Neith's solution	204
23	Shadow of despair	215
24	The watching universe	228
25	The night of the Thing of the Night	240
26	Revivification	244
27	The boundaries of existence	249
28	The final truth	252

1

Tomb machine

WILSON RYDER STRETCHED HIMSELF out on a camp bed in the thick, textured darkness of a tomb, a bow and quiverful of arrows at his side and a dog at his feet. Nothing came except memories of Janet. He turned on a torchlight and flashed a yellow eye around the decorated ceiling.

It was like a painted spaceworld. The ceiling was black, and over it stretched a horde of golden stars and images of Egyptian gods and goddesses and boats with sheerly raised bows and sterns — day barques and night barques — spaceboats to transport the dead through the afterlife.

The young Egyptologist directed his torch beam at the downturned face of a sky goddess on the ceiling of the burial chamber and felt her pagan stare. Under an elongated eyebrow, the broad Egyptian eye, rimmed with *kohl* like the painted outline of a fish in profile, was dark and impenetrable as the tomb world itself. Her skin was golden, her hair thick and blue-black — so different from the fairness of Janet, his archaeological partner. The goddess had looked down for thousands of years, first on the sarcophagus of the original occupant of this tomb — the priest Ani — then on Janet, and now on him.

The dog at his feet sighed. Ryder raised his head and turned the beam onto the animal. Snakeback was a Rhodesian Ridgeback or African Lion Dog, a sturdy breed with a snake of fur running along its back in the opposite direction to its sleek, wheaten-coloured coat. Bred from European mastiffs and the African Hottentot hunting dog, Snakeback was tough and protective, a dog built to attack lions, with a deep muzzle, long straight legs and the ability to run all day in the heat of the sun without a drink of water. The dog's eyes glowed in the beam and its long, tapered tail flicked lazily. Snakeback didn't see anything peculiar in Ryder's behaviour. The animal's presence gave the situation a reassuring sense of normality.

Ryder wondered again at how he and his dog came to be lying here in an ancient Egyptian tomb.

The morning had started out normally enough. He'd been practising archery in the desert not far from their campsite, a favourite escape from archaeology. He recalled lifting his bow, a big, sculpted-looking weapon, dragging the arrow to the familiar anchor point at his chin before taking aim into the bright sky. It was a modern composite bow, without the protruding stabiliser arms, sights and counterweights of the target bow — he preferred instinctive shooting — and it was able to shoot a seventy-five centimetre metal alloy arrow with the penetrative power of a bullet. A bow like this could have turned the course of ancient battles like Kadesh, he thought. A few well-directed arrows from long range would have sent Pharaoh Rameses and his Egyptian chariotry, archers and foot soldiers and his

Libyan and Shardana mercenaries scurrying in retreat. Those that were still alive.

Ryder was a dark, lion-chested man, with a strong upper body. His twenty-two kilogram draw-weight bow was heavy tackle by any bowman's standards and required considerable strength of arm to draw. He let fly. The arrow blurred from the bow and shrank as swiftly as a departing swallow in the sky.

'Fetch!'

Snakeback gave a bark and took off across the sand. He watched the dog stretch itself in a run. The dog had sighted the arrow and had locked on its flight. The arrow must have gone about three hundred and fifty metres, Ryder estimated. He had lost sight of its fall. Snakeback would be gone for a while. It would come back with the shaft of the arrow gently held in its jaws, looking as if it had been shot through the muzzle, with the fletching sticking out on one side of its mouth and the arrowhead on the other and its round amber eyes flashing a challenge, warning him not to shoot the arrow again, but secretly hoping he would.

With the dog safely out of the way, Ryder took another arrow from the quiver at his side. He nocked it fluidly to the bowstring, bent the bow and swung at a target he had set up earlier, a black bag filled with sand, perched on top of a sand dune. He imagined it was Pharaoh Rameses attacking in his fast, lightweight chariot, drawn by a span of horses. Making a heartbeat adjustment for range and windage, he let fly. The broadhead arrow snapped home into its target. *Thwack*. Slightly to the right of the pharaoh's heart, he estimated. In rapid fire he loosed four more arrows, making a creditable grouping around the pharaoh's heart.

Mildly critical of his performance, he went to the

target and retrieved his arrows, slipping them back into the quiver. He watched Snakeback bounding over a sand dune, its muscular back legs kicking up dust in its haste to retrieve the arrow. He sat on a rock and rested the bow on the sand beside him.

'We're a long way from home, Snakeback,' he said quietly, looking beyond the dog into the plain.

It was only an hour after daybreak, yet the heat of Egypt was gathering its forces. Wilson Ryder turned a glance up at the barren limestone cliffs that flanked this deserted, stony place. The archaeologist in him still wondered about those cliffs. Were there more finds waiting to be made? Were there more eternity seekers at rest in the cliffs in their secret 'houses of millions of years'?

Don't be greedy.

They'd already found one tomb. That tomb took his attention now. His eyes travelled up the cliff to focus on a doorway slanting into the pink cliffs.

It had been an intact tomb, yet to the mystification of the excavators, the mummy had never been found. When Ryder and Doctor Janet Nancarrow, fellow university archaeologists, had opened the tomb, they had discovered an empty basalt sarcophagus. Yet there had been no sign of an earlier entry to the tomb. The unbroken seals of the Necropolis priests were still in place on the plaster doorway. It was a great mystery, a mystery that had been the cause of speculation of a rational and irrational kind. Had a sham burial taken place in this tomb, designed to throw off tomb robbers? Or was there another explanation, one of a supernatural variety, one that Ryder had resisted? When all possibilities were exhausted, you had to consider *impossibilities*, his partner said. The explanation Janet had in mind was an astounding one, coming as it did from a trained archaeologist, but he recalled that sensationalism had always had an ability to exert a powerful hold on her imagination.

One morning at breakfast in their campsite, after a night spent alone in the tomb examining the inscriptions, Janet had shared her amazing theory. Had the mummy, she suggested, without a hint of a joke in her voice, been transported *bodily* into the beyond? At the amused widening of Ryder's eyes, she had defended her notion: 'Egyptian tombs weren't actually graves or monuments,' she reminded him, sipping her Egyptian coffee and chewing on some stale bread and dates. 'They were magical machines — "tomb machines" as I prefer to call them — designed to transport the dead into eternity to meet the gods among the stars. This tomb in particular.' She showed him a notebook with some notes she had made of a hieroglyphic text on the wall. She read out her translation:

I, Ani the Justified One, shall journey from this place to dwell in the Land Of Osiris for millions of years. I know all the secret sanctuaries and amulets of power of Osiris, hidden by the Evil One, Apophis, the primeval serpent of chaos and outer darkness who is in league with Seth — these amulets being the Djed column, the buckle of Isis, the scarab beetle, the Heqet frog, the *ankh*, the menat necklace, the flail, the crook, the *uraeus*, the *was*-sceptre, the amulet of the heart, the sacred headrest, the sacred adze for opening of the mouth. I know the locations of all, except for the Eye of Horus, stolen by Seth, the enemy of Osiris. I go ahead to prepare the way for him, Mighty of Bows, who comes to win back the Sacred Amulets of Power so that Osiris may rule forever in the land of Amenti and his son Horus may rise to avenge him.

Then it described the sites in the land of Osiris where each relic was to be found.

He'd shaken his head at the idea. 'It speaks of a spiritual journey, not a physical one.'

'But it's gone. The body has slipped into eternity.'

'It's not a laundry chute, Janet. Things don't vanish in a sealed tomb.'

'Be black-and-white, if you like,' she had said, losing patience with him. 'But rational explanations aren't getting us very far, are they?'

His mind went over the events, the excitement and glare of attention that had followed their discovery of the tomb. Two years later the fuss had died. The tomb had now been stripped of its artefacts, part of the finds going home, the choicest pieces remaining in Egypt. Yet on Janet's insistence they had returned to the site for one more season. 'I've got a bee in my bonnet about this tomb and I want to do some work on the wall inscriptions.' Janet Nancarrow, despite her youth, was an expert in hieroglyphics, and she had written textbooks on the subject. 'I also want to do something else, something difficult to explain.' And here she'd smiled a little awkwardly, her eyes warning him not to laugh. 'I want to spend an extended period alone in the tomb. I've studied the surfaces of the tomb,' she said, 'and now I want to explore its inner life — if the word "life" can rightfully be attached to tombs — and I believe it can, especially this tomb. I want to soak up its vibrations and observe its secrets with the inner eye.'

It sounded like New Age nonsense to Wilson Ryder, who had a more earthy view of the ancients, seeing the Egyptians as intensely practical people, but he had nevertheless indulged her as had the Egyptian Antiquities Organisation. She had been in the tomb for a week. By the time she came out she would have the ghostly pallor of a seedling starved of sunlight.

But now the term was coming to an end. The days had passed by in a dull ache of monotony. He had filled the time by writing a follow-up book to the one that had announced and revealed their discoveries, by practising his hobby of archery and by exploring the rocky cliffs with Snakeback.

She was due to emerge at noon. Janet would come out of the tomb, as if back from the dead. Had the experience changed her? He found himself giving an involuntary shiver. He still did not understand why she had chosen to put herself through such an ordeal. He loved life too much to shut himself away. The thought was particularly abhorrent on a morning like this one. He recalled the words of an ancient Egyptian hymn written in praise of the morning sun:

> Thou arisest beauteous in the horizons of heaven, O living Aten, beginner of life, when thou didst come forth in the eastern horizon and didst fill every land with thy beauty. . .
>
> Being afar off, yet thy rays are upon the earth. Thou art in men's faces, yet thy movements are unseen. When thou settest in the western horizon, the earth is in darkness after the manner of death. . .
>
> How manifold are thy works. They are mysterious in men's sight.
>
> Thou sole god, like whom there is none other.
>
> Thou didst create the earth after thy heart, being alone, even all men, herds and flocks, whatever is upon the earth, creatures that walk upon feet, which soar aloft flying with their wings, the countries of Khor and of Cush, and the land of Egypt. . .

The hymn to the sun god bore more than a passing

resemblance to the Bible's Psalm 104, he thought, as many had noted before. It was the finest thing Ryder had ever read in the Egyptian religion, composed by Pharaoh Akhenaten who had advanced the idea of monotheism. Mostly the ancient Egyptian religion was a load of mythological rubbish in Ryder's view, a creaking cosmology that over the millennia had gathered accretions like barnacles, one idea conflicting with another, with no idea ever being abandoned. They simply piled new ideas on top of the old.

The confusion was best exemplified by their view of the dead. The dead soul was thought to travel in the sun-boat with the pharaoh, to join the imperishable stars, to reside in the World of Osiris, to rest in the tomb with the mummy and to visit its favourite haunts on earth in the shape of a soul bird. All at one and the same time!

His amused scepticism had infuriated Janet. 'Don't you think they were trying to reach for deeper ideas in these symbols?' she said in her quietly assured voice. 'You are too linear for my comfort sometimes, Wilson. You have no grasp of plurality. But think. Ice, snow and water are all one and the same thing, but different. Do they sound contradictory? Do they clash?'

'Ice and water,' he said dreamily wiping his forehead as he lay in the heat of the tent. 'No, come to think of it, they don't clash. They tinkle. I can hear them tinkling in a tall, frosty glass. Feel like a drink?' She had thrown a book of Egyptian mythology across the tent at his head.

He pictured her as he had seen her last, a young woman with an adventurous air, dressed in khaki fieldclothes — a skirt and top and desert shoes. She was erectly pretty, with short fair hair and shining eyes, a tall girl who was conscious of her height and determined to carry it proudly. His cheerful cynicism was a challenge and a trial for her.

Snakeback broke into his thoughts. The dog had returned without the arrow in its jaws and an embarrassed, downcast tilt to its head.

'Where is it?' Snakeback rarely lost an arrow. Ryder was surprised. Had it landed in an animal hole? The dog wagged its tail in a slow, guilty way.

'Lost it, boy?' The dog whined softly. Ryder shrugged. He ran his hand along the snake-ridge of fur on its back. 'Don't worry. We'll take a walk and see if we can find it.' Snakeback wagged its tail in relief that Ryder wasn't angry.

The archaeologist picked up his bow and the two of them set off along the flight path of the arrow. A languor stole over Ryder's body as he walked. Snakeback was breathing easily and rhythmically, panting — a sleepy sound. The sunlight dazzled on the plain. How far had the arrow travelled? They came to the spot where he believed the arrow had fallen. Snakeback sniffed the ground, looking puzzled. They searched the area. Where could it be?

Ryder detected a blur of movement from the tail of his eye and looked around to see a dark-haired young woman emerge from an outcrop of rock and hold up his arrow. She had a second arrow in her other hand. She paused to direct a challenging stare at him, then added his arrow to the second arrow in her hand, crossing them, so that she held both in one hand at her side. Then she walked towards the cliffs, carrying the two crossed arrows. She climbed a rocky path up the cliff. Who was she? What was she doing?

Wilson Ryder snapped out of his daze. Snakeback

had seen her too, but instead of growling it was wagging its tail and its eyes sparked the way they did when it was daring Ryder to shoot an arrow in the sky, eager to go on another chase.

It was an exhausting climb up the steep path of the cliff. Ryder passed into a dull zone of tiredness. He kicked a stone with the side of a boot. The stone rolled off the path and clattered hollowly down the cliff to the desert floor below. Snakeback turned its head to watch it fall as though tempted to go after it.

Why had the girl taken the arrow? Where was she going with it? The stranger seemed oblivious to gravity. She climbed the steep path ahead of him in lithe, smooth-flowing movements, taking his arrow further and further from where it had landed. She turned off the path and went to the tomb — the tomb where Janet had shut herself away. Then she passed into the deeper shadow of the entrance and vanished. But the tomb was locked. Ryder felt a tingle of warning.

He hurried to reach the shadow in the cliff face. The girl had gone, yet the tomb gate was still in place, still padlocked. Had she gone inside? How? He grabbed the iron bars and shook them. Impossible. Had he imagined that she'd gone in here? Had he imagined her? He called into the tomb. 'Janet!'

Echoes beat back. Perhaps she was asleep. He would go back to the camp and get the spare key.

He felt a growing prickliness under his field clothes and a knotting of his stomach as he made his way back after getting the key. The feeling wasn't entirely caused by the heat and the effort of his second climb up the cliff path. Was it nerves? An eagerness to see Janet again? He had been aching for this moment to rejoin her, but now that the time had come, now that he was on the spot where he'd said goodbye to her a week earlier, an unexpected fear of what he would meet grabbed at his insides. The mysterious girl with the arrow had added to his unease. There was something spectral about her appearance, like a warning figure in a dream.

As his eyes adjusted to the shadow of the entrance, he saw the familiar iron gate with a steel padlock on it barring his way. Still locked, he noted. The tomb entrance, the deeper shadow behind the bars, looked dark and drowning as a well. Why hadn't Janet come to the entrance to meet him?

'Janet!' His voice funnelled into the passage and beat back. Echoes from an empty tomb, he thought. But it shouldn't be empty. Janet was in there. Asleep still? She probably had no idea of the time, the sojourn in the tomb upsetting her body clock, he reasoned. He hoped she would be all right and not disturbed by her experience. He had heard of cavers on extended stays underground who had started hallucinating as a result of sensory deprivation and loneliness. But Janet had taken plenty to read and notebooks for her translations.

Ryder reached into a pocket to retrieve the key. He slid it into the padlock, rattled it around and the lock jumped open. He swung the gate open on its hinges. It gave an iron groan. Snakeback slipped into the tomb. Ryder followed.

After the glare of the sun, coolness settled on Ryder's skin like dew. He produced a torch from his pocket and its beam was like a yellow, steady eye that split the darkness. The silence swarmed in his ears.

'Janet!' he called again. Edgy now, he sprayed a fan of light over the tomb passage. Where was she? Ryder swallowed hard. He glanced at Snakeback. The dog seemed relaxed, a lolling tongue giving its mouth the appearance of a smile as it panted.

'C'mon boy, time to wake up the dead.' His light beam moved on, coruscating along the rectilinear walls. Scenes sprang into view as if he had switched on a slide projector. Images, painted bas-reliefs that had faded with the passage of thousands of years gave a dim echo of life to the walls. He passed a banquet scene, a line of symmetrical dancers, a female harpist. He passed a row of goddesses standing on the backs of serpents. The goddesses were narrow-hipped and serpentine.

He dropped his cone of light to the stone floor of the passage and went deeper into the tomb. The layout was impressed in his memory as well as the layout of his home half a world away. A fifteen-metre passage led to a doorway and an antechamber. An annexe to the right ran off the antechamber with entry gained by another doorway. It was used as a makeshift washroom by the archaeologist and was fitted with portable facilities and water supply. To the left of the antechamber, another doorway gave onto the burial chamber and another chamber they called the storeroom.

Surely she could hear him coming?

The animal disappeared into the antechamber. A lick on the cheek from Snakeback would be sure to wake her up — as long as she didn't think it was Anubis, jackal of the dead, come to claim her, he thought grimly.

Ryder followed Snakeback to the doorway. He bumped into the dog coming back. The long muzzle of the dog reared in his cone of torchlight. Why wasn't Snakeback barking and licking her joyously? Why had it come back?

'What's the matter, boy?' he said. The words came out in a tight whisper.

Snakeback whined. Wasn't she there? Maybe she

was in the washroom. He checked it. A clean whiff of soap and disinfectant greeted his nostrils, but it was empty.

'Janet!' He went to the burial chamber, his torch beam shining around it, peering for an explanation that must surely greet him here. Dust motes shredded the beam. No Janet. Maybe she was hiding from him to tease him. Maybe she had come out of the tomb already. She had her own key. Had he missed her on the way down? Unlikely. A dank panic snaked around his chest.

'Janet!' His torch beam swept the burial chamber again, probing the darkness short-sightedly. His searching torch found her camp bed on the floor. Empty.

She must be in the storeroom. He went to look. He dashed torchlight around the room like water from a hose. He came out, puzzled, went back to the burial chamber. The dog gave a low, morose whine, circling Janet's camp bed warily and squatting at the end of it.

'Janet — where are you?' The tomb took his cry and rattled it around.

2

Corridor

THE TORCH BEAM REVEALED A BLACK, oblong shape on the floor beside the camp bed. He turned the light on it. It was Janet's microcassette recorder, a compact, hand-held machine. Ryder knelt to retrieve it. Did this hold an answer to the mystery? Had she left a message on it? Scent echoes of Janet rose from the camp bed. What could the machine tell him?

The archaeologist crawled to the wall and squatted on the floor with his back against it. Snakeback flopped heavily against the wall beside him. Ryder left the burning torch on the floor, flooding light over the stone like an abandoned water hose. He saw a beetle scurry into the beam, turn green in the glow, then disappear. With numb fingers he felt for the serrated reverse knob on the microcassette recorder. He jabbed it. The machine whirred into life, the tape lisping through the tiny machine towards the head of the tape. That should be far enough. He fumbled for the 'play' button.

He held the machine to his ear. There was a shuffling sound then the low, conspiratorial voice of Janet Nancarrow filled his ear. '. . .had the dream again. It woke me up. I heard things. . . silvery, shimmering sounds. . . like the sistra instruments shaken by the priestesses in ancient ceremonies. A perfume brushed over my face like bird's wings. Then the tomb slowly started to turn as though wheeling through the painted heavens of the ceiling above me. A feeling of vertigo gripped me as if I were being sucked to the edge of something. I felt myself slipping from my body but, as on the other occasions, I held back, frightened to let go. I thought of you, Wilson. Where would it take me?'

The tape clicked, went dead then came to life again after a pause. The voice held a tremor of excitement. 'Well, here goes. I've decided. I'm letting go. I'm going to go along with it, wherever it takes me. I just hope I can get back. . . at least I think I do. Wilson, if you hear this and if I don't come back, forget about me and don't even think about trying to come after me. It's my choice and I'll be all right. Unlike you, I see a radiance behind this darkness. But I know you won't understand that. You have such fixed ideas on things. I'll be all right. Please believe it. Goodnight, my love. . .'

The machine clicked and a soft, empty roar filled the gap where her voice had been, but it did not fill the void that opened inside Wilson Ryder.

The sun had glared accusingly as he left the tomb with Snakeback beside him. He felt as if he were abandoning Janet. He stumbled down the cliff path, half in a daze. He forced practical details into his mind. He needed to advise the Egyptian authorities and Janet's family back home. What would he tell them? What would they think? There was no way to explain it to them. There was no way of explaining it to himself.

It had all turned savagely wrong. A stupid experiment. He had spent his adult life digging in tombs, observing the funerary customs of another civilisation, without ever considering final separation as a shocking event. Now the loss of someone close hit him with the force of a slamming door and he wanted to rip that door off its hinges.

Where had she gone? He looked up into the bright sky. A falcon planed the thermals. Where are you, Janet?

Snakeback whined. The dog was a comfort. There was a watchfulness like concern in its eyes. Ryder thought of Anubis, the jackal-dog god of the Egyptian underworld and the Lord of the Wrappings. Dogs, old bones and death — they seemed to go together.

A memory flashed into Ryder's mind of shooting an arrow into the dawn sky for Snakeback to chase. It had flown like a departing swallow, or maybe a departing soul.

He pictured the mysterious girl who had taken his arrow. There had been something ghostly about her appearance. Had she been an omen?

He wanted Janet back. He wanted her to be walking down the cliff path with them, the way he had pictured it and longed for it to happen every hour of every day of the week they had been apart.

He remembered shooting an arrow into the black bag of sand, imagining it to be an attacking pharaoh. He heard again the solid force of its hit. But there was no fighting this. He was powerless against this empty, stinking silence.

Janet's whisper filled his ear: *'If you hear this and if I don't come back, forget about me and don't even think about trying to come after me. . .'* How could he go after her? He remembered other times when her voice had filled his ear, loving times, when there had been the warmth and humid mist of life behind the murmurs: *'I'll be all right.'*

He found his eyes drawn to the sky again. Where are you, Janet? She had been convinced that the tomb was some kind of machine, a corridor to the beyond — but to what beyond?

He did not know what she really believed about the beyond. Surprisingly she had never stated her beliefs definitively even though they had often discussed the subject. She had always mixed her beliefs with what he felt was a kind of reckless syncretism, as if religion were a field of flowers and you could pick the flowers that appealed to you to make a pleasing arrangement. Wilson Ryder didn't see it that way, never had.

'Don't sit on the fence,' he would say.

'You're too black-and-white, Wilson,' she would complain. 'You think about things with the simplicity of a child sometimes. That probably explains why you won't go anywhere without your spiky-backed dog and why you enjoy firing bows and arrows into the sky.'

'You can't fire an arrow. You *shoot* an arrow. Anyway, I just happen to think some things *are* black-and-white. Darkness and light. You can't have aesthetic shades of grey in everything. There are some distinct boundaries to existence. Picking the best from religions is usually just a way of accepting the benefits of each but not the rigours imposed by any, a way of copping out. . .'

'Egyptian tombs weren't actually graves or memorials. They were machines — "tomb machines" as I prefer to call them — designed to carry the dead into eternity to meet the gods and join the stars.'

But it wasn't a laundry chute.

Ryder allowed gravity to topple him down the last

few metres to the desert floor. He turned in the direction of his campsite.

Why had he let her go? Why was he letting her go now? something asked him. But was he letting her go? What else could he do? He wasn't abandoning her. She had gone. God alone knew where, but she had *gone*. His tall, willowy Janet had stepped into perpetual night.

Ryder and Snakeback reached the tent. Ryder's parked Land Cruiser sat sheltering under a pool of shade created by a canvas awning braced on poles and tethered by ropes. He opened the tent fly and went inside the tent. The empty tent jeered at him. His bow and quiver of arrows sat at the foot of his camp bed.

A photograph of Janet caught his eye. He had put it up to comfort himself in her absence, hanging it on the tent pole. The slender, daring face smiled fearlessly out at him.

He looked at the bow again.

Was he even *thinking* this? The loneliness, the heat and now the shock of this loss had pushed him too far. It was madness. But a primal instinct to fight back had taken over. He calmly attached the quiver to his belt, picked up his leather bracer guard and tab and pocketed them. Then he picked up Janet's photograph before pocketing it along with a few other things he might need.

All he knew was that a week ago she had been there and now she was gone and the vacuum left by her going exerted an irresistible tug.

The mummy had vanished, too. They had found an empty basalt sarcophagus.

He grasped the bow by its handle. Its weight comforted him. Snakeback growled hopefully. If there was a breath of chance — a swallow's breath of chance —

that he could reach her, or understand what it was that had taken her, he was going to try — in the face of all he knew and all he believed, at whatever risk it meant, even crossing the boundaries of time and reason and maybe sanity. I'm going to find out what happened in there.

'You should never swear, either by heaven or earth or with any other oath', a book with soft black covers had once told him. It didn't stop him now.

'I'll try, Janet, I swear by all that's in heaven and earth and in hell — if I can get to you, I will.' Hang on, I'm coming.'

He left the tent. He crossed one of those sharp boundaries between shadow and light as he left the shade of the tent and went out into the sunlight. The sun wasn't accusing any more. Instead, it glared at him and there were spangles in the shimmering plain like the weapons of a facing army. The bowman and the dog went up the cliff path to the tomb.

'Come, boy, let's fetch.' The lion dog's tail slapped eagerly against his leg.

3

The Opener of Ways

HE WAS MISSING THE SUNLIGHT already. Like a pharaoh of old, he lay stretched out in a tomb, with his most prized possessions around him, his dog and his bow and arrows.

The dog he could explain. He couldn't leave the animal behind. Snakeback would never be parted from him. The bow and arrows were harder to deal with. He had reached for these weapons in a reflex action — a primitive grasp for protection and power. A modern composite bow and a quiver of arrows could be no defence against what had happened here, against shadows.

Maybe it was just the pharaoh complex. Years of studying the funerary habits of the Egyptians had made it seem natural to take his treasures with him. That raised another question. Did he think he was going to die? How long would he wait here to see what happened? Until his strength failed and he crossed that boundary?

Maybe Janet's New Age fancies were having an effect on him, he thought. He was behaving like a pagan.

And yet there was reassurance in feeling the length of the bow beside him and in the breathing presence of the dog at his feet.

He switched off the torch. Darkness rushed in. The beam left an afterglow in his eyes that slowly faded, as if his eyes were reluctant to let go of comforting light and wanted to trap it in his memory.

A languor stole over his body. Snakeback was breathing peacefully, rhythmically, a calming sound. He realised that he had been lying with his eyes open. What was he hoping to see in the womb-like darkness? He shut them now.

Let go. Go with it. If sleep wanted to come, follow it. He saw himself bending his bow and shooting an arrow and watching it shrink in the sky. Snakeback ran after it and he followed the dog this time. The dog ran on and on. He hurried after it. How far had the arrow travelled? They came to the spot where he was sure the arrow must have fallen. Snakeback was standing on the spot, looking puzzled. They searched the area together. Ryder looked around and saw a dark-haired girl emerge, holding his arrow, felt the challenge of her stare, then watched her walk away from him, carrying it to the cliffs. She climbed the rocky cliff path to the tomb entrance.

She disappeared into the dark mouth of the tomb. Ryder and Snakeback followed. Ryder passed into an even darker zone and into sleep.

It was an exhausted sleep with no shimmering sounds of sistra rattled by the temple priestesses, no wheeling through the heavens — just the image of the girl carrying his arrow further and further along an endless dark passage. Where was she taking it? When would she drop it? Where did she want it to fall?

Who was she? A goddess? She wore a white sheath halter-necked dress like an Old Kingdom divinity. There were bangles at her wrists and on her upper arms. The sight of her made him think of Neith, the goddess, whose hieroglyph sometimes included a pair of crossed arrows and a bow. His arrow swung in her hand. She turned to throw a backwards glance at him. He quaked inside at the shock of her glance. She disappeared around a bend in the passage. Ryder and Snakeback quickened their pace, rounding the corner.

The girl was running. Snakeback gave an excited bark. They broke into a run. They could see her clearly in the darkness of the passage. She glowed like one of the golden figures on the ceiling. What ceiling? He had left the tomb far behind him. The girl ran lithely as a cat. He thought: no arrow of mine has ever travelled so far from my bow.

Hour after hour they ran. Time stretched into infinity like the perspective lines of the passage they followed. He wondered whether it was his arrow or his soul that she carried in her hand. Her sandalled feet flew underneath the haze of her dress. She never tired and neither did they. They stayed with her.

Now he guessed where she was taking them. It had to be *there*. They were running across space and time. Keep on her trail. He mustn't lose her, something urged him.

She turned and waved, but not to him, he felt. She seemed to be calling to the dog. The animal yelped, put on speed and flashed ahead of Ryder. It caught up with the running girl. It ran happily beside her. She turned her head again to throw a smile of victory at Ryder.

She had taken his arrow and now his dog. An unreasonable anger grabbed Ryder. He drew an arrow from his quiver and nocked it to the bow as he ran. I'll give her a warning shot. He let fly. The arrow leapt down the corridor towards the girl.

But now the arrow was him and his consciousness was wrapped around it and he felt himself pass into her — not into flesh, but into a star-lined space where she had been. He was tumbling into a void. Something tried to hold him back. He looked over his shoulder. He was linked to something behind him by an endless, elasticised silver string, attached like an umbilical cord. But he kept falling. The cord stretched and snapped.

I'm dead, Ryder thought. Wilson Ryder and Snakeback landed on a stone floor, the bow clattering, the arrows spilling out of the quiver. He fumbled for the torch in his pocket, pressed the switch and tore a yellow hole in the darkness. He was back in the tomb, he saw with bitter disappointment. Had he fallen out of the camp bed? He fanned light around the tomb, looking for the camp bed. He was out of the tomb chamber, in the main passage. Had he been walking in his sleep?

Relief and disappointment converged in his mind. He retrieved the arrows and picked up the bow. Snakeback stood up, a bit shaky-legged.

'Back to earth, Snakeback. Let's get out of here.'

He left the burial chamber and went along the remaining length of the corridor to the entrance.

How long had they been inside the tomb? Ryder saw dim, golden light beyond the entrance. He went out with Snakeback at his side, took one sweeping look around and came to a halt. The world turned around his head. This wasn't the entrance. Gone was the cliff and also the plain below. He had stepped out into a green marshworld at the edge of the Nile.

But there were no papyrus thickets like this on the river near the campsite — there were none like this left in Egypt. The papyrus clumps encircled them like a mysterious wall. Whispers rustled among the tall plants, the heavy umbels bending like heads to confer. Mist swirled on the water beneath them. He lifted his head to look over the reeds and he saw a boat further out on the water, its sail bellying in a breeze.

The passage had somehow brought them down to the river, much lower down. Had they stumbled onto another entrance? Perhaps it explained where Janet had gone. Yet there was something else that jarred. It was the time of day. The sun was only just beginning to rise. Could so much time have gone by? A whole day? It had been mid-morning when he and Snakeback had gone into the tomb.

Then he saw that what he had taken to be a felucca was something shockingly else. It was a boat in the archaic papyriform style, swept up at stem and stern. It had a trapezoid sail and a deckhouse with sides of mats in a chequered pattern and twin steering oars held by two steersmen in loincloths. It was a sight Ryder had never expected to see, except in a tomb painting.

He began to understand. 'We're a long way from home,' he whispered in a shaken voice to the dog.

4

Primordial dawn

WILSON RYDER WAS AFRAID in the way only a person with a religious sense could fear. His soul was afraid. It wasn't a fear of personal danger, but rather that he was about to experience something hitherto unknowable that could shake his beliefs to their foundations. It was like the attenuated moment before the impact of collision.

He was about to meet with something horrifyingly else, something that was other than what he knew and trusted. This was not only an unknown place and an unknown time. It was also, he sensed, an unknown reality.

He blinked at the dense thickets of tall papyrus plants that thrust their heavy umbels into the sky around them. There was a youngness and diffused glow to the light, softened the way memories of the distant past are softened, like dreamy memories of childhood. The air was filled with the smell of green, growing things. Waterfowl honked in the sky. The Nile sparkled in blue-green patches between the mist. Insects and frogs filled the misty river with a ratcheting throb. It was like being at the scene of the original dawn, as if the bank in front of them had just emerged from the waters, like the primordial mound, still streaming with the ooze of creation.

Words from the first chapter of Genesis leaked into his mind: 'The spirit of God moved upon the face of the waters. . . And God said let there be light and there was light. . . and God made the firmament and divided the waters which were under the firmament from the waters which were above the firmament. . . and let the dry land appear. . . And God said, Let the waters bring forth abundantly the moving creatures that have life, and fowl that may fly above the earth. . .'

If this was the place and the time that his retreating senses told him it was — was that other presence here? Was there a time before that redeeming presence? Was there ever such a time — surely that hand was behind everything?

The boat had altered course to head towards him, he noticed. It was still a way off, but already he could see people gathering on the prow, craning their necks. He saw the glint of light on metal, swords and speartips. Some of the figures were pointing. Some held objects with the distinct curve of bows.

There was a rustling sound of something moving through the thicket of papyrus and the tall stems swayed. Ryder cautiously slid an arrow from the quiver and nocked it to the bowstring. Snakeback growled, more a cautionary warning to him than a dare for him to shoot.

A figure parted the stems and came out. It was the girl with his arrow. Wilson Ryder's breath caught in his throat. Snakeback ran to her, giving an excited bark of greeting as if it had known her of old.

The stranger bent and ran her hand along the back

of the dog who wagged its tail delightedly. 'Hello, Hound with a Snake on its Back,' she said affectionately. 'See, the hound knows and likes me. We are old friends. We have run together in dreams, following the arrow's flight.' She spoke in a low, thrilling voice that was thickened with an accent — not Arabic, he thought, but something softer. It was as though she was speaking in another tongue, and yet he understood her words.

Ryder lowered the bow. 'Who are you?' he demanded. 'How did you bring us here?' He said it roughly, yet he was reassured by the dog's welcome of the stranger.

'I dreamed you here, Bowman from Tomorrow,' she said. Ryder swayed like a reed as if a breeze had buffeted him.

She came nearer. 'Why did you take my arrow?' he said.

She held it out to him. 'You may have it now. You will need this arrow — and more — for your quest. You have battles to fight.'

She looked faintly leonine with her shining mane of hair, parted centrally and falling forward in lappets, from behind her ears, in the ancient style. Her body shimmered in a fine, white sheath dress. Her beauty was almost repellent, he felt, swallowing. Yet there was something purely natural about her, like one of the lotus blossoms growing at the edge of the river.

'I'm not here on any quest,' he said to her, 'except to get someone back who vanished from the tomb.'

'Your Lost One. You cannot get her back — not yet. First you must complete the quest. The one whose power could help you is helpless himself. The land is under the thrall of his brother, the Usurper.'

'Who are you?'

'I am Neith,' the girl said lightly as if he should have known. 'The Opener of Ways, Mistress of the Bow and Ruler of Arrows. I will come with you on your quest, although I may not help you in your struggles,' she said. 'It is your destiny to advance the struggle of Osiris. Come quickly. We must begin the search. I can help you regain your Lost One, but only after you have completed your quest.'

'I'm not here on any quest. I told you.'

The girl shook her great mane sadly. 'For too long you have been a loose arrow, happy merely to watch its flight and to share its freedom in the air. But you must learn that the true meaning and joy of life is to commit yourself to a great cause, a cause for others — a cause worth dying for. You must have a target, Bowman, not clouds.'

Neith. How could it be?

'Am I dead?'

'If you think you are dead then you must think I, too, am dead. Do I look like a corpse?' She made an amused face at the strong, dark bowman.

She didn't look dead. There was a humid gleam in her eyes. 'No, perhaps not,' Ryder said. 'But perhaps I am dead.'

'You do not feel dead, Bowman,' Neith said, touching his arm with fingers as cool as marble. What was he in the presence of? Evil? Was this breathing creature with the cold touch a pagan divinity; was she malignant? Why did he feel drawn to her?

'We must go quickly; we have little time.' There was a whistling sound and an arrow zipped overhead and clattered against the rocky entrance to the tomb. Ryder threw a glance at the approaching boat.

'Who are they?' He took the arrow from her and

slipped it into the quiver, but with one hand still kept the first arrow nocked to the bowstring.

'They are the confederates of Seth. They will kill you. Hurry, I will take you to the supporters of Osiris, to where the child waits in a thicket of the Delta near Buto. There, the Mesniu will help us. They are men of the dwarf god Ptah. They are smiths, cunning workers in metal, and will make arrows for your struggle.'

Ryder ducked as another arrow whizzed across the reeds. He swung his bow at the boat and drew. Two archers stood on the prow. He hesitated in surprise. One had the head of a jackal, the other a crocodile.

'They are demons of Seth,' Neith said. The girl seized his arm. 'Spare your arrows until the Mesniu have made you more. Come with me; my boat is waiting.' She ran to the reeds and Snakeback chased after her.

The boat was drawing near. They would soon be landing. Snakeback slipped into the reeds after the girl, wagging its tail as if on the scent of an arrow. 'Hurry,' Neith called over her shoulder.

Ryder went after them. The mist thickened near the water's edge. He heard Snakeback's soft whine. It was a muffled sound in the thickness of the reeds. He parted the reeds, pushing his way through. He came upon a raft of papyrus bundles, swept up at stem and stern. It was bobbing. The girl and the dog were already on board, squatting on the top. He followed them on board, making the small craft rock.

'Down,' the girl instructed him. 'Take an oar.' Two oars with flared tips like spears and decorated in lotus pattern design lay on the deck. Ryder slipped the bow over his shoulder and grabbed one. She took the other.

They paddled away from the bank. The girl pointed. They headed left and went into enveloping mist.

'Watch the dog,' the girl said. 'His tail will guide you.' Snakeback stood at the prow. 'See his tail turn.' The dog slid its long tapering tail to the right. 'He knows where we must go. This is the land of the lost arrow and he is enchanted here. Follow the sign of his tail.' Ryder opened the blade of his oar and the girl paddled hard, turning them in the mist. They narrowly slipped past an island clump of reeds. The dog's tail went straight. They kept the boat nose ahead.

She dreamed me here. Perhaps that was the only thing that explained it. I am in a dream, but not a dream of my own making. He gave a shiver as the mist wrapped around him.

There were far-off shouts where they had been.

The dog and the girl led them on through the mist, taking them between island thickets of papyrus plants.

Something heavy dragged itself through the reeds and entered the water with a splash. Snakeback growled. 'Crocodile?' Ryder whispered.

'Fear not,' Neith said. 'Crocodiles will not harm a papyrus boat. They fear it is Isis still seeking the body of Osiris.'

Isis. Her search was one of the first great struggles between good and evil. Osiris was murdered by his evil brother Seth, the Egyptian devil. Seth tore his brother's body in fourteen fragments and scattered them in the river, but Isis, his devoted wife, travelled the length of the Nile in a papyrus skiff on a quest to recover each part. Then, along with her sister Nephthys, Isis worked 'magic with knotted cords' on the dead king's body and re-formed the broken parts of his body, anointing and bandaging him as a mummy. By her magic she was then miraculously impregnated and so gave birth to Horus, the hawk-headed one, who was to be his father's avenger.

Neith referred to it in a matter of fact way as if it were an event that she accepted had actually occurred. She believed it, but it was myth. Could he believe that it had actually happened? Only in myth. But did that make it a lie or a greater truth? Did myth have a reality in some part of the universe — in this part of the universe?

What's happening to me and what will it do to all that I believe in? Ryder wondered.

5

Horus and Seth

'LOOK, THE HOUND IS TELLING US to alter course,' the girl whispered. They adjusted course, then straightened, settling into an easy pace. The mist thinned and they came upon a small village at the edge of the thicket. It was raised on stilts and lay dreaming in the early morning sunshine.

A small person, like a child, but thickly set and squat and wearing a leather kilt, came running to the edge of the bank. A dwarf. He struck a gong, a tube of metal suspended on a pole. They were approaching a landing stage made of reed bundles. Others came running.

'These are the Mesniu,' Neith explained, 'dwarfs of the dwarf god Ptah.' They were stunted, blackened and grimy as if they had come straight from a forge. Ryder looked up and saw smoke issuing from a mud brick kiln.

Eager hands dragged the boat to the edge and steadied it. Neith was the first to go ashore and they parted respectfully to let her through and then Ryder noticed something else about these people with the squat bodies and bulging faces. They did not speak, but crackled like electricity, communicating with each other by means of sharp, electric-sounding clicks of their tongues. Yet their blackened faces were split by white-toothed smiles of welcome.

'Come with me to the child,' Neith said, leading the way through the tiny folk who clicked excitedly. Snakeback eyed them warily. It was like walking through a swarm of grasshoppers. One, a grey-haired man, ran to catch up with Neith.

She took Ryder and Snakeback through the village. Dogs slunk around the huts, eyeing the stranger and his dog with suspicion. Children shrank shyly into doorways, their big eyes watching them pass. The reek of native beer and woodsmoke, livestock and primitive shelter filled Ryder's nostrils. On the other side of the compound of mud and thatched buildings on stilts, Neith brought them to an even denser patch of papyrus. It rose like a fortress. They passed through it and then into a clearing.

'The nest,' Neith said. There in the clearing of papyrus, resting under a small pavilion made of reeds, a woman sat on a reed bed suckling an infant, attended by a second woman, a nurse.

'This is the hope of the world. A baby in a humble shelter.'

Wilson Ryder shuddered as the collision he had dreaded occurred. It was the impact of something other, something that shouldn't have been. A mother and child in a humble setting. The image shimmered in his brain.

'This is Isis, her infant Horus and her sister Nephthys, the nurse.'

The woman looked very regal holding the boy on her lap and natural in her maternal pose and did not stop in her suckling as if their arrival were expected and the most natural thing in the world. She did not wear her customary headdress of a throne-crown on her head, nor a golden girdle at her waist.

Isis. The name screamed like a trapped bird in his brain. Was he standing in the presence of the Mary of the ancient world, seeing the image of the suckling mother and child that was to be echoed thousands of years later in portrayals of Mary and Jesus?

Ryder looked at the child. It was no helpless babe in arms. Although the child's face was hidden, from its body he could tell that it was a boy of six or seven, yet in accordance with ancient Egyptian custom he was still being suckled by his mother.

'The bowman from tomorrow is here to help us,' Neith said.

'Welcome, Bowman,' the woman smiled and nodded her head in a gracious way. Her eyes sparkled like green waters. 'We have waited for your arrival and now the whole universe waits to see if you can prevail. But first we must arm you. Soneby, you must fashion more arrows for the bowman.'

The grey-haired dwarf who had accompanied them bowed and withdrew.

Now the woman took the child away from her breast and turned him around to face the new arrivals. 'Look upon Horus, the son of Osiris.'

Ryder gave a gasp. The child, as unbelievable as it may seem, had a curved beak and a flashing eye — the head of a young falcon on a human body, with swaddling clothes around his waist. She handed the child to the second woman and rose to address the new arrivals.

'Do you know the nature of your quest — why you have come?'

'I've come to get somebody back.'

'The Lost One,' Neith put in.

The mother of the child shook her head sadly. 'That is not possible just yet. The lord of the dead is not the lord until his son has succeeded him. The reign of Osiris was a golden age when men were changed from cannibals and taught to plant grain and grow crops and live in the light. But now he is dead, murdered by his brother and his confederates, and the land is in his thrall — I speak of the usurper, Seth. He has turned the Land of Osiris into a tombworld where the living must hide like the dead below the earth in tombs. He holds the land in his cruel thrall and is working powerful magic even now to find my child Horus and bring about the destruction of the rightful heir. If the dead king were to forever remain in his unresurrected form, the outlook for him and for the world would be desolate. He only remains in this condition, however, until his son and successor, Horus, has vanquished his enemies and ascended his throne. Seth, you see, is death and his confederates are the demons of decay and dissolution.'

Wilson Ryder felt a protest rise to his lips. The salvation she spoke of was old and surpassed. Another saviour had come and changed the world. But before he could open his mouth, a mighty shaking in the thicket turned their heads. Something vast was crashing through the reeds.

Neith gave a warning cry. A giant black boar burst squealing out of the tall reeds like a boat breaking through the green of a wave. Nephthys screamed, enfolding the child in protective arms.

It came like a black evil wind, thirty-centimetre tusks flashing, rushing at the child and the nurse.

Wilson Ryder whipped two arrows from the quiver, nocked one to the bow while holding the other, pulled back and aimed just in front of the target, sustaining the lead for a few metres before releasing the arrow in one smooth action. *Thwack.* The arrow hit the boar behind the point of the shoulder and it screamed and veered, but beat a new angle to the woman who was trying to lift the boy protectively in her arms.

Ryder notched the second arrow. *Thwack.* This time a neck shot — central on the neck. It should have dropped any animal, but the squealing creature merely veered off again and redirected itself at the nurse and the child in a line that faced the bowman.

Ryder took another arrow from the quiver, feeling panic now, but trying to keep steady. Would nothing stop it? He aimed between the black hulk's deep-set eyes. With the pace of the boar, at about twenty-five kilometres an hour, the arrow would hit slightly higher in the forehead and strike the brain. Ryder loosed the arrow. It sped across the gap and hit home with a sound like an axe going into hardwood and there it quivered.

The black boar threw up its head and its front legs crumpled, but momentum carried it on like an express train with locked wheels. It continued to travel, running into the nurse and child and throwing them to the ground. The woman fell back and the child flew to one side.

Ryder saw a wicked flash of a tusk as the boar gouged at the child. The child gave a scream of pain and clutched his eye. Then a black hand went over the sun and the world plunged into partial night. Silence closed in. The boar was still as a mountain. The child lay whimpering in the arms of the kneeling Isis. Nephthys, dazed, climbed to her feet.

Neith was quivering like a reed in a breeze. 'Now you

see why we need you, Bowman. No-one else has ever landed an arrow or a sword on this enemy. This is Seth who has taken the form of a wild boar and found us.'

'Then your problems are over — he's dead.'

'No, not dead. The boar is dead, but the one within it has sped back to his true body. You see, he dare not come here in his own shape.'

Isis set up a wail in the tremulous eastern way like a kite of the desert, a sound that seemed to shred the air with sorrow. 'The eye of Horus is lost,' Neith said in a dead voice. 'Seth has taken it and now he has the most powerful amulet of all. The eye of the sun will not shine again until the eye of Horus is restored.'

Ryder looked up at the sky. An eclipse had cut a dark hole in the sun, leaving only a glimmer of light around the edges.

'What must we do?'

'Seth's power rests in fourteen sacred amulets, hidden throughout Egypt, just as the body parts of Osiris were scattered and hidden, so these are hidden in strongholds guarded by traps and demonic foes. You must gather them all. Here are the fourteen amulets you must find.' She now recited them as if she expected him to commit them to memory: 'The Djed column, backbone of Osiris, the buckle of Isis, the scarab beetle, the Heqet frog, the *ankh*, the menat necklace, the flail, the crook, the uraeus, the *was*-sceptre, the amulet of the heart, the sacred headrest, the sacred adze for opening of the mouth. And finally, the eye of Horus. . .'

Ryder dragged his arrows from the hulk of the boar. The beast gave off a loathsome reek. He rinsed the arrowheads at the edge of the river.

The Mesniu brought Ryder bread and a jar of beer that had the consistency of watery porridge, but was refreshing and bracing. They gave Snakeback a hunk of venison. They were in awe of the dog and pointed, their tongues clicking, staring with their bulging eyes at the snake of fur on it back. One gave a loud hiss that made the others scatter and they all enjoyed the joke hugely. They couldn't talk, but they could laugh, Ryder noted. That was something in their favour.

6

The radiance of the past

THE MESNIU PROVIDED A SAILBOAT and crew for the next part of their journey. It was a small boat, again in papyriform shape, but this time made of wood, small pieces of acacia cleverly morticed together — good ship-building timber was rare in Egypt, even in pre-pharaonic times, Ryder noted — with the length of the craft hog-trussed by a cable that tied the swept up stem and stern together, giving it longitudinal stability. It had a deck-house and a stepped mast and sail that could be lowered quickly, allowing the boat to be rowed into the reeds and hidden at the first sight of an enemy vessel.

Ryder, Neith and the dog boarded the boat and the crew set an orange trapezoid sail. They sailed, hugging the reed-fringed river bank, in the pall of the eclipse. The Mesniu had fashioned more arrows for Ryder which he wore in a second quiver on his back. They were well-made broadhead arrows, considering they were of wood, with fletching made from the tail feathers of vultures and angled to increase the spin of the arrow in flight and reduce the effect of wind.

Neith went into the small deckhouse that was enclosed in screens and sat, neat as a cat on a grass mat. A small oil lamp flickered on the floor and caught flashes in the paint-rimmed lustre of her eyes. Ryder joined her and sat opposite her. Snakeback flopped in a corner and promptly went to sleep.

'Where are we going?' he said.

'Across the river to the west to the first nome of desolation. There, hidden in a tomb of the priest of Seth is the first amulet, the Djed column, which represents the backbone of Osiris.'

'How do you know it's there?'

'I am Neith, the Opener of Ways.'

'Are you divine?' he said, sensing a danger in asking the question.

'You think so. You are drawn to my beauty. You are especially attracted to my shining hair, are you not?' It should have sounded like vanity and assumption, but she said it with such conviction that it seemed pointless to deny it.

'You are beautiful, yes, incredibly so,' he said. 'But I want to know about your nature. Are you divine?'

'You think so.'

'I mean, do you have powers?'

'What woman does not?'

'Powers greater than mankind?'

'Every woman has that.' She had a bright wit. He shouldn't be surprised. He reminded himself that Ancient Egyptians were great lovers of wit and wordplay.

'Are you a holy person?'

She smiled. 'Not when I am angered. You don't want to discover how unholy I can be.'

'Are you immortal, then?'

'We are all immortal,' she said lightly. 'Isn't that what you believe?'

She was right. He did. But her answer left him puzzled. It led him to wonder exactly what was meant by divinity. How did he define it?

'Are you a goddess, with special powers to influence?' he said, trying to pin his meaning down.

'Were there none called goddesses in your time, Bowman from the Future?'

'Well, yes, there were some that were called by that name.' He thought of the women who had been called goddesses by the media — Greta Garbo, Marlene Dietrich, Marilyn Monroe. . .'

'And did they have special powers to influence?'

'Well, I suppose they did, but not in a magical way.'

'These goddesses had no magic?'

'I suppose they did, in one sense. They were what we called stars.'

'I, too, am an imperishable star,' she said. Is that all the gods of ancient times were, he wondered — people with a greater luminosity in their lives? No, it wasn't that simple. This girl did more than shine with a brighter light — she had led him in a chase across space and time. He wanted to know about her powers. Did she feel emotions like other women?

'I am baffled by you,' he confessed.

Neith smiled. 'I will tell you this about myself. I am everything which has been, which is and which shall be, and there has never been any who has uncovered my veil of secrecy. Now I have a question for you. This Lost One that you wish to recover — is she beautiful, Bowman?'

Nothing he had ever seen was as beautiful as the girl sitting in the deckhouse opposite him. He felt dizzy in the scented pool of her presence. 'Janet is beautiful to me in many ways. She was worth crossing the great divide to try to get her back.'

'Are you sure you crossed for her and not another?'

'Who?'

'Never mind, Bowman.'

But he was intrigued. 'Who else could you mean?'

'Think of your love of Egypt. What lay behind your love of it? Was it a place or a person? Who was it who lay behind your thoughts — who shimmered in the Egypt of your mind and the Egypt of your soul? Do you remember your first journey to Egypt? What did you come to find? Recall it now. I will conjure the picture of it in the darkness of your mind. What do you see?'

Sparks danced in her dark eyes and then flashed into his brain and illuminated memories that lay half-forgotten there.

*   *   *

Wilson Ryder had a fear as he sat on his Egyptair flight out of London bound for Cairo. He was eighteen and it was his first visit to Egypt, although he had read about it since he was a child.

'What if the Egypt of my boyhood dreams isn't there?' he had thought. 'The Egyptians believed in parallel Niles — the real Nile on the surface and the parallel Nile of the underworld below. Maybe they will still be there today. The abysmal one may be the one on the surface, the postcard Egypt, and the radiant one may be the one deep below — the Nile of the mind, the soul and eternity.'

He looked out of the window at the first dusting of the lights of Egypt appearing in the darkness far below him. He lifted his eyes, pausing on the eagle-headed emblem of the god Horus painted on the engine pod of the Airbus A-300, the symbol of Egyptair, then went still higher to the stars in a velvety sky. He called silently to boyhood images of Egypt. He had to call to them; they weren't there. With an effort of will, he evoked an image of the sky goddess Nut in the heavens: he imagined her golden body stretched across Egypt, her toes touching one horizon and her fingertips the other, and stars spangling on the vault formed by her body.

Egypt, Kemet, the Black Land and the Red Land, the Nile, the Land of the Dead — of magic, of pharaohs and mummies who had undergone their 'night of ointment and bandages' thousands of years ago. He recited this like a prayer, trying to get in touch with something that transcended the reality of sitting in an aircraft seat. Why didn't he feel anything? He could be landing at any airport in any country in the world, but he was landing in Cairo, in Egypt, in *his* Egypt.

The intercom crackled and the captain spoke in Arabic. Then he spoke in accented English that was very little clearer: 'Ladies and gentlemen, we are now making our descent into Cairo airport. Please fasten your seatbelts and observe the no smoking signs. We hope you had a pleasant flight and thank you for travelling Egyptair. . .'

Ryder crammed his face to the glass of the window for a glimpse of Cairo. They landed. He saw apartment blocks quite close to the airport and airport buildings and lights and moving vehicles like any other airport in the world. The Airbus played bland musak over the intercom as they taxied to the terminal building. Why musak, here? Why not a haunting lute or the shimmer of the sistrum played in a dim Egyptian temple? The magic isn't here.

He left the plane. It was winter in Egypt, yet the Cairo air was laden with moisture and wrapped itself warmly around him as he went down the stairs. Two modern transit buses waited to take the passengers to the terminal building. The buses were walk-on, walk-off affairs, the drivers standing behind driving consoles. The buses were filling up quickly with passengers ahead of him.

He paused as he reached firm ground. You're here. Ryder felt numb. Egypt did not reach to him. Maybe it would come later.

They rode to the terminal. They held onto ceiling straps, their bodies swaying with the movement of the bus as it picked up speed, heading towards the terminal building. In the arrivals hall, they gathered in long lines to go through customs. In a neighbouring hall, he saw people who looked like Bedouin, sprawled on the floor, waiting serenely with luggage, boxes and packets spread about.

Maybe it will hit me later, he thought.

They went by coach, passing through Heliopolis. Their Egyptian licensed guide, a matronly lady, who wore a heavy black cardigan in spite of the heat, informed them harshly over a microphone that the mythology of Egypt was born right here in Heliopolis and that this was now a fashionable suburb of Cairo. Not that fashionable, he thought. It was filled with high-rise apartments, many with balconies like open drawers in cupboards and with drying laundry tumbling out. He saw a goat on one of the balconies.

'The President lives here,' she said, 'and security is very strict. If you live in this neighbourhood and want to have friends visit, you must first get permission from the authorities.' Clearly, the Egyptians had not forgotten about the assassination of President Sadat.

They travelled along Corniche Road. Traffic cut in and out, hooters blared. One car cut in front of their bus and the driver swerved. Some of the passengers gasped, others chuckled uneasily. Tales of Cairo drivers were not exaggerated, Ryder discovered. Traffic lanes were mere theoretical barriers.

The guide noticed their amusement. 'After our cruise to the historical sites of Egypt, you must pass a written examination. Those passengers who fail the test will be forced to drive a car in Cairo.' She laughed breathily into the microphone. 'However, you will see very few accidents in Cairo. Cairenes are very safe drivers. If you do see an accident, it will be settled quickly before the police come. If the police come, they impound the cars.'

They reached the city and passed a statue of Rameses. 'Here on the left you will see a *hyooge* big statue of Rameses the Second,' the guide informed them. 'This is an original statue of Rameses.' Poor Rameses, he thought. Not a favourite pharaoh of mine with his megalomaniacal obsession for scale. The 'huge big' statue of Rameses sat dwarfed between flyovers and beset by a stream of honking traffic that was enough to make the monarch's head spin.

They turned off near the Rameses Hilton, then crossed a bridge over the Nile to their hotel on the island of Gezira. Their hotel for one night was to be the Marriott, a former palace of the Khedive Ismael which formed the central building with accommodation towers built on either side of it. A haze lay over the streets. Cairo seemed to be in the grip of a fog, he noticed as he went into the hotel. The group checked in. Their passports were ferried away, not to be returned until they left Egypt.

Settled into his air-conditioned hotel room, Ryder went out onto a balcony. The warm night air enfolded him. To his left, the city lights shone on a hazy Nile. To his right lay the hotel's sculptured gardens, conceived in the formal European style for the visit of the Empress Eugenie at the opening of the Suez Canal. Haze hung over the gardens.

Pollution. *The abysmal Nile is the one on the surface.*

The haze gave Cairo a mystery he did not feel.

After breakfast, he joined a group who were visiting the Cairo museum. A young girl dropped into a seat beside him. She introduced herself as Janet Nancarrow, a university student. She told him about the museum they were about to visit. 'I've always liked the Cairo museum,' she said. 'It's a complete shambles, like a bulk warehouse of history. Nothing's very well showcased at all. Not like the Louvre, or the Metropolitan. But that's the pleasure of it. It's full of the most marvellous hidden surprises as well as the more notable treasures. I spent a day there once and only saw half of the place.'

They crossed the bridge from Gezira Island and they were soon at the Cairo museum. Maybe he would feel something here, Ryder thought as the coach pulled up, joining a throng of other rattling, honking coaches outside the gates. Pharaonic statues stood like trees in the gardens outside the domed building. The girl had brought a camera and was directed to a kiosk inside the gates.

'You got cine-camera?' a bored-looking Egyptian girl said at a window of the kiosk.

'No cine-camera — stills camera.' The young girl held up her automatic Pentax.

'Ten Egyptian pounds. No flash!' It was as well she hadn't brought a cine-camera. A sign said the additional charge for cine-cameras was a steep 100 Egyptian pounds. Egypt was a land of ticket offices.

They went up the steps into the entrance hall of the museum building. It was as busy as a railway station with various Egyptian guides rallying their groups of visitors. The Egyptian guide in the sweltering black cardigan held up a blue and white rolled umbrella and directed her group to gather around another 'huge, big' statue of Rameses. Ryder and the girl slipped away, leaving the group of visitors to be hammered into submission by the ringing voice of the Egyptian guide. It was a voice that fell like chisel blows as if the guide were once again hacking Rameses out of a block of stone.

Ryder hurried away from her, going further into the crowded building, heading left. The girl quickened her pace to keep up with him.

This was better. A statue of the old kingdom monarch Zoser greeted him. The builder of the step pyramid. His eyes had been hacked out. The hollows were as mysterious as caves.

The young girl, Janet, saw Ryder staring at it and lined up her camera, taking a snapshot of Zoser and Ryder together, then one of Rameses and later Pharaoh Mentuhotep with his big black, solid legs. 'I hope you don't mind posing for me,' she said. 'It gives some scale to my pictures.' He didn't mind. The click, click of the camera was reassuring. He hoped it might stitch him into the scene, into the fabric of reality. I really am here, he thought.

They went upstairs. A black-uniformed museum guard insinuated himself into their presence. He waved to the girl slyly as if he were about to offer her illicit antiquities. 'What does he want?' Ryder said uneasily.

'Maybe he wants to sell us the treasures of

Tutankhamun,' she joked.

'Mummies, mummies,' he said with a shy grin to the girl. She glanced a little anxiously at Ryder, but followed the man into a darkened room. Ryder went after them, puzzled. Mummies? This couldn't be right. The real mummy wing, the resting places of Seti and Rameses and the other famous eternity-seekers, was permanently closed. The Muslim government had difficulties with the concept of parading their dead forebears before the eyes of foreigners, although it was rumoured that this difficulty might be overcome and the wing re-opened for visitors, with the introduction of a suitably hefty entrance fee.

Now he saw where the guide was leading them and smiled. They found themselves in a gloomy room crammed with unlit cases. Mummies surrounded them, but they were not the mummies of humans. They were the mummies of animals — ibis birds, crocodiles, dogs, cats, even rodents. Shabby, forlorn bundles, Ryder thought, looking around. They had none of the optimism implicit in human mummies.

Janet Nancarrow shuddered as her eyes met the narrow-eyed stare of a mummified baboon who was sitting up on his haunches in a case. His bandages were unspooling around his feet. She left hastily. Ryder handed the guard at the door an Egyptian pound for his trouble.

'You are welcome,' he said, reaching out for the money and already turning his eyes away to look for another prospect. They visited the treasures of Tutankhamun next. To Ryder, it was like looking at postcards of too-familiar scenes.

Beyond the Tutankhamun display, another uniformed guard sidled up to Ryder, this time leading him to see an object in a large case. It was the sarcophagus of the princess Merit Amun, lying on her back, an outer coffin. Others had once nested inside it. It was bigger than a telephone box.

'I've seen pictures of her in books,' Ryder said. 'I'd never realised it was so big.' The outer sarcophagus was made of coloured and gilded cedar wood and had a beautifully sad face with inlaid eyes that shone as though tears had sprung into them.

'Thankyou,' the girl said to the museum guard, taking Ryder by the arm and moving him on.

'Shouldn't we. . .' He threw a glance at the guard.

'There must be over a hundred thousand exhibits in this museum,' she told him. 'We can't hand out a pound every time somebody points at something.'

'You are welcome,' the guide said, moving on. Ryder turned to go downstairs. He had missed something.

'Where do you want to go?' Janet asked.

'To look for Pharaoh Khafre.' He found what he was looking for at the back of a hall. It was a statue of the pharaoh seated on a throne, a majestic work in veiny black diorite stone. A falcon, the Horus-symbol of kingship, rested on the chair behind his head, its wings enfolding the king in its divine protection. The eyes of the king seemed unafraid as they contemplated the prospect of eternity.

'Will you stand in front of it?' she asked. Wilson Ryder posed beside him.

'You don't really think I want you to be in every picture just to provide some scale, do you?' she said teasingly.

'Not for a second,' he said, smiling. She lined up the picture.

Then he saw her.

She stood near the door. The echoing voices of the visitors and museum guides in the hall seemed to thin away for Ryder. A hush settled in his ears. It was the white statue of an Egyptian girl. Her slender form was revealed by a clinging sheath dress, so sheer that it revealed the depression of her navel. He started towards her.

'Stand still. I haven't taken the picture yet.'

'Sorry.'

The camera froze Ryder and Khafre in a one-dimensional slice of time. He went past her. She turned to see what had taken his interest.

The statue was that of a young woman, Middle Kingdom, in appearance. She had long hair, goddess-style, centrally parted and falling forward on her chest in two rounded lappets. The hair was hooked behind her ears and so had the effect of pushing out her ears. It was a Middle Kingdom artistic convention. Prominent ears were an earmark of the period, literally. He checked a sign beside her. The statue was a much later piece than it appeared, a hard limestone statue, maybe of XXVIth Dynasty, although Middle Kingdom in style. Was she a woman or a goddess?

An Egyptologist had once described the appearance of ancient Egyptian women in tomb frescoes and in statuary, as possessing 'slender profiles like precious vases'. She was certainly precious to him, he thought.

She has given it back to me. Egypt. The Egypt of his boyhood affections glimmered in the rippled whiteness of her form.

He went closer. 'This'll be good,' his companion said. He turned and posed for a photograph. She smiled as he went so close to the statue that it seemed they were holding hands.

'I have this thing about older girls,' he joked.

'I think that one's a bit too old to be jealous about,' she said, chuckling. They left the hall, Ryder reluctantly.

His eye was ambushed next by a winsome figure of a girl in stuccoed and painted wood. It was a servant girl, bearing offerings. She held a duck by the wings in one hand and balanced a basket of offerings on her head. She was Dynasty XI, twenty-first century BC.

Is my love of Egypt romantic at heart, he wondered sadly, an attraction to mysterious allure? He recalled the biblical allusions to the 'fleshpots' of Egypt. Was it the sensual nature of ancient Egypt that attracted him? The thought depressed him. He had always believed it was something deeper, more spiritual. Egyptian art, it had seemed to him, expressed a unique grasp of eternity, especially the eternal in woman. He had always felt attracted to girls who were passive and static, cool ladies of mystery, women with an unattainability. And yet the girls he met and liked were always lively and direct, like this young girl who had attached herself to him.

Ryder found another marvellous statue in a central glass case. Again it was a lady. It was the head and sinuous standing figure of the wife of an Egyptian General Nakht-Min. She wore an intricately carved wig, in the New Kingdom style, ears hidden, and her body displayed by a pleated, form-fitting dress. Her small, exquisite face was dominated by broad swept-up eyes and a neat cat-like mouth. She held the sacred *menat* necklace in her hand. . .

Was it true? Was it a female radiance that attracted him to Egypt, a pagan femininity?

*   *   *

He returned now to a heightened awareness of the girl who sat with him in the flickering lamplight in the deckhouse of the boat. 'You saw your love of Egypt,' she said, 'or at least an echo of it... did you not?' Yes, but he had seen Janet, too. I've come to find Janet, he reminded himself and he would do anything that he had to do to succeed.

They crossed the river to the west and left the boat in the reeds. The Mesniu crew stayed on board. Ryder, Neith and Snakeback went ashore.

7

The backbone amulet

THEY LEFT THE RIVER BANK and made their way into stony desert. 'We are lucky the eye of the sun is blind,' Neith said. 'We can slip through the Necropolis guards with less fear of detection.'

'Where are we going?'

'To a tomb and a maze. This is your first challenge. I do not know the danger, Bowman, but it is a trap, you can be sure. The first amulet, a small Djed pillar or backbone of Osiris, lies at the other side of a maze.'

She led him to a shattered place of stones. It had once been a quarry. The tomb entrance was a shaft that had once been covered and hidden by stone chippings, but the entrance had been cleared and somebody had been down it recently, very recently. In fact, they were probably still below.

Wilson Ryder and Neith went to the entrance to the tomb.

He looked down. Between his dust-covered desert boots, a length of *halfa* grass rope, a rope that shouldn't have been there, ran along the rubble-strewn ground and slid over an edge into a rock-cut shaft, disappearing into the darkness of a tomb. It was as shocking as finding a snake under his feet. 'Somebody has gone after the Djed pillar ahead of you,' Neith said, alarmed. Snakeback sniffed at the rope and slowly wagged its tail. It whined. Was it hungry for another chase?

'Tomb robbers?' Ryder suggested. The rope was anchored to a boulder.

'Not in this tomb. None would dare. It is a tomb of a priest of Seth and reeks of evil.'

Wilson Ryder looked around the site. He was standing at the base of a cliff-quarry abandoned in even more ancient times than these. A blur of movement caught his eye. A falcon sailed over the shattered cliff. Its desolate cry bounced off a million limestone fragments below. Thieves? The archaeologist pictured predatory fingers tearing at the contents of the tomb.

He knelt beside the rope, grabbing it in his fingers and giving it a soft, testing tug to see if there was any weight on the end of it. Nobody there. It moved freely. How long had they been down there? He squinted into the pit, hunting for lights.

Should he stay up here and wait for them to come up? Or go down? I'll go down, he decided. He took the bow off his shoulder and removed the quivers of arrows.

'Are you coming down?' he said to Neith, who squatted neatly like a cat at the mouth of the shaft.

She shook her head.

'I have led you here — that is the limit of my power. Good luck, Bowman, but be very careful. Be mindful that nothing will be as easy as it seems. You will need all your wits to succeed.'

Snakeback did not intend to be left behind. The dog pawed excitedly at Ryder's leg. 'Okay, boy.' The dog could be useful in a maze. The archaeologist picked up the dog and supported it over his shoulder, then went to the edge of the hole. The dog knew how to hook onto his shoulder with its front paws.

Flakes of limestone crunched under Ryder's boots as he went to the edge and grabbed the rope. He marvelled again at the cleverness of the Egyptian who in ancient times had chosen this shattered place to be the site of his tomb.

The secret of this tomb was like a jigsaw in a million pieces. Chippings, like those underneath him, were the betrayers of secret tombs. Even the most careful excavations by the ancients left tomb chippings behind, like thousands of little calling cards, invisibly written notes on ostraca. But the tomb robbers knew how to read them.

The owner of this tomb had devised an ingenious solution. Why try to hide the tomb chippings, the fatal evidence of a tomb's construction? Instead, he chose a place that was already a sea of chippings. A worked-out quarry. Who would think to look here? And even if they did, how would they find the tell-tale tomb chippings? It would be like looking for a needle in a mountain of needles. Yet somebody had beaten him to it.

The archaeologist and the dog went over the edge. He let himself down carefully, hand over hand. Snakeback hung onto his shoulder. The dog had descended with him into tombs like this many times before. It was not a particularly deep shaft and it opened up into a vault. He felt something brittle and dry crunch underneath his foot. Probably a mummy. He winced, not out of any squeamishness, but regret. The archaeologist in him regretted destroying a clue to the past. Mummies held no disgust or terror for him. A man steeped in the funerary practices of ancient Egypt, he had a distanced view of death. He had slept in tombs with mummies under his camp bed. Egyptology was a matter of cool, almost mathematical problem- solving to him — and he loved problem-solving

He put down the other foot, gingerly. Snakeback wriggled over his shoulder and jumped to the floor behind him. The tomb shaft entranceway, lit by a fall of dim light from above, had evidently been used as a secret mummy cache in more recent times. Then it had been shut up again, he guessed.

He took a torch from his pocket and turned on a spurt of yellow light. Dust danced in the beam. The beam revealed decorated walls and a clutter of wooden mummy cases, some open and with the bandaged occupants peeping out.

The vault was an entranceway. To work his way through it, he would have to press between mummies and cases. Snakeback went eagerly ahead of him and Ryder squeezed through after it. His shoulder jarred the side of a sarcophagus near the image of a pair of painted eyes and the wood crumbled away. The occupant — a mummy lying on its side — protested, jaws apart in a soundless scream.

'Sorry,' Ryder murmured. Dust swirled in his beam. There was an entranceway just ahead. It was a square doorway going into blackness. He had to bend to go inside, following his prowling torch beam. It wasn't another chamber. It was the entrance to a maze. He felt himself pass through an unseen barrier that minutely resisted his progress, like a spider's web. It was a cautionary fear. Ryder did not underestimate the builders of this tomb and he had been in mazes before.

It was possible, without the help of a good guide, to lose oneself for hours.

How deep did the maze run?

Snakeback, growling uneasily, looked up. They heard a rushing sound, like wheezy laughter above their heads. Something was shifting. A sudden shower of fine chippings rained to the floor and a pile of dust billowed up. Was the tomb caving in? He flashed his torchlight up at the ceiling. The torch beam steadied and froze like a horrified stare. It wasn't a cave-in. At least not a natural one. Neith's words came back to him. '. . .*I do not know the danger, Bowman, but it is a trap, you can be sure. The first amulet, a small Djed pillar, or backbone of Osiris lies at the other side of a maze.*'

Neat apertures had opened up in the stone roof and were admitting showers of fine chippings. The maze was going to fill up like a deadly hour-glass, but not in an hour — within minutes. Something had triggered it off.

Snakeback barked anxiously, shrill notes that rang through the tomb like chisel blows. 'Snakeback! Wilson! Is that you?' It was a cry of the lost that had lost all hope. The cry hooked into Ryder and spun him around.

Janet. Here. How? The joy he should have felt was smothered by another shower of chippings that hissed down. He swept the branching passages of the maze, hunting for a glimpse of her.

'Janet!' he shouted. 'I'm here. Where are you?' Pieces rushed out of the darkness, a roar of grating laughter, muffling his shout. A thin voice from another world filtered through the din. 'I'm here. . . at the other side of the maze. I found my way through. . . but I'll never get back in time. Help me, Will! Hurry!' The archaeologist's eyes widened in the glow of the torchlight. What could he do? Think, brain. Two choices. Rush in and try to find her. But even if he found her, would he be able to find the way back with her before the maze filled up? Or, alternatively, find something to mark a trail behind himself so that he could use it to find the way out again. But what? He was wasting time. Limestone dust filled his nose. He tasted it in the back of his throat. There was no time to look around. What he needed was a ball of thread to unwind behind him, just as Theseus had used to escape from the maze of the Minotaur. Would the *halfa* grass rope serve the purpose? He dismissed the idea. The rope was anchored to a rock outside the shaft. It probably wouldn't be long enough anyway.

'Wilson, I can't get through. . . where are you?' She was on the run, trying to find her way back. Two options; neither of them might save her. Wilson Ryder was pinned by indecision. Yet the longer he took, the more the passages would fill. I've found her again, only to lose her again.

Ryder flashed his light back to the entrance. The light revealed the body-shaped lids of mummy cases. 'Good luck, Bowman,' Neith said. 'But be very careful. . . You will need all your wits to succeed.'

He saw the one he had broken. The mummy's head angled towards Ryder as if it were trying to see him through the wrappings. A sprinkling of sand hissed on Ryder's boot. Ryder was not seeing the mummy, although his eyes were fixed on it; his attention converged as if he were taking aim at it with his bow and arrow. Ryder saw a possibility. A child looked at everything in terms of its opportunity for creative use and, like a child, Ryder had never lost that ability to discover fresh uses for things. He saw the mummy with new eyes. He ran to it. He shoved the painted mummy lid aside and hooked an arm around the mummy's waist, hauling it out.

'Sorry, old friend. You're our guide today.' It was the body of a full grown man, but light as *papier mache*. Mummies lost three-quarters of their body weight in the blasting drying-power of natron and it weighed no more than a child.

He held it fast under one arm and ran back into the maze. He felt for a loose end of bandage as he ran. Don't think of it as a body. Think of it as a ball of thread. But where did the grisly bobbin of thread begin? Some mummies were impossible to unwind, the bandages black and hardened with resin, but his fingertips found a rough, cracking edge like a dried leaf.

He grabbed the edge, with fingers extended around the handle of the torch. The wobbling beam lit the face from beneath the opened mouth, like crude 'spook lighting' in a horror movie, turning the bandaged features into glowing rims and dark pools, but the crumbling form under his arm was no film prop. He pulled on the edge. It broke.

His fingertips hunted for another tag to grab. There, another roughened edge met his fingers, on the mummy's head; it was loose and frayed, but not as brittle. His fingers clamped on it and he tugged. The bandage ripped from the head with a sound like a kitchen paper towel coming off a roll along its perforations. A faintly sweet odour of mummification spices rose to Ryder's nostrils.

Using the mummy like a giant bobbin, Ryder unspooled a length of bandage as he went. Snakeback barked warningly. They ran into a blank wall. The maze went three ways. Ryder made a choice, went into the middle one and followed it, winding out the bandage behind him, beginning with the mummy's head.

'Keep calling!' he yelled to Janet. 'I'm coming!'

'It's filling up around me. Quickly!'

Ryder's weaving light flashed off stone walls, then flared on a blank wall. He had run into a dead end. Snakeback whined in frustration. They doubled back, tripped over the bandage and snapped it. Oh no. This was no time for running repairs. But his plan couldn't work unless the thread remained intact. He swiftly knotted the broken ends together. A shower like sand hit his shoulder. He doubled back to where the corridor branched.

Try the left one.

That worked. They were running deeper into the maze. Another choice of passages. Left or right? Snakeback seemed to want to go right. Ryder followed, pulling on the human spool. The mummy, while light, made an awkward load, its legs and feet jamming in the corners and squeaking against the walls. He tugged and heard a sharper rip as the end stuck. The bandage came free. He looked down. The exposed face of the mummy stared back at him, shocked.

The mummy looked even more shocked when Ryder knocked off its head with his fist. Now he fed out a bit of bandage from around the mummy's neck and shoulder, tying it to the loose end. He ran on. Losing the head made the mummy smaller and easier to get around corners. Another dead end.

He went back, careful not to break the yellowy-brown trail on the floor. Left this time and along a rectilinear passage, filling fast with chippings from the ceiling. Another choice. Could I be wrong again? Luck had to be with them eventually.

Luck.

Maybe he was supposed to think that. Maybe the malignant owner of this tomb wanted to play with him a bit more. Ryder's light and his hopes dashed on another blank wall. A dead end? No. A free standing wall. There were passages behind it, to take him on. He had spooled out most of the bandages from the mummy's shoulders. Small protective amulets — faience udjat-eyes and a heart scarab — flew out as the mummy unwound and the chest cavity broke with a dry snapping sound. Only the bandages had been holding it together. Now the arms were hampering him. He ripped them off, leaving them on the floor, pointing the way out of the maze.

He headed left and down another long stretch, shedding thread like a spider. Dust, some of it mummy dust, thickened the air. He was breathing heavily and he felt dry particles swarm in his lungs and settle there, blocking the air. He coughed.

'Janet. . . where. . .?' He dodged as a thunder of chippings descended from the ceiling and he pulled the dog to one side.

'Will. . . oh please. . . hurry!' She was near. Just behind a wall, but which wall? He finished unspooling the trunk and reached the legs. He broke them off at the pelvis and took one, leaving the other on the floor. The smaller circumference of the leg slowed him. He turned a corner. He was down to the knee. He broke the knee, now running with just a lower leg and foot. She'd better turn up soon.

A shower of dust rose like a cloud and through it stumbled Janet Nancarrow behind a torchbeam, a small carved pillar in her hand. She threw herself gratefully into Ryder's arms. Snakeback barked at her in uproarious joy.

'Snake boy! You, too! Thank heavens. We've found each other. Now quickly, Wilson, just show me the way out of here!'

Ryder waggled the mummy's foot under her nose. 'Just follow the mummy.' Then Ryder noticed that the bandages had come off the fragment of mummy and all that he now held in his hand was a bare, withered foot. 'Have you lost your mind, Wilson? How's a mummy's foot going to help?'

Janet gaped at Ryder as if he had taken leave of his senses.

'You're right. It's useless.' He tossed it disgustedly over his shoulder.

'Then what, Wilson?' She was scared and demanding. He hardly felt it was the time to ask her what she was doing down here ahead of him.

'Follow the trail,' he said roughly, yanking her arm.

'What trail?'

'The mummy trail.'

'You can't be serious.'

'It's unravelled.'

'You're unravelled.' He reached the trail of linen. It wasn't yellow any more. It was white, quickly vanishing under dust and limestone chippings.

What was the rest of the trail like? Had it vanished already? He almost yanked his archaeological partner around a bend in pursuit of the swiftly vanishing trail. It vanished under fragments. Snakeback picked it up on the other side and sped after it.

'You're ripping my arm off, Wilson,' Janet complained. A pile of tomb chippings rose in front of them. They ran over it. It crunched under their feet. The trail was buried. They had lost it. No, there it was on the other side.

It was much easier going back. They were making good time, Snakeback following it with ease. But now the trail ended. Snakeback gave a whine of frustration and scurried in circles, looking in vain for the covered trail.

A discarded knee peeping up through the rubble pointed the way. Snakeback set off again. 'Thanks,' Ryder muttered as he dragged Janet after the dog into a new passage. This time a gruesome pointing leg revealed the way.

Now the trail vanished under a sea of tomb chippings. They were piled halfway up the wall. Snakeback detected a single mummified fingertip showing above the rubble. It pointed the way. They scrambled over the pile, following its line of direction.

But now the trail had gone and it wasn't just in this passage. It was in the next and the next. Were they still going the right way or going around in circles? Snakeback stopped and attacked the surface with its front paws, vigorously scratching the pile as though digging for an old bone, sending a shower of debris out through its back legs. The animal yelped in excitement. It dug its long snout into the pile and came up with a mummified hand in its jaws and dropped it at Janet's feet.

'Great, Snake boy, but what does that tell us?' Janet said. She gasped as a shower of dust from the roof hit her head.

'It tells us we're going in roughly the right direction,' Ryder said. 'Now let's see; I think we go right from here.' He changed his mind. 'No, maybe that way. . . I'm pretty sure. . .'

'Wilson, we're going to *die*! Following bits of mummy cloth around is a lunatic idea — especially with all this stuff coming down on top of it.'

'You've got a better plan?'

'No.'

'Then let's keep going. And if you want to point fingers, it was pretty lunatic of you to come down here alone in the first place. . .'

She screamed. A roar of chippings came at them like a wave, throwing them both off their feet. She dropped her jewelled pillar and she scratched around for it. 'Get up. Run!' he yelled.

'Not without the amulet!' Now she was digging for the amulet like the dog on all fours. 'Got it!' She pulled it out.

Chippings, pouring from the ceiling, trapped Ryder's legs. He pulled one leg free, then the next and took Janet's arm, hauling her up. She spat grit out of her mouth. The air wheezed in Ryder's lungs. They ran on.

Then, blessedly, they were out of the maze. There was a dumping sound behind them like a big wave landing on a beach and it made the floor tremble. A tidal wave of chippings and dust rushed at them and swirled around them as they ran for the rope.

Janet went up first, careful to tuck the Djed column amulet safely away before mounting the rope. Ryder swung the dog over his shoulder, where it clung by its forelegs and he followed Janet up the swaying rope. Dust from the collapsing maze rose like smoke around them.

But they had succeeded. He had found the first amulet and the biggest surprise of all — he had found Janet Nancarrow.

The backbone amulet/71

I don't believe in coincidences like this, he thought, clambering up to the fresh air. I think she has some explaining to do.

8

Janet

THEY RESTED IN THE DEEPER SHADOW of the quarry and caught their breath.

Janet recovered enough to sit up first. 'I'm sorry, Will. I nearly ruined everything didn't I?' She took out the Djed column, which she had stuffed into her blouse on the rope climb, and leaned against the rock to look at it. Even though she was still struggling for breath, her eyes shone. 'But we have it!' It was a small object like a palmette column with four capitals, one on top of the other, looking like a section of vertebrae. It was made of white alabaster.

'You always did want to be first to everything,' Ryder said.

Neith, who had vanished into the quarry, came to them and looked imperiously down her nose at the lanky, boyish woman in dusty khaki fieldclothes who sat against the rock.

'Who are you?' she demanded. 'Are you the Lost One?'

'Who are *you*?' Janet shot back at the spectral girl standing over her. Janet feared her intentions and held the Djed column protectively to her chest.

'This is Neith, Opener of Ways, Mistress of the Bow and Ruler of Arrows,' Ryder said. 'And this is Janet Nancarrow,' he continued.

'Neith, did you say?'

'Yes.'

'*The* Neith.'

'That's what she claims.'

'Then I'm Nefertiti,' Janet said. 'Neith is a goddess.'

'Something you are evidently not,' Neith said, sweeping her eyes disdainfully over Janet's clothing. 'What were you doing in the tomb?'

'Yes, what were you doing down there?' Ryder said.

Janet deflected the question by going onto the attack. 'What were you doing coming here after me? Didn't I tell you not to try to follow? Didn't you listen to my tape?'

'I did. But it didn't stop me.'

She surprised him then by throwing her arms around him and hugging him demonstratively. 'That was the maddest, bravest thing you've ever done, Wilson! Thankyou for not listening to me. I've never been so grateful in my life! You don't know what a relief it is having you and Snakeback here. Now you're with me, I know I can succeed.'

'Succeed at what?'

'Gathering the sacred amulets of Osiris, of course. Do you know what concentration of power comes with them? The holder of all fourteen will have the power of a deity. A real deity,' she said, throwing a sceptical glance at the girl.

Neith stiffened. 'The power is not for you. It is for Horus and Osiris. . . only by these means can Seth be overthrown and the mummy of Osiris be restored to full life in the Land of the Blessed.'

'Power that can raise the dead from the tomb. Think of it!' Janet exclaimed.

'All I want is the power to be able to take you back,' Ryder said. 'For some reason that can't happen until the job is done. I have to regain the amulets first.'

Janet looked appalled. 'Going back is the last thing on my mind. Think of what we've discovered by coming here!'

'I don't care about that right now. I just want to get you back.'

'As black-and-white as ever. Don't you know what our coming here means? We've uncovered something far greater than truth. We've spent years as archaeologists digging up the past in search of the truth, when in fact just beyond our excavated tombs and restored temples lay something of far greater significance and radiance. Myth. And we've found a way into it.

'Myth isn't just myth, don't you see? Myth has a parallel reality, like another dimension. It had to have a reality when you think about it. How else could the same basic creation stories and myths of dying gods emerge in every civilisation, the same patterns endlessly repeated? They have leaked through into race consciousness, through the dreamers, the true priests who mediate between the two universes. Myth is the ultimate truth at the back of reality. Myths are dreams that we struggle to reach throughout our lives, but never can — but *we have*. By some freak of circumstance, we have stepped through a doorway into the realm of myth — into one of the most ancient myths of all, a primordial Egypt in the age of Osiris.

'The ultimate reality behind the universe is not just another dose of reality — it is something far different and more radiant. It is myth itself. Heaven is myth and that's the most wonderful discovery of all.'

'I believe in truths.'

'Do you? How do we know that myth isn't God's language to man? Think, Wilson,' she said passionately. 'Would Adam, Eve, the Garden of Eden, Noah, Abraham, Joseph, Moses, the Exodus — for which, we know there is no shred of archaeological evidence — David and Solomon be any less significant if they were proved to be myth? Myth is the truth of the spirit.'

'I'll stick to simple truths. You came here and I want to take you back. That's what I came for and that's what I'm going to do.'

'Back to a world where myth is dead? Why would I want to go back? Why would you? Don't look so angry, Wilson. I know you've probably put yourself to some trouble coming after me, but we *are* scientists, let me remind you. We must explore this universe. We must learn every little thing there is to learn about it.'

'How did you know where to look for the Djed column?' Neith said.

'It was written on the walls of a tomb of Ani, the priest of Osiris.' Janet pulled out some folded paper from a pocket. 'I've got the whole list here.' She consulted her notes. 'Now let's see what's next.'

'You found it alone, from that?'

'With some help from Ani. I found him. The tomb gave me clear instructions of where he would be. Ani provided me with a guide to lead me here, a dwarf who wouldn't come down with me into the tomb, but instead ran away.' Janet put the tomb transcription away and looked up at the blackened sun.

'What happened to the light? It can't be night yet. The morning sun was shining when I went down.'

'It is the blind eye of Horus,' Neith said, as if Janet ought to know.

'An eclipse,' Ryder explained. He told Janet when it had happened and how he had killed the wild boar to protect the child.

'Very good. But it's a pity you weren't able to stop the boar from stealing the eye of Horus. That's the most important of all the amulets and you could have saved me — I mean us — some trouble.'

Neith frowned. 'The Djed column is not yours. You must give it to me,' she said.

'I'll keep it, thanks. I risked my neck going down there for it.' Janet slipped the small amulet into a drawstring canvas bag on her belt.

Neith gave her a stare as if trying to decide whether to press the issue. There would be time enough to obtain it later, she seemed to decide. She gave a faint shrug. 'Then take no risk with it. But we must go quickly now in search of the next amulet which is. . .'

'The buckle of Isis,' Janet put in. 'See, I'm ahead of you.'

'No-one is ahead of the Opener of Ways,' Neith corrected her. 'You must follow me.' Then she turned and left, heading back in the direction of the river. They got up to follow. Ryder collected his bow and quivers of arrows.

'Trust you, Wilson. You wouldn't be parted from Snakeback and your precious bows and arrows.' They left the shattered place of stones and followed the girl.

Janet directed a stare at her. 'Is she really Neith?'

'She's unearthly,' he said. 'She frightens me.'

'Good. Don't forget that. Remember she's a pagan entity and you know your horror of paganism. Or is it really horror, Wilson? Maybe it's fascination. Anyway,

I think she could be useful as a guide. Rather quaint and exotic, isn't she? Look at that mound of hair and vase-like figure. From behind, she reminds me of a wooden statue of the lady Nai in the Louvre. Did you notice her eyes? Dramatic slashes of *kohl*, like the eyes on a mummy lid. And her perfume could drug a honey bee.'

The dog loped happily beside the girl. 'Snakeback has made a friend,' Janet said pointedly, 'and so have you, I think.'

'What happened to you in the tomb?' Ryder asked, ignoring the remark. 'I want to know.'

'I told you in my tape. That's the way it happened. I don't know how, but it did. What happened to *you*?'

He shrugged. 'It began with the girl who appeared like a ghostly visitation. We saw her in the desert on the day you were supposed to come out of the tomb.'

'I did come out of the tomb. I just happened to come out on the other side of it. Anyway, go on.'

'I was practising archery and shot an arrow into the air for Snakeback to fetch, but he couldn't find it. This girl appeared with the arrow in her hand and carried it off. We went after her, but lost her. Then later, after you went missing and I was lying in the tomb, I saw her again. I was dreaming, I think and, when she appeared, I simply followed her here.'

'I thought you came here after *me*,' she said.

'Well, what do you think? '

'I wonder. You're staring at her awfully hard.'

Was he? He was unaware of it. 'Of course I came after you. But what are you planning, Janet? Why are you trying to gather these amulets for yourself? You can't mean it. Just accepting for a moment that there is some kind of pagan influence surrounding them, is that what you want? Magical power? Where are your beliefs? You're not a heathen. You'll need to cling to your beliefs more than ever in this place.'

'I don't know what I believe in, Wilson. But I know I don't believe in the powerlessness and workaday reality of my life as it was. There has to be more mystery to life — more magic and more power. We are opposites. I want myth, magic and mystery. You want to cling to simple beliefs and you dread any collision with anything else.'

Now it was Janet who frightened him. The daring face held a fierce determination. A glitter-bright purpose had entered her eyes. When the willowy Janet set her mind on a course, she turned into tensile steel.

Neith led them back to the reed boat and they continued southwards with Ryder and Janet standing on the deck in the ghostly light of the eclipse. Janet ran an arm around his shoulder and hugged him. 'Thank you for coming to rescue me, even though I didn't really want rescuing. But I did need your help.'

He turned and held her by the shoulders. 'What are you saying, Janet? Don't you want to go back? Don't you want your life — with me?'

'Now I've upset you. Of course, I want a life with you, but why does it have to be there — prosaic *there*. Why not magical here? Doesn't your heart hunger for mystery?'

'It does, but I have found a greater mystery.'

'Ah, your beliefs. And you think your God and Saviour is here, do you?'

'He is everywhere, even here where these people are reaching out from their darkness and ignorance.'

'There you are wrong. There are entities here who live in radiance. Your lady guide is one of them, possibly. You have always loved that mysterious radiance. Don't think I haven't noticed. And don't think I didn't notice it the first time I met you, when we walked around the Cairo museum together. I saw what it was that held you captive. I could not compete with that then, nor can I compete with it now, except here, where the possibility of transcendence is possible. Here I could gain that very power and mystery that attracts you. Think how much more you would love me if I were more than a woman.' The tall young woman shook her boyish head sadly. 'You're always looking for something more.' She took his face in her hands. Her touch was not cool like Neith's. It was firm and possessive. 'Help me, Wilson and I — we — can be more than we dreamed and love each other more than we dreamed.'

'If you don't want to come back, why should I go through with the quest to find the amulets?'

'You have no choice. You can't go back until the quest is completed.'

'Without you, what must I go back to?'

'Back to reassuring reality and your faith in an historical truth. But there is another higher reason for you to succeed. This quest is a cosmic struggle between opposing powers of darkness and light. If the light fails here, what repercussions might ensue throughout history?'

He remembered then his shock at the sight of Isis and her child, and about Neith's reference to the child as the saviour of the world. It had seemed pagan and eclipsed by the incarnation that followed, yet could the myth of Osiris — a man-god who suffered and rose from the dead — and the myth of the mother whose child was born in a humble setting, but who was to be the saviour be pre-echoes of what was to come? Could their failure in this quest reverberate to that later incarnation and disturb it? Was the working out of this saga a part of the other great working out, the great expiation of the evil in the world and in the souls of men?

Ryder watched a pair of Mesniu dwarfs hauling on a rope to trim the sail. Another stood at the stern manning a long spear-tipped steering oar. Their signals to each other, sharp clicks like insects, carried clearly across the boat. What did these stunted men with their bulging faces and eyes know about God and eternity? They believed in a creator god named Ptah who created man on a potter's wheel.

Ryder hadn't prayed in a long time, but he said a quiet prayer for illumination and strength in this darkened world of eclipse.

9

The demon charioteers of Seth

THEY BERTHED AMONG THE REEDS on the river bank and set off into the Western desert, with a supply of food and water in bags hitched over their shoulders, although Neith took neither. The crew remained on board.

Neith did not strike out ahead this time, Ryder noticed. He soon found out why as they reached a plain. Beyond it, in the gloom of the eclipse, lay the smudges of mountains. 'This plain is patrolled by the demon charioteers of Seth,' she warned him. 'In the darkness we may be fortunate and escape, but we are open to attack at any time. Keep your bow ready, Bowman.'

Ryder was puzzled, as much by the new threat as by the nature of it. The archaeologist in him was curious. 'Charioteers?' he said. 'But the horse and the chariot were only late introductions into Egypt, appearing somewhere around the fifteenth Hyksos Dynasty. The Egyptians improved the chariot and made it faster, but it was certainly unknown in early pharaonic, let alone pre-dynastic times.'

'You are thinking in lines,' Neith said critically. She was starting to sound like Janet.

'Myth is eternal,' Janet said. 'It can draw on the past or the future, just as it has done with you.'

'And with you.'

'Perhaps, but I have an idea I am not supposed to be here. I was merely a means to bringing you here.'

Snakeback growled low in its throat. 'They are coming,' Neith said in a low voice. 'Two of them, very fast.'

The group had just passed a big outcrop of rock and faced a bare stretch of plain. Ryder stopped and peered into the gloom. The dark silhouettes of twin-horsed chariots were running an oblique line towards them, throwing up ribbons of dust. Ryder was struck at once by their speed. Demon charioteers, she had said. They were certainly travelling at demonic speed. But then the Egyptian chariot was a lightning fast and deadly weapon. Egyptian innovation had taken the cumbersome Aryan invention and made it skeletal, lighter and infinitely more nimble. The chariots ran between two horses at breathtaking speed so that they became high-speed launching platforms for the missiles of their occupants — arrows and spears.

Ryder handed his shoulder bag of food and water to Janet and slipped his composite bow off his shoulder. 'Get behind that rock,' he told them. Snakeback's tail beat against Ryder's leg. Janet was happy to obey, but Neith merely climbed the rock so that she could gain a better view.

Ryder thought of times when he had stood at the edge of the desert with his bow, taking aim at some stationary target that he imagined to be a pharaoh attacking in his chariot. But that had been make-believe and the target had been stationary — usually a bag of sand. These targets were not only moving; they were coming to kill. He saw the curve of bows in their hands. He saw something else. They did not have human heads, but shadow heads. One had the pricked ears of a jackal. The other the curved beak of a vulture. They were skilful riders, able to ride alone with the reins lashed around themselves while shooting a bow.

Ryder felt their intent hit him like pressure waves. He slipped on his bracer and tab. He chose an arrow from the quiver, not one that the Mesniu had fashioned. They were well made, but were wooden and imperfect and could not give him the accuracy and length of cast he needed now. He took two broadhead alloy arrows and kept one arrow in readiness in his hand, while nocking the other to the bowstring.

He drew the arrow to the anchor point at his chin. Ryder felt that unique convergence of senses that the marksman knows. The world reduced to his targets. Their place on the horizon and the line his arrow would take, bisected like cross-hairs. He felt the space that lay between them, swept the emptiness like radar and then searched for the solidity of the target. His senses computed distance, windage, the speed of his assailants.

He had chosen the charioteer on the left, the one with the jackal head. He felt all these factors converge down and down to the point of an arrow. He released.

They were around three hundred metres away and couldn't imagine themselves to be under threat yet. Egyptian bows had a range of around two hundred metres at best. The arrow blurred across the gap. He saw it climb, lost sight of its fall, but knew it was true as if his mind had gone out with it. The jackal-headed one clutched his chest and snapped out of his chariot like a leaf taken by a gust. He saw the surprised twist of the head of the other beaked one and then sensed the flash of fear and hate as he looked back at Ryder.

The chariot swiftly closed with Ryder. He was now in range of the charioteer's arrows. The vulture man took aim.

Ryder put the second arrow in place and knelt, making a a smaller target of himself. The empty chariot, driverless, careered in a wide circle, gradually losing speed. Vulture head shot. An arrow zipped harmlessly overhead. The charioteer did not wait for Ryder's response. He took evasive action, swerving. Ryder's arrow struck the frame of the chariot, a hand's breadth from his body.

The charioteer lost his fight and sped towards the horizon. 'Don't let him escape,' Neith called from the top of the rock. 'He will bring others back with him.'

Ryder had another arrow in place and drew it to his chin. But he hesitated. He couldn't shoot at a fleeing man — even one with a vulture head.

He'd try to catch him instead. He slipped the bow over his shoulder and made a run for the abandoned chariot. It had stopped and the sweating horses were standing, pawing at the sand. Ryder had been harness-racing once as a youth. It couldn't be much different, except that in harness-racing you sat. This would need more balance, especially if he needed to use the bow. Maybe it would be better to cut one of the horses free and ride bareback. No time. The charioteer was getting away. Ryder leapt up into the basket and grasped the reins. He flicked them over the horses' backs and they reared, sensing an alien presence. He flicked the reins again and they took off after the fleeing charioteer.

The base of the chariot was a semi-circular frame

across which were stretched a web of leather strips. These bobbed like springs under his feet absorbing some of the shock as the wheels struck bumps along the ground. Many depictions of pharaohs in battle showed the pharaoh alone in his chariot, despatching his enemies. Archaeologists believed that this was an artistic convention designed to make the king look more heroic, and that he would have needed a charioteer to steer while he fought.

The demon charioteers had given lie to this and now Ryder would find out for himself if it were possible for a man to guide the flight of two horses and arrows from a bow at the same time.

The fleeing charioteer gave a glance over his shoulder. He had evidently planned to race back to his base for reinforcements but, seeing Ryder in pursuit and aware of the vulnerability of his exposed back, he thought better of it and turned to engage. Ryder set his course for the vulture-man and lashed the reins around one arm. The desert plain was nothing like a harness-racing track, he discovered. The uneven sand, at greater speed, made the chariot as unstable as a surfboard in choppy waves. With the reins over one arm, he groped for an arrow from his quiver and put it unsteadily to his bowstring. The hard wooden wheels hit a bump. The speeding platform bucked. Ryder flew. Without free hands to steady himself, he hit the rail. He clamped the arrow to the bow with one hand and grabbed for the rail with the other. Another lurch, this time in the opposite direction, threw him back into the basket. Perhaps the archaeologists had been right. It was hard enough to stay on the moving platform, let alone use a bow from it.

Demon-head had not failed to notice his ineptitude.

Ryder saw the flash of his beak as he laughed. They were closing swiftly. Ryder tried to take aim. The charioteer was doing the same. He noticed something else. The Egyptian's bow was much smaller than his, giving him freedom of movement. Ryder's heavy tackle was unwieldy by comparison. The lower limb of the bow hit the rail as he tried to lift it. He was going to be late.

The charioteer shot. This may not have been the best idea in the world, Ryder thought, ducking. His horses reared and whinnied. The charioteer flashed past, turned. Ryder lost the reins and the horses veered, snapping him to the floor of the basket. He straightened. The horses were out of control, whinnying and bucking. He saw why. The charioteer was having sport with him. He had hit one of Ryder's horses. An arrow protruded from the flank of the contorting animal. Ryder struggled to turn, but the horses were out of control.

He looked over his shoulder. The demon charioteer had no compunction about shooting him in the back and was already taking aim as he came at an oblique angle. The bow was bent, the arrow ready to fly. This time the arrow was aimed at him. Ryder jumped. He hit the sand and rolled, holding the bow over his head.

Sand burst up into his mouth and eyes. The force of landing knocked the air out of his lungs. Had the charioteer shot his arrow? Ryder scrambled to his knees. The charioteer didn't need to shoot the next arrow. He was simply going to run Ryder down.

Ryder saw a streak of brown with flashing teeth run at the horses' legs as Snakeback flew at them. The horses shied. Ryder dived and rolled, the thunder of the hooves shaking the earth under his body as it passed. The charioteer turned in a surprisingly tight circle and raced back to finish him off. Ryder got up. The horizon spun. The swiftly-growing chariot and span of horses twisted as if in the shimmer of heat, sliding out of focus. Ryder shook his head to clear it. Amazingly, he had clung to the bow and still had the end in one hand, but he had lost the arrow. He felt for another one.

His hand slapped an empty quiver at his side. His metal alloy arrows had fallen out. Luckily, a few of the rougher-hewn Mesniu arrows remained. He nocked one to his bowstring, taking swift aim. The rapid convergence of target and arrowtip told him that he was too late, that even if he struck his target full in the heart, it would be too late to deflect the arrow that was about to leap from the charioteer's bow. The arrow was aimed at Ryder's heart.

Ryder flicked the aim from the jackal-man's heart to his bow hand and shot. The arrow snapped through flesh and nailed the hand to the handle of the bow. It was enough to deflect the aim a few degrees so that the arrow flashed past Ryder's shoulder, so close that the fletching hissed across his sleeve and it went by like the black wind of a bullet. The charioteer gave a scream like an enraged animal, but he remained in control of the chariot. He ripped out the arrow that pinned his hand to the bow handle and reached with his good hand for a spear. Enough of this, Wilson Ryder thought. He hit the demon charioteer full in the chest with his next arrow. The vulture-man fell.

Ryder patted the dog who had saved him from the charging horses of the demon's chariot. 'Good work, Snakeback.'

He collected his arrows with Snakeback's help and went after the attacker's chariot. It had come to a stop near an outcrop of rocks. He climbed into the chariot and rode it back to the first chariot with Snakeback running happily beside him. Only one horse was standing. The other, shot by the charioteer, had died in its traces.

We now have three horses and a chariot, Ryder thought. This would quicken the pace. He found a scythe-shaped sword in a sheath inside the chariot and used it to cut the remaining horse free from the chariot. He used the reins to tie the horse behind his own chariot and climbed back into it. With a flick of the reins, he sent the horses galloping back to the rock where Neith and Janet waited.

'Not bad, Wilson,' Janet said, coming out from behind the rock. 'Where did you learn all that stuff? Not in archaeology.'

He drew in the horses.

'You did magnificently, Bowman,' Neith said with shining eyes, smiling down at him from the top of the rock. 'I can see now why you were the one chosen by the Universal Lord, the High God, from the beginning of time. We must hurry to the mountains. When the patrol does not return, others will come looking.'

'That's why I brought the chariot and the spare horse. With these we can move much faster. Maybe I should cut my two free and we can all go on horseback. There's a horse for each of us.'

Neith looked appalled. 'Only barbarians and Asiatics sit on horses,' she said contemptuously. 'No Egyptian would think of it.'

Ryder shrugged. 'Sorry, I forgot.' Horse-riding was taboo for the ancient Egyptians.

'I shall travel in the chariot with you,' she said, imperiously. 'The Lost One can go on the horse's back.'

'That's handy for her, being squeamish about horses,' Janet said, suspiciously. 'She wouldn't happen to want to ride alone with you by any chance?'

'You know how they were about riding on the backs of horses,' he reminded her.

'Funny about that. They never seemed to have any trouble riding on donkeys,' she said sceptically. 'They rode happily on the backs of donkeys in all periods of history. I often wondered if it really was a taboo about horseback riding or merely because the Asiatic horse was too small in stature.'

'Well, now you know.'

She shrugged. 'She probably couldn't stay on a horse anyway. I'll take it. I used to ride bareback as a kid. It holds no terrors for me.'

10

Stronghold of the lioness

NEITH'S HAIR TRAILED BEHIND her in the wind as the chariot swept over the sand towards the rapidly approaching line of mountains.

'What will face us there?' Ryder said.

'The demon priestess of Sekhmet, the slayer of men. She guards the sacred headrest.' Sekhmet was the marauding lioness goddess of the Western desert, believed by the Egyptians to be the hot breath of sandstorms, a goddess of war and chaos.

'A lioness or a woman?'

'Both. Her yellow eyes will be watching us already.' Grains of sand hit Ryder's face and a wind buffeted them.

'Look,' Neith said. Smudges of billowing sand were rushing across the plain to engage them like an army. 'The breath of Sekhmet. She knows we are seeking her.'

'Where will we find her?'

'In her lair, in a mountain with a peak that is itself shaped like a headrest,' she told him.

Brown swirling dust enveloped them, turning the already darkened sky into the colour and texture of hessian. Janet reined in her horse to gallop beside the chariot so that they would not become parted and lose contact in the dust. She rode very surely on the horse, even without a saddle. She held herself erect with an air that managed to convey her scorn for the Egyptian standing in the chariot beside Ryder.

The wind made a whining sound. It sounded like the complaint of a ravenous animal. 'I will guide you,' Neith said. 'Give me the reins.' Ryder handed them over to her. He could see nothing now. The dust and wind plucked at their clothes and swirled around them like a whirlwind.

Neith changed course and Janet followed. The Opener of Ways had the ability to see through the dense columns of dust that marched in against them. The wind seemed to be gaining in strength, but Neith pressed on. Without her, they may have travelled in circles, but suddenly the wind abated and they were across the plain and running along the foot of a mountain towards a ravine.

They looked up to the head of the ravine. A peak, shaped like an ancient Egyptian headrest, dominated the skyline. At the base of the peak lay the small dark shadow of a cave entrance. Neith slowed the horses as they reached the mouth of the ravine. The horses whinnied and reared. 'They are afraid,' Neith said. 'They can smell her.'

'Sekhmet?'

She nodded.

Snakeback was uneasy, too. Until then it had run happily beside them. Now the dog stiffened and the spine of fur sat upright on its back. It was not called a Lion Dog for nothing. It could smell cat.

They dismounted from the chariot and secured the horses to a stunted tree. Janet slid off her horse with a practised air and hitched it to a nearby bush. They would go the rest of the way on foot.

Although there was no sign of danger, Ryder could feel a presence in the silence of the ravine as palpable as the challenge of a sentry and it immediately set his nerves tingling. He cautiously put an arrow to his bowstring.

They went carefully into the ravine. Ryder swung his head slowly from side to side, feeling for an attacker's presence just as he felt for the solidity of a target when aiming his bow.

Sekhmet, the powerful, the slayer of humankind. All Egyptian goddesses were forms of the one great goddess and Sekhmet was an early form of the great goddess Hathor, in her phase of destruction before she became the lady of love, music, dancing, wine and pleasure. Sekhmet was sent by the sun god Re to punish humanity when he discovered that they were plotting against him and turning towards the Dragon of Darkness. He sent the goddess in the form of a giant, marauding lioness. By day she stalked humanity, killing and devouring in such a rampage that the Nile turned red with their slaughter and the river banks turned soggy with blood like red marshes. By night she hid in the hills and rocks of the desert. Her hunger for blood became unquenchable.

Fearing that no living soul would remain to serve him, Re had a change of heart and devised a trick to stop her. Overnight, he had red ochre, the colour of blood, brought from the island of Elephantine beneath the first cataract, and mixed it with barley mash in a vast quantity of beer. This he used to fill seven thousand jars which were poured out over the ground to a depth of three hands. When the goddess awoke to complete her task of destroying humanity, she saw the red liquid and roared with savage delight. Taking it to be the blood of her victims, she bent and drank deeply, but the sleep-inducing beer intoxicated her brain so that her rage passed and humanity was saved.

They had gone no more that fifty metres when a scream of terror from the horses broke in upon them. They turned to see a tan, smooth-stretching streak run from the hillside and strike at the nearest of the chariot horses. In a blur it tore the horse down as if it were no bigger than a calf, spilling the chariot as it sank claws and fangs into its neck. The other horse fell with it, kicking its legs in the air and whinnying.

Ryder took quick aim and shot. The arrow nicked the shoulder of the lioness, but plunged into the dying horse. The attacker let go of the horse and roared, the sound rolling down the ravine like a rockslide. It turned yellow-eyed flashes of hate at the bowman before she loped arrogantly up the hillside, tail stiff and twitching, losing herself among the boulders.

'What do we do now?' Janet said. 'Leave the horses to the mercy of that thing?' Now only two horses remained.

'We must continue,' Neith said. 'If Sekhmet thinks we are more concerned about the horses than the prize, she will keep us here. We must go on. We must gain the sacred headrest before Seth's squadrons of chariots come after us.'

It was a hard decision to make. If they stayed, they risked capture. If they went on, they risked losing their transport back to the river and without horses, even though only two remained, their chances of avoiding capture were slender.

They moved on. Curious, Ryder thought. Snakeback hadn't warned them of the cat's impending attack. It was a lion dog and this was its enemy. Maybe the lioness had cleverly stalked the horses, staying downwind.

The defile seemed to sit up and stare at them. Ryder felt an intent, yellow-angry stare as they progressed towards the base of the peak that was shaped like an Egyptian headrest. There were boulders on the hillside, good cover for the lioness. It might spring at any moment.

'Stay close together,' he murmured. He was thankful for the presence of the strong-shouldered dog loping along beside them, its tail held out and quivering, its nose plucking the air. This was what Snakeback was built to do.

A piece of tawny mountainside detached itself from the rest and flew at them. Snakeback gave a warning bark and bravely flew at their attacker. The dog stood no chance. The cat was the size of a cow, yet the dog's fearless charge slowed the beast, giving Ryder a chance to loose an arrow. A good, solid, straight hit. He felt it from the moment the arrow left the bow but, unaccountably, it missed.

The cat made a glide to one side, seemed to change its mind about attacking and flew across their path and up the other side of the ravine. Snakeback was built to run down lions until they dropped from exhaustion, but it came back happily to Ryder's side, panting, its tongue lolling from its mouth, seeming content with its effort. Why hadn't it given chase? Where had the lioness gone? There was no sign of it climbing the hillside. Was it crouching behind the next boulder?

Ryder prepared with another arrow. He gestured the others to slow. He stepped ahead and with the bow ready, swung around the boulder. He lowered the bow in puzzlement. Where had it vanished to?

'It is a demon of death and destruction,' Neith reminded him.

Evidence of this came to offend their noses as they proceeded up the ravine. The stink of death rose like the clouds of flies. There was soon not only the smell of it, but the sight of it. Dead animals, gazelles, bulls, an ape, an ibex — even a headless man stuck in the fork of a low acacia tree. Flies fretted around the corpses like the sound of worry and despair. It was a valley of carnage.

'Don't look to either side,' Neith told them. 'This is a display meant to strike terror into us.'

'It's succeeding,' Janet muttered.

They reached the end of the ravine and climbed up a narrow path towards the darker shadow of a cave entrance. 'This is the cat's lair,' Neith said.

'What chance have we got if we go in there?' Janet said in a low voice to Ryder. 'Once that cat's got us caged, there's no escape.'

'There is no other way to gain the headrest,' Neith said.

They entered the cave. Death came out like a foul wind that rushed around their legs and made them shiver. Ryder and Janet produced their torches. Neith looked surprised by the appearance of their lances of light. They cautiously followed the passage which opened into a haughty chamber. 'You will not need those,' she said. 'Look.'

Dim light like moonlight, from the eclipse, shone down from a hole in the mountain onto a slab of basalt.

On the slab, as shocking as a smear of blood, lay the Lady of Bright Red Linen. She wore a decorative wig threaded with gold and her head was supported by a headrest of carved ebony, with its base in the shape of the god Shu, her slender neck bent gracefully. Her feline profile had the pallor of sleep — or death — and she did not stir at their approach. Her mouth had the faintly downturned slant of a cat.

'The sacred headrest is around her neck,' Neith whispered. It was an amulet in gold, shaped like a headrest and threaded on a fine chain.

'What do we do?' Janet said eagerly. 'Just go and drag it off her?'

The decision was made for her by a growl like the grating of stone. It came, not from behind them, but from one side. The cat was here in the chamber with them. But how had it entered without their seeing it? It had not gone ahead of them or passed them. Was there another way into her lair?

Ryder put an arrow to the string. He glanced at Snakeback. The snake of fur had risen on its back, but its deep snout was pointed not at the lioness, but at the sleeping woman. The grating-stones rumble of the lioness drew closer and now it came into view — flattened, baleful yellow eyes, ears back, body crouched low, ready to pounce.

'Shoot now,' Neith whispered. Ryder swung the bow.

'Not at the lioness — at the woman.' Ryder had baulked at the idea of shooting a fleeing charioteer. He recoiled now at the suggestion of shooting the sleeping girl.

'Shoot.' The lioness broke from the shadows, running at them. This was the danger, not the sleeping girl.

In a bound, it would be on them, tearing with claws and fangs. Snakeback broke too, but it flew not at the lioness, but at the girl on the slab of basalt.

The lioness or the girl? 'Bowman — believe!' Neith cried.

Against all his instincts, Wilson Ryder pivoted and shot the arrow at the girl, going for the slender curve of neck. The arrow struck, the girl sat up on the slab and turned shocked, hate-filled, tawny eyes at him.

'Again!' Neith shouted. Ryder fluidly took another arrow. He saw the flying shadow of the lioness. Snakeback leapt at the girl. Ryder shot again, this time going for the heart.

The figure on the slab flashed, seemed to suck the flying shadow of the lioness into itself and then shrank into two angry eyes that threw light across the cave, then went out. The headrest amulet fell tinkling onto the basalt surface and all was silent.

'We've got it,' Janet said, running to the slab and scooping it up. 'That's two amulets down!'

They returned to the horses to find that the attack of the lioness had damaged the harness of the chariot.

Ryder cut the living horse free. It was pinned by the dead horse and by the upturned chariot. It rose, shaking and snorting, to its feet.

'We'll have to go on horseback from here,' he said.

'I will not ride a horse,' Neith said firmly.

'Then I'll ride it and you can ride with me,' he said.

'How very convenient. I think she's planned all this,' Janet said with certainty now. 'She's getting closer to you by degrees.'

Janet mounted her horse and Ryder mounted the other one and held out his hand to Neith. 'The charioteers will be coming,' he reminded her. 'They'll overtake us unless we ride.'

She shuddered, not at the thought of the charioteers, he guessed, but at the barbarity of riding on a horse, but she allowed him to swing her up in front of him, where she sat, side-saddle, her back stiffly erect.

He had never been this close to Neith before and her nearness robbed him of air to breathe. It wasn't her heady perfume that caused it, but a sense of falling into the drowning depths of her femininity. I could die in her mystery, he thought, and it would be a blessed oblivion. Up close, the refinement of her body was like a snake, sinuous and cool. She turned her head in profile and he wanted to shake his head in wonder. She was a living frescoe — a wonderfully painted profile, blue-black tresses, elongated Egyptian eye under an arched eyebrow, faintly curved nose and neat mouth and chin. His heart quaked.

'Be strong, O heart,' he heard the words spoken, not aloud, but in his mind. 'Do not tremble to your foundations. Fear me not.' But he *did* fear her. She frightened him more than the lioness.

'Aren't you two coming?' Janet said peevishly, setting off at a canter. Ryder caught up with her, Snakeback running at their side. He hoped it was not too degrading for Neith to find herself balanced on the back of a horse. She had never ridden on a horse before, that was certain, but she looked no less regal and she balanced herself by holding onto the horse's mane. It would take more than a bareback horse ride to rob Neith of her glowing divinity.

11

The Heqet frog

PERHAPS THE DUSTSTORM HAD DELAYED discovery of the fate of the two demon charioteers who had attacked them on their journey to the lair of the lioness. While they kept a cautious eye on the horizons for the appearance of chariot squadrons, none came in pursuit of them.

They rejoined the boat hidden in the reeds and continued south. Ryder and Janet rested in the deckhouse after their exertions, lying on reed mats on the wooden floor. Neith squatted, her knees drawn up under her chin, stretching the linen of her sheath dress like an Egyptian block-statue, her eyes fixed on the flame of a lamp, but turned inwards to commune with something unknowable inside herself. Ryder lay watching Neith and wondering what she was thinking. He felt drained by his proximity to her on the horse, like one who has been overlong in the glare of unbearably bright light. He was grateful to crawl into the darkness and escape.

He listened to the gentle slap of water on the hull and the aching creak of the timbers and allowed himself to think some of the thoughts he had dared not think while

Neith had been close. He had sensed that Neith was attuned to his every thought and that her serpentine body would vibrate like a tuning fork to his slightest attention.

Janet had fallen asleep by the look of her. She lay on her side, her hands tucked under her cheek, her legs drawn up and a small frown on her forehead. Janet pursued everything, even sleep, with the determination, the concentration of a hunter. Snakeback lay on its stomach like a wearied sphinx, paws outstretched, long muzzle lying flat on the floor.

The figure of Neith reminded Ryder of one of those charming depictions of Maat, the goddess of truth. Her shape, in profile, was like a familiar template in his mind that filled a shadow-space that had always waited to receive it. Contemplating her was peculiarly satisfying and soothing. He closed his eyes for a moment, just for the sweet denial of losing her image, and his pleasure was deeper when he opened his eyes again to find her still there. Are you my heart's desire? he thought. Should a man dare to want that much?

A moth circled the flame of Neith's lamp, then dived into it. Its wings spurted dry sparks briefly before it dropped, dead. There are greater dangers to me in this place than demon charioteers and monster guardians, he thought.

Ryder reluctantly let the image of Neith slip from his eyes as sleep carried him away like the boat that swept them steadily southwards.

Eventually the boat had stopped. 'Bowman.' Neith shook his shoulder. Ryder came back from a long sleep, a sleep that was not only lengthy in time, but stretched to boundless distances.

'What is it?'

'The next amulet. We have reached the island of Sobek.'

Janet sat up. 'We need the Heqet frog next,' she said, instantly alert and eager. 'A green-glazed steatite frog on a necklace. I dreamed about it.'

'I am sure you did — and about the power it and all the rest will bring when they are assembled,' Neith said critically.

Ryder gathered his composite bow and quivers of arrows and went out yawning onto the darkened deck. Am I really here? he thought. Am I here on this boat, on the most ancient river, in a time so distant it's before the age of the pharaohs?

They had anchored in the stream, a short way off from a small, sandy island. On the island was a single sycamore and a lone ridge of green rocks. The rock shifted and split as a mouth opened to reveal a canyon of teeth. It was a crocodile of heart-stopping proportions.

'Do you see it?' Janet whispered beside him on the deck.

'I could hardly miss it,' he said. 'It's like a dinosaur.'

'Not that. I'm talking about the necklace with the Heqet frog on it. It's hanging from the branch of the sycamore. Hurry, Wilson, fetch it.'

'You seem to be overlooking the small matter of the crocodile,' he said drily.

'Don't let that distract you.'

Ryder hadn't seen the necklace. He wasn't even tempted to look for it. He couldn't take his eyes off the crocodile. It was bigger than a papyrus raft and had plated skin like the reinforced metal of a tank. Would arrows do the slightest damage to it? he wondered. The eyes. He could always go for the eyes, he supposed. It may not kill it, but it would rob it of its fight long enough to allow him to go ashore and retrieve the necklace.

'Why don't we take the boat to the shore of the island and then we'll see what we can do,' he suggested.

Neith shook her head. 'While an enemy to the Mesniu, the crocodile is also sacred to them. They feel they have already gone further than their inclination tells them — they will do no more to offend it. You must do the rest.'

'What am I supposed to do?'

'Get the Heqet frog,' Janet said as if it were the most obvious thing in the world.

'Yes, but *how* — with that thing lying out there?'

'Fire a bow at it.'

'You don't fire a bow.'

'Well, you know what I mean — fire an arrow.'

'You don't fire an arrow either. You shoot it.'

'Do whatever you do with the silly thing, but hurry. It's crawling into the water.' The beast, swinging its head and tail in a grotesque waggling run, hit the water and pushed out, spreading a bow wave like a powerboat. It sank low into the water until just the bulges of its eyes, its nostrils and the jagged plates of its tail cut the surface. Each plate was the size of a shark's fin.

'Just perfect,' Ryder said.

'Well, you shouldn't have dithered about,' Janet said unsympathetically. 'You had your chance to fire at it.'

'Shoot.'

'Don't be annoying, Wilson. You'll just have to take your chances now and swim out there. We'll warn you if it comes.'

'What good will warning me do?'

'You'll know you have to swim faster.'

'I can't outswim a crocodile.'

'How do you know? I think you'll move surprisingly fast with that thing behind you,' Janet reassured him.

'We must have the Heqet frog,' Neith said firmly.

Ryder looked from his archaeological partner to the Egyptian girl. Were they both equally intent on killing him? 'Don't *you* care if I get eaten?'

'I have faith in you, Bowman, as did the High God of old.'

'You mean nothing can happen to me?' he asked hopefully. 'This is all pre-ordained — and I can't get killed?'

'Possibly,' Neith said, dubiously. 'You may be spared if that is the High God's plan, but you may, of course, lose a limb. I just hope it is not an arm. It may stop you from completing the quest since you will need to use your bow.'

'Don't stick your arms in its mouth, Wilson.'

'Thanks, Janet. You mean losing a leg is all right? I'm supposed to hop around the rest of this suicidal quest on one leg?'

'I was only making a joke,' Janet said. 'We'll be watching out for you.'

'I think I'll try to blind him first.'

Ryder nocked an arrow to his bow. He swung the bow, lining up with one of the eyes breaking the surface like twin rocks. The crocodile sensed danger to itself and sank. The arrow punctured the surface.

'We must be quick,' Neith warned him. 'A boat of Seth might arrive at any time.'

'Yes, get moving.'

Ryder's glance again travelled in amazement between the cool dark Egyptian and the daring-eyed Janet. He found no shred of concern or sympathy in the faces of either. Were they equally careless of the risk to him? Perhaps it was women like these that made heroes of men, he thought. They simply expected you to do impossible things and, in the face of their provoking expectation, you simply went out and did them anyway — or died trying. He looked around the deck. A Mesniu dwarf, the captain, shuffled his feet and avoided his eye. What would he take for protection against the crocodile? A sword? The blade would probably bounce off its scaly armour. Then what — a bow? Useless.

What else? 'Don't stick your arms in its mouth, Wilson,' Janet had said. He imagined the power that hinged the saurian's jaws and snapped them shut on their prey. The thought at first chilled him, but then he brightened. Into his mind came the memory of a peculiar detail about crocodiles.

He took a pair of arrows from a quiver — not his own arrows, but barbed arrows fashioned by the Mesniu. He found a piece of *halfa* grass rope lying on the deck and he separated it into narrow strands. Then he placed the two arrows together, fletching to fletching, and bound the overlapped shafts together so that he formed a small spear with barbs at each end.

'Is it magic you are making by joining the arrows together?' the Lady of Crossed Arrows said.

'I don't know about magic, but I'm hoping it'll be lucky for me,' Ryder said. He stripped the shirt off his back and kicked off his boots. He lowered himself over the side into the cold mystery of the Nile and struck out for the island, swimming breaststroke so that he could keep his head above water. He watched for any swirl or streak that might betray the rush of the crocodile. Would he see it coming? Perhaps it was submerged far below and propelling itself at him with powerful sweeps of its tail. Ryder felt dread wrap itself like cold weeds around his waist, chest and arms.

'Faster,' Janet coached him. 'This is no time for a leisurely paddle. That crocodile could pop up at any second.' She's a consolation, Ryder thought.

The water was green and impenetrable. He mustn't think about the crocodile. He thought about the river instead. I'm immersed in the most sacred and ancient of rivers, he thought, the seminal stream of time, myth and legend. The Nile in its infancy. It was like swimming in the cooling afterbirth of creation. This water will carry history on its surface — carry pharaohs, queens, pyramid stones, golden images of gods and goddesses. It will flow through the imaginations of humanity for thousands upon thousands of years.

He was nearing the edge of the island. Shallows rose underneath his grateful feet and he waded ashore between the reeds in soft, black mud.

Where was Sobek? Was it circling the island patiently, allowing him to relax and grow careless? Was it delaying its attack, preferring to strike when he swam back with the amulet?

Ryder swept the water for a sign of it. The water was still — barely a ripple. He saw Janet give a cheerful wave from the boat. Neith stood unmoving as a statue. Mesniu crewmen clambered onto the roof of the deckhouse and up into the rigging for a better view. They clicked excitedly among themselves, adding to the early morning stir of birds, frogs and insects in the reeds.

Ryder approached the solitary sycamore tree, searching among the spreading branches.

He heard a rumble and a heavy squelching sound as the crocodile broke the suction of the mud bank and made a jagged run across the island towards him.

106/The Heqet frog

Ryder scrambled up the tree, still holding his two arrows.

'Wilson!' Janet yelled. The warning came a bit late, he thought.

'It's all right; I've seen it.'

It wasn't a warning, it turned out. It was a complaint. 'Don't waste time climbing trees. Grab the frog and get out of there.'

The reptile, wet and black with mud, dragged itself up to the base of the tree and settled. Its belly flattened under its weight, the skin of its back spreading out like a scaly green net, ready to catch him. A foetid smell of decay rose up to Ryder's nostrils. There was some commotion aboard the boat, Ryder now saw. The dwarfs were jumping up and down and banging a small gong.

'Sorry if I'm tormenting your sacred crocodile,' he muttered to himself. 'Maybe you think the pious thing to do would be to offer myself as breakfast.' But the squat little men weren't pointing at him. They were pointing upstream where a large trapezoid sail had come into view above the reeds, around a bend. A Seth boat.

'This is all I need,' Ryder thought.

'Are you going to carry on fooling around up there or come down?' Janet said in a cranky voice. 'There's a boat coming.'

'I'm stuck here!'

'Stop playing around. Make a run for it, but get the frog first.' The sail and now the swept-up prow of a boat reared above the reeds.

The frog. He'd almost forgotten about it. He peered among the branches. There it was, a green frog threaded onto a necklace and suspended over the end of a branch. He crawled to it, reached out and took it and shoved it into a trouser pocket.

Here goes. He swallowed hard, then inched his way down the tree. The crocodile couldn't believe its luck and moved away, giving him generous room, encouraging him to come down.

Ryder dropped the rest of the way and landed barefeet on the soil beneath the tree. Down on the ground, the crocodile was of such a size that it could frighten a man to death before it opened its mouth, Ryder thought, feeling the slit-pupils nail him with their stare.

He held out the arrows that were lashed together like a double-ended spear. It seemed a very puny weapon to use against a thing of this size.

The creature did not even bother to run, but ambled up to take the prey that was rightfully its. The jaws opened like the gates of hell. That's when Ryder rammed the twin-tipped spear into its mouth like a tent pole. The jaws snapped shut on the arrows. The metal tips on either end sank deep into flesh. One end came through like a new nostril as the jaws snapped shut. The crocodile tried to open its jaws, but now the barbs of the arrowheads bit deeply, clamping the upper and lower jaws.

A crocodile had powerful jaws for biting, but remarkably weak muscles for opening its jaws. It was trapped. It rolled in a flash of white belly and green scales, its tail flailing as it tried to free its jaws from the imprisoning barbs.

Ryder ran to the shore and dived into the cold green water. He swam hard, not caring to look around. Willing hands of the Mesniu dragged him aboard. They had lowered the mast and were running out oars so that they could propel themselves into the shelter of the papyrus thicket on the river's bank.

'You nearly ruined everything,' Janet complained. 'Now give me the Heqet frog.'

'You get your own,' he said.

'Don't be silly. Give it to me,' she said like a demanding schoolgirl, holding out her hand. 'We must keep them together. With you jumping around and putting on stunts, you're likely to lose something.'

'Yes, my life,' he said, dropping the little green steatite frog on its necklace into her eager hands. She had the first two amulets, he thought. She might as well keep them all.

Neith, watching them, frowned and went into the deckhouse.

12

Tombworld city

THERE WAS NO SIGN OF LIFE on the river banks; only marching walls of papyrus. They passed a plateau with pyramids in the distance. Ryder wondered how pyramids could be there in a time before the dynasties. Was Janet's explanation right — that myth could borrow from any time? If it could, it would explain why the pyramids were there. They were legendary creations belonging as much to the realm of myth and mystery as to reality.

They travelled for two days, it seemed to Ryder's calculations, stopping only occasionally to refresh themselves in the river. They ate and slept on board.

On three occasions the Mesniu had to lower the mast and the sail and paddle into the reeds to seek refuge from an approaching vessel of Seth. 'This is as far as the Mesniu will go,' Neith said at length as the crew took down the sail and rowed them to the shore. 'We are reaching Tombworld. Others will help us from here.'

'What's Tombworld?' Janet asked.

'It is a home of the followers of Osiris. Because they

are followers of Osiris, the lord of the underworld, they are made to take refuge underground, like the dead, in a network of passages and vaults beneath the cliffs. They are forced to do this by the evil vizier Seker whose legions of animal-headed demons patrol the land, killing or enslaving those they find. Only the useful are kept — or the beautiful, who are taken to stock the harem of the vizier.'

'Harem?' Janet said. 'How exotic. What does this vizier Seker look like?'

'He's a man with the head of a snake,' Neith said coldly.

'Perhaps not my kind,' Janet said.

Neith thanked the Mesniu for their help and for the use of their boat. 'Go back and prepare weapons for the war of freedom that will come one day if we can succeed,' she told them.

They went on foot and approached a mud-brick city. There were people to be seen for the first time; cowed people, who kept their heads downcast and went about their business with a guarded air. Most were carrying boxes and vessels like beasts of burden. They passed fishermen fixing their nets and others scaling their fish, scales flying up in fine clouds.

'Be careful,' Janet warned him. 'Scales can stick to your eyes and blind you.' Ryder shielded his eyes. Janet's father was an eye surgeon and presumably she knew about these things.

They approached a market with meagre produce on sale and a few half-starved wretches running it. Their bones were protruding from their flesh as if they were the survivors of a famine.

'This is a market for the slaves and workers. We may not walk freely here,' Neith said. She took a ring from her finger and gave it to a half-blind woman at a market stall. In exchange, the woman gave Ryder and Janet long loose linen tunics to throw over their clothes and headcloths to cover their heads. They put these on over their clothes and slipped the sandals into their bags until they had further use for them. The tunics, not unlike galabias, came quite low, hiding their feet.

Neith also bought two empty jars and a staff and she told Ryder and Janet to shoulder the jars while she held the staff.

Her plan soon became clear as she shepherded them into a side street.

The tramp of marching feet approached. It was a squad of soldiers, hyena-headed men with ox-hide shields, war axes and sliding, ravenous eyes. Neith gave Ryder a crack with her staff and used the other end to nudge Janet along the street. Janet gave her a murderous glare.

'You should beat that one,' the commander of the soldiers growled. 'She has a defiant eye.'

'I shall,' Neith said.

The leader of the patrol stopped and unsheathed his teeth in a grin at Neith. 'You are a pretty one to be in charge of slaves. How is it that a pretty one like you is not herself a member of the vizier's House of the Secluded?'

'It takes a pretty one like me to go where the pretty ones are hidden and to seek them out for our master,' she told him.

The hyena-headed commander nodded. His attention had been diverted by the sight of Snakeback. The ridgeback bared its teeth. 'I will have your hound,' the captain said, admiring it.

'Then you will have death,' Neith said. 'See, it is a

bewitched animal — it has the sign of the great serpent Apophis on its back.'

The hyena-headed soldier bent to touch the dog's fur and the spine of hair rose warningly. The soldier thought better of it and withdrew his hand. He bowed. 'Life, health, strength to Seker and to our Lord Seth!'

'Life, health, strength,' Neith replied, 'but not to you, Dog-head,' she whispered, moving on.

They came to a grove of palms and acacias and beyond the treetops bulked the mud brick walls of a palace.

Neith led them through the grove until they came to an adjoining building with pylons and even higher walls. There were crenellations on top and the glint of speartips as soldiers patrolled the battlements.

'Seker's House of the Secluded,' Neith explained. 'Here the flowers of maidenhood are imprisoned. And here, Seker's favourite dancer, Meresankh-Amun, wears the sacred girdle of Isis, the next amulet we must recover.'

They stopped directly opposite the entrance to the House of the Secluded and hid in the deeper shadows of the grove. A squad of ibis-headed soldiers, armed with sickle swords and spears, guarded the gate. They had strong legs and deep chests and their heads and necks looked obscenely small on their shoulders.

'One of us must find a way inside,' Neith said. Her glance travelled between Ryder and Janet. 'Entry is forbidden to the House of the Secluded — only women, eunuchs or blind musicians may go in there.'

'This may be your chance to experience a harem,' Ryder said to his archaeological colleague.

'Don't look at me,' Janet protested. 'I know about ancient Egyptian harems. They weren't the indolent palaces of the pampered that people imagine oriental seraglios to be. There wasn't much pampering or lolling on cushions. They were factories where the inmates were like bondswomen who earned their keep by weaving and crafts — in between entertaining their lord and master with their songs and dancing.'

'What about you?' Ryder asked Neith. 'You can go in there.'

'I am the Opener of Ways. It is not in my power to recover the sacred amulets.'

'Then it ends here. Our quest is over. We have no other option.'

'Not quite,' Janet said thoughtfully, a perturbing gleam entering her eye. 'She did say eunuchs and blind men were allowed inside.'

'What are you thinking? I'm not either.'

'Yet.'

'Now just a minute.'

'Would you ask him to submit to the knife?' Neith said, only slightly shocked.

'I don't think it's very much to ask.'

'Janet!'

'Where's your sense of humour, Will? I'm only joking.'

'Well, you're joking about a delicate subject.'

'Sorry. Actually, I was thinking of something less drastic.'

'Like digging my eyes out instead?'

'Something like that. We saw something on the way here that now gives me an idea.' She told them her plan. Ryder's horror abated, but not his scepticism. Neith was in perfect agreement.

'It is a good plan, Lost One. It fits in well with the plan I propose,' she said. 'We have spies who go into the House of the Secluded each day — a group of blind musicians. Bowman can go in with them. One of these musicians, the leader, is the blind harpist, Paibekkamun. He has a giant, big-bellied harp which is hollowed inside and which has been used to smuggle certain noblewomen from their imprisonment.'

'Why don't I hide in it?' Ryder suggested.

'You are too large. It is a space made to fit the body of a young girl, not a man.'

'Pity,' Ryder said.

'Stay here,' Neith said. 'I will go and speak with Paibekkamun and also see others for the things you will need.' She left them.

'I don't believe this,' Ryder said.

'Trust us.'

They sat in silence for a while. Ryder took the bow from under his cloak and removed the quivers and stretched out to rest. 'Do you really think this outrageous plan can work?'

'It's not as outrageous as sticking a couple of arrows into a crocodile's jaws. You're lucky it didn't take your arm off.'

'It's nice of you to be concerned now,' he said bitterly. 'You didn't show much concern for me at the time.'

'I was only trying to stop you fretting over the crocodile. It was a stupid plan. If you'd lost your arm you could have ruined everything.'

'Is that all you care about — getting those blasted trinkets?'

'You know they're a lot more than that. They are the fourteen amulets of power.'

'And you think scraps of alabaster or gold or steatite have the power to do anything?'

'They do here.'

They heard a rustling in the grove behind them. They thought that it was Neith returning, but a dark skinned young man leapt at Janet and held a sickle-shaped sword to her throat.

Ryder's hand stretched out for his bow. 'Do not move or she will taste her own blood,' the young man said. He had the angry eyes of a bird, a man driven to extremes, yet his hand was steady with the knife and he was well in control.

'What do you want? Do you want to rob us? We've got nothing to give you.'

'I want your attention. I don't want to rob you. I want to rob those who have robbed me.' He jerked his head towards the palace building. 'Many times I have tried to get in. I was hiding in the grove today and I heard your plan. I, too, have a treasure in the vile Seker's House of the Secluded. It is my betrothed, the lady Bint-Anath. You will use the harp to rescue her or I will send your fair one into the land of the blessed. Say you agree — or she dies.'

This was not a complication they needed, Ryder thought. 'Say we agree,' Janet gurgled, her eyes popping with fright.

Ryder relaxed, although the young man looked capable of doing anything he said he might do. 'Who are you?' he said conversationally.

The man wanted something — something badly and he was not about to ruin his chance of getting it — unless he was certain of failing and Ryder wasn't about to deny or threaten him. 'If we're going to band together, I'd like to know who you are.'

'Ryder, this is no time for pleasantries,' Janet gurgled as the knife pressed harder against her throat.

'I am Benwese, the soldier.'

'A soldier — of Seth?'

Benwese spat. 'Of Osiris. My father was the nomarch — as I should be in his place, with my chosen one Bint-Anath as wife beside me. But they have taken her.' Ryder noticed the wiry, muscled youth had the duskiness of a man who had lived his life outdoors. Didn't he live underground like the others? Was he part of an active resistance group?

'I want Bint-Anath. You will get her back for me or I will spill the blood of this Long One.'

'Long One,' Ryder said thoughtfully. 'Like that description of you, Janet?'

'Wilson!'

'Do you agree to help?' Benwese said.

'I suppose we could. What do you think, Janet?'

'I'll kill you, Wilson.'

The man withdrew the knife from her neck. 'Will you help?'

'I'll help, but only if you'll join up with us. We could do with a soldier on our side.'

'Agreed.'

Neith returned and regarded the calmly squatting young swordsman and the glaring Janet with puzzlement. Ryder explained what had taken place.

'I am Benwese,' the man said.

'The swordsman,' she said, nodding. 'Yes, I was expecting you, although I did not think you would crawl out of the bushes with a knife in your hand. Welcome. We will have need of your skills.'

She turned to Janet. 'I found that which you require. The salve is from a physician and will afford protection.'

'Then let's get to work,' Janet said. 'Wilson, you are about to lose your sight.'

'I suppose it could be worse,' he said philosophically.

13

House of the Secluded

RYDER STRETCHED HIMSELF OUT on the ground. Neith bent over him with a small jar of salve in her cupped hand. Janet, who had recovered from her attack, also attended, holding a collection of small objects in her hand. She chose one and held it up to examine it. It was a fish scale.

'First put some salve in his eyes,' she instructed Neith. 'We don't want the scales to adhere permanently. The salve will also give the scales a cushion to ride on and so prevent it from scratching too much.'

Neith held up his eyelid and dropped a cool drop of oily salve into each eye. The world blurred and the bent faces of the two women swam. Now Janet came closer, one forefinger held above his right eye. The finger descended, something clamped with a feeling like suction over his eyeball and smudged his vision into a murky haze. A feeling of breathlessness rose up in Ryder.

'It is good,' Neith said with satisfaction. 'See, the pale scar of blindness lies over his eye. It is the eye of a blind

118/House of the Secluded

man. Just like the eyes of Paibekkamun.'

'Okay, so it works,' Ryder said, sitting up and feeling suffocated by the scale clinging to his eye, 'but you're forgetting something. How am I going to pass as an ancient Egyptian musician? I can't play an instrument and I can't sing.'

'You can chant and beat a drum,' Neith told him firmly.

'Yes, don't be difficult, Wilson. We need the buckle of Isis. You must snatch it from the dancer Meresankh-Amun.'

'And you must rescue my lady, Bint-Anath,' Benwese reminded him, watching the medical procedure with some amusement.

'How will I know Bint-Anath among a harem full of young women?'

'She, too, is a dancer, a dancer of exceptional skill and will almost certainly dance with Meresankh-Amun. She has green eyes like the Nile and a crescent moon mark on her neck.'

'How am I going to see it if I'm blind?'

'The same way you're supposed to see the knot of Isis. With your eyes. Once you have passed the inspection of the guards, you must slip the scales off your eyes.'

'When you see Bint-Anath, you must use a secret phrase,' Benwese instructed him, 'which I will give you. Say these words to her and she will know you have come from me and will follow your instructions to the gates of doom.'

And so it was that the string of musicians, led by two girl singers, approached the gates of the House of the Secluded. There were lamps burning on poles to illuminate the gateway.

The ibis-headed guards recognised them and greeted them with a derisive cackle. 'The blind worm approaches.'

Ryder was helping the stout Paibekkamun carry his harp. The guards opened the gates, swinging them open on hinges that groaned. The singers and musicians filed through.

'Halt!' a guard said harshly. The soldier had blocked the path of Paibekkamun, Ryder guessed, for the old man had stopped abruptly almost dropping his end of the harp. Had they guessed the secret role of the outsized instrument? 'What have we here, blind frog?'

'Only my harp,' Paibekkamun croaked.

'Do you think we are blind like you?'

'Not like me, Lord,' Paibekkamun said with a subtle insolence that went over the head of the soldier.

'You have a new group member. What is the qualification of this one: is he a eunuch or a blind one? He looks a healthier specimen than the rest of you who have grown sleek and fat with your easy living.'

Ryder tensed. He felt a cold metal tip of a spear dig into his neck.

'Come into the light and let's look at you,' he heard a harsh voice say.

Ryder lurched in the opposite direction to the light. 'He is a blind servant, just as I am,' Paibekkamun assured the guard hastily. The guard grabbed Ryder's arm and spun him around. Ryder dropped his end of the harp on the ground, ready to run if he must.

'Open your eyes,' the voice said. Ryder opened his eyes and heard the guard's hiss of disgust. Ryder could imagine the sight of the two milky moons of blindness that lay over his eyes. He closed the eyes again, before they streamed. The scales were irritating his eyes and they were filling with tears.

'Get inside and don't open your eyes with the vizier's young women around — you'll frighten them!'

They were led along passages until at length they were met by a majordomo with perfumed breath — a eunuch, Ryder guessed — who searched each of them bodily. Then they were led on into the echoing space of a hall.

Ryder bumped his shoulder on a column. 'Set up here,' a girl singer whispered, 'next to a column. They are coming soon.' They set up the harp and drums. Ryder was given a pair of gourd-shaped rattles that were meant to produce a shuffling sound not unlike a South American rhythm.

Ryder slipped behind the column where he hoped he was hidden from view by any in the hall. He raised an eyelid with a finger and used his thumb and forefinger to slide the scale off his cornea, making a grab for it before it slid under an eyelid. He pinched it and took it out.

The world swam into view. But the scale had left a blur and his eye streamed. He saw the dim rise of columns and thought he saw a gathering of shapes on a dais at the back of the hall. Perhaps it would be safer to leave one scale in place, he thought.

Ryder blinked and the scene glimpsed through one tearfully protesting eye cleared. As well as the two girl singers, he saw the bulking form of the blind harpist with his great harp. It stood higher than the harpist and had twenty strings, a wide frame and a bulky resonance chamber at the base. The base was decorated with the carved head of Hathor, goddess of music and dancing. It was this section that opened, allowing a small person to slide in and lie upside down with their body in the resonance chamber and their feet and legs running up into the hollow stem of the harp. Lamps stood on small stands around the musicians, like stage lights.

A hush of expectancy fell on the hall, signalling the beginning of the performance. It began with a beating of a drum, much like a Nubian drum, Ryder thought. Then the two girl singers wove a tremulous interplay of vocals in the Eastern way.

The song was a love song, filled with Egyptian passion and despair:

> Lost! Lost! Lost! O lost my love to me!
> He passes by my house, nor turns his head,
> I deck myself with care; he does not see.
> He loves me not. Would God that I were dead.

Ryder squinted across the hall at the dais, where seated figures were dimly emerging in the gloom. His attention focused on a man — or creature — lolling in a richly glinting inlaid chair. The man had powerful shoulders and legs, but a shuddersomely thin snake's neck and head. A cobra's hood flared out behind the squat head like a pharaoh's *nemes* headcloth. Female attendants, fan bearers and eunuchs, some of them armed, stood around him. Was this repellent creature the vizier Seker?

The girls sang two more verses that ended with the sad avowal:

> Come! Come! Come! And kiss me when I die,
> For Life — compelling Life — is in thy breath;
> And at that kiss, though in the tomb I lie,
> I will rise and break the bands of Death.

They finished their song and in the silence that followed, Paibekkamun whispered to Ryder: 'Play as I begin with the harp.'

The harpist plucked at the chords and the chamber shivered with voluptuously rich sounds. Ryder shook the rattles in a measured shuffling rhythm. Now the lute plucked notes in the air and the sound thickened.

The audience on the dais stirred expectantly and now Ryder saw why. A dozen girls, dressed in girdles and ornamental collars, ran into the chamber and proceeded to do acrobatic cartwheels across the floor. Leading them was a ravishingly beautiful woman with a buckle of gold on her girdle. The audience applauded.

Meresankh-Amun, Ryder thought, the favourite of the vizier Seker and wearing the buckle of Isis on her girdle. He could almost hear Janet's voice saying, 'It's here, Wilson, the next amulet. Right in front of you, waiting to be grabbed.'

But first he would have to locate the other girl, Bint-Anath. Green eyes. How was he expected to notice green eyes amid these spinning, flying forms? The girls cartwheeled back and forth, some flying close to the musicians.

Not that one, she's a Nubian. Not that one. She has eyes like coal. A small girl took her place, cartwheeling up to the musicians. She slid to the floor as they all did. The instruments suddenly stopped their playing — but without warning to Ryder who discovered himself playing the rattles alone.

'Cease your playing,' the harpist hissed. Ryder stopped.

The girl on the floor raised her head, a mildly curious look in her green eyes. Ryder saw a sickle mark on the curve of her throat.

It was Bint-Anath.

'The swordsman has come for Lady Sheath,' he

whispered to her. 'When chaos erupts in our performance, run to the pillar beside me and I will hide you in the chamber inside our great harp.'

Now the drums throbbed and the girls, flattened on the floor, rose in slithering reptilian movements. The music resumed and the girls now wove and parted in a complicated dance with much waving of arms. The girl with the girdle of Isis came close.

Now. Ryder made a grab for the secret handle on the resonance chamber of the harp and flipped the lid open. Brown, squeaking entrails poured out onto the floor.

Rats.

They scurried across the floor in all directions, running among the dancing girls who leaped in every direction. Screams split the air and girls ran everywhere. At the signal, the two girl singers knocked over the lamps and several running girls from the harem helped with the others.

Ryder dropped the rattles and flew at Meresankh-Amun who had frozen on the dance floor. He made a grab for the golden knot on her girdle, twisted it and it came free. A running girl nearly knocked them both off their feet. It broke Meresankh-Amun's frozen thrall and she ran off screaming with the others.

Green eyes was waiting at the harp. 'Climb inside,' Ryder said.

'Not in there. You had rats in there.'

'Benwese said you would follow me to the gates of doom if I said the words he gave me.'

'Yes, but I'm not going in a harp where rats have been.' Ryder scooped up the kicking girl and jammed her into the harp, thrusting her legs up to the top. A rat that had been too shy to emerge, jumped out with a squeak of protest and there was a bottled scream from

Bint-Anath as Ryder slammed the lid shut.

The eunuchs were thrown into as much a state as the dancing girls by the plague of rats. Where had they sprung from? Nobody knew. In the chaos that followed, the performance was summarily cancelled and the group of musicians expelled from the building.

Bint-Anath, thankfully, had fainted. There were no more protests from the belly of the harp. But they now had the sacred knot of Isis.

Janet, Neith, the soldier Benwese and Snakeback greeted them with excitement and relief in the grove. 'I think I'm blinded forever,' Ryder complained as Benwese drew the girl from the harp and into his arms.

'You shouldn't have been looking around in a harem anyway,' Janet told him. The girl in Benwese's arms opened her eyes, saw the face of her loved one and wept with joy and gratitude.

Bint-Anath was ferried across the river. Benwese gave her into the hands of a supporter, a fisherman who promised to take her back to her people. 'Beware of the charioteers,' he warned her, enfolding her in his arms one last time before letting her go.

'Where are her people?' Ryder said as the waving girl and the old fisherman set off across an empty plain.

'Under the ground like the dead. The realm of the good king Osiris is now a tombworld where we must live in rags like mummies in tunnels beneath the earth. We dream one day of being free and coming again into the light when the sun will shine again on the mummy king's realm.'

Benwese joined the group for the continuing journey south.

Neith had promised after the departure of the Mesniu and their boat that others would help from that point onwards; these others turned out to be secret supporters of Osiris. A baboon-headed ship's captain, while officially in the employ of the pharaoh Seth, carrying cargoes of supplies for his troops, secretly aided the cause of the resistance. They were taken by boat to their next challenge.

14

The sacred beetle of chalcedony

BEFORE THEM LOOMED AN ABANDONED TEMPLE dedicated to not one but two deities — the serpentine goddess Renenutet, where a golden *uraeus* amulet adorned the crown on a statue of the goddess, and the adjoining temple of the beetle-headed god Khepera, where a sacred beetle of chalcedony lay hidden in the innermost holy of holies.

'If it's an abandoned temple, where is the danger?' Ryder asked Neith.

Benwese, their new recruit, answered for her. 'It is abandoned by humans, but not by serpents who throng in their thousands, and other assorted guardians such as beetle-headed demon creatures,' he said grimly.

Ryder suddenly felt grateful to have the wiry swordsman at his side. A strong sword arm might be useful against demon creatures, although slithering serpents in their thousands were another problem. Neither arrows nor a sword would provide much protection. How would they get past them?

Neith described the layout of the temple and Ryder made preparations for the task, collecting things he would need.

The group left the boat on the eastern bank of the river and set off for the temple. The temple lay abandoned, the papyriform pillars at its entrance half-buried in sand. A stone carving of *khepera*, the scarab beetle, stood on an obelisk in a sand-covered forecourt. A winged serpent looked down from a lintel over the entrance.

The temple interior was as dark as a cave. They had brought torches — staves with heads of linen dipped in oil — and these they lit before they advanced into the temple, passing between bulky papyriform columns. Neith led them through the columned hall.

Ryder kept a watch on the floor, eyes on the alert for snakes. He hoped the flaming torches in their hands would keep all but the most aggressive reptiles away.

Twin temples were not uncommon as Ryder knew. At Kom Ombo there was a temple with a shrine split into two, one half dedicated to the crocodile god Sobek and the other to Horus, but he had never come across a temple shared by a snake and beetle deity, although they shared some religious symbolism. The beetle represented the sun and the *uraeus* snake was often depicted with a sun's disc on its head.

Which shrine would they enter first? Neith led them to the left. They entered a hallway with great curving ramps at either side. The ramps led up to doorways that were plugged with boulders. Ryder wondered what lay behind the boulders and why the passages were sealed. Were they catacombs, tombs of long-dead priests of the temple?

Snakeback growled as it walked. Its tail was held low and its head swung uneasily from side to side, its round amber eyes warily sweeping the plugged passageways.

They went further into the hall, the light from their torches throwing twisting shadows. Sand lay on the floor, blown in by the endless winds. It crunched under their feet.

Snakeback rumbled and this time its rumble was drowned by an even deeper rumble, one that shook the floor. Benwese shouted a warning. A boulder rolled down a ramp towards them, thrust by a pair of giant spiky legs. Janet screamed.

Now more boulders were working free from the doorways and rolling down the ramps towards them. They froze, bunched together like skittles in a bowling alley, not knowing whether to move forwards or backwards or to stay where they were.

A ball of granite of crushing size went by with a rush like a comet, the slipsteam of its passing tugging at them. Another ball rolled towards them from an oblique angle. It threw up sparks like spiky hair. Ryder and Benwese each tugged one of the women aside and Snakeback jumped to avoid it.

More were coming from other directions. Two boulders collided just ahead of them with a thunderous crack, striking sparks like lightning as they exploded into fragments of flying stone that rained over them. They were trapped with no way forward, backward or to either side. A boulder ran into a column and it crumbled and crashed. Slabs of stone slammed down from the temple roof.

Ryder slipped off his bow and snatched an arrow from his quiver, an arrow attached to a length of cord. This in turn was attached to a coil of *halfa* grass rope in an open-necked bag on his back. He aimed at a stone block that spanned two columns and shot the arrow.

The cord streamed out of the bag. The arrow passed over the block and dropped neatly down on the other side, taking the cord with it. The arrow swung on the cord. Ryder caught it. He pulled on the cord, taking the rope over the block.

'Hurry!' Janet shouted as a boulder came with ground-jarring force at them. They leapt to one side.

The rope was over the stone support and snaking down the other side. Ryder tugged it down. He joined the ends together and pulled it tight. He didn't have to tell the others to climb.

Janet went up first, then Neith, followed by Benwese. Ryder followed, sweeping up the dog and throwing it over his shoulder, clear of the bow. The animal wriggled a bit higher so that it could balance itself and steady, hooking its forelegs over him in the accustomed way. Ryder took a firm grip on the rope and hoisted them both clear of the floor. The rope creaked and twisted. Snakeback whined anxiously. Would the rope hold their combined weight? It should do. It was ship's rope of the kind used to truss keels. Ryder used his strong upper body to haul and his legs and feet to clamp and hold.

'Climb up higher, Wilson!' A grey ball grew in his vision. It was a boulder as big as a hillside and it was going to hit them. His hands gathered in the coarse rope like reels, yanking them higher. The ball rushed up to fill his eyes with whirring greyness and sparks. He snapped up his legs to avoid it. It grazed the sole of one shoe like an orbital sander, but they were still hanging on.

The ball took the loose end of the rope and sent them swaying across the hall, before it swept away into the darkness to meet a wall with a crash that made the darkness shake. They had dropped their torches and only one was still burning on the floor. From their vantage point on the rope they saw below them a scene of mass collisions like a battle of asteroids. Dust and fragments of stone flew up as the boulders smashed together with bangs and showers of sparks. Nothing down there could have survived.

The hall grew quiet and they were in darkness, their ears still ringing. The rope still trembled. Was it a reverberation from the violent collisions below — or their fear?

They came cautiously down. Ryder and Janet produced their pocket torches. They were able to find only two of the oil torches in the rubble. Janet produced a lighter and ignited an oil-soaked head. They held up the spurting light and looked around at the scene of ruin. Benwese pointed to the top of the ramps.

'The beetles of Khepera!' he whispered. Gone were the giant boulders that had plugged the doorways, but the doorways were still blocked, now with living plugs — the vast heads of shiny black scarab beetles, waving their mandibles and grinding the planes of their palpus plates in frustration, for the passages were not wide enough to let their bulk through.

In mythology, a great dung-rolling beetle was believed to roll the sun across the heavens and these guardians rolled balls of doom. Ryder undid the rope and dragged it free and they went on into the holy of holies.

They found the amulet, a tiny scarab made of shining chalcedony, sitting on a quartzite plinth. Janet palmed it eagerly.

Ryder wished they could leave this place, but they still had the hall of Renenutet, the lady of serpents, to go. I think I prefer flying boulders, Ryder thought. At least they can't climb up ropes after you. Benwese shared his uneasiness. He drew a sickle-shaped sword from the belt at his waist.

They kept their eyes turned down, slowing as they approached shadowy cracks that took on the appearance of snakes on the floor, always alert for the scribbled death-threat of a snake on the slither, but they should have been watching the columns instead, for from behind one sprang not a snake, but a female creature with the neck and head of a snake. Ryder saw the flash of a knife as she raised her arm to strike.

Benwese swung his blade at the scaly neck and the fanged mouth flared briefly, then the head was gone and the figure slumped to the ground. Ryder wished he had brought a sword. He nocked an arrow to his bowstring, one of the rough-hewn arrows of the Mesniu. These were good enough for close combat.

A blur of movement from another column. A man with a squat snake's head grabbed Janet's arm and pulled her after him. Ryder swung with the bow and let fly. The arrow took the attacker cleanly through the head. A hiss like gas escaping under pressure blew from the snake-head and the creature spun off to fall in the darkness.

'That was risky using an arrow,' she complained, the torch shaking in her hand at the narrowness of her escape. 'I was about to singe its eyebrows off.'

'Snakes don't have eyebrows.'

'They do have deadly fangs, however,' Neith informed her. 'Serpent guardians possess poison of a virulent brew. One bite and not even the magical skills of Isis could save you.'

They closed ranks, except Benwese who dropped back, sword brandished. He had seen something. Knives flashed in their torchlight. Attackers, two of them, closed in on him. Benwese's blade flew in a wide shining arc and lopped off both of their blunt heads. He was a nimble youth with a sword, Ryder noted with gratitude; not an adversary he would care to come up against.

Now a snake-head leapt at Neith, grabbing her arm, its mouth open, its fangs unsheathed to strike. Janet blocked Ryder's way, preventing him from using his bow. Benwese was too far away to help her. Neith stiffened and turned her eyes on the creature who let go and stepped back. A sigh, like leaves caught in a sudden gust, rustled in Neith's throat. Now tears of light blazed from Neith's eyes and the creature screamed. Covering its head with its arms, it fell to the floor where it shrivelled and grew still.

The others took a step back from Neith in surprise. When she turned, the glow still brimmed like tears in her eyes and just as suddenly it went out. She had destroyed with a look. The display came as a shock, a reminder to Ryder that Neith was not like others. She probably had an infinite capacity to destroy. How lightly she could have killed me or all of us, he thought. The proximity to such otherworldly power made his skin prickle under his fieldclothes. Could this lovely, slender vase of femalehood contain more lethal danger than any guardian he had faced? Why had she hidden her powers until now? There was one possible explanation. She had not been involved until now, never threatened directly.

'Why can't you do some of that stuff for us?' Janet complained to Neith, yet with respect seeping into her voice.

'Don't provoke her,' Ryder whispered, 'unless you

enjoy living even more dangerously than you normally do.'

Ryder went ahead of the others, walking alongside Neith, but keeping his distance from her. He felt vaguely humiliated by her display of power. It held an implication that she had been toying with him up until now, carefully hiding her superiority. Hadn't she wanted to discourage him? I wonder if she's been secretly smiling at my efforts? Ryder thought. She could have overcome all of the challenges herself, with ease, but she had chosen to hold back, content to look on like an indulgent teacher, as if this were all some set-piece devised for his benefit. Either that, he thought, or she doesn't care enough to help and doesn't give a damn what happens to me.

'Do not shrink from me, Bowman.'

'The other times when I was in danger, when all of us were in danger, you did nothing. I don't suppose you cared what happened,' he said in a low voice.

'Cared. Of course I cared. The amulets must be recovered if Osiris is to rise and his son Horus is to take his place.'

'I mean about me — us.'

'Why? Do you think I should?' she said. She was a woman again, playfully slapping at his assumptions. 'Is there something about a tomb robber from the future who has a bow and a hound with a snake on its back that should arouse the compassion of the Opener of Ways?'

'No, I suppose not. I wonder why you brought me here at all.'

'To complete the quest. What else?'

'Nothing.'

'Say. What else, Bowman?'

'Why didn't you step in before? In the tomb maze? Against the lioness? Or the crocodile? You left it to me. Why didn't you use your powers to help?'

'You don't know what you are asking.'

Maybe I don't at that, he thought angrily. I'm asking a pagan creature to care. 'I suppose the answer is clear.'

'You do not know the risk. You cannot know. This is your quest. If I became involved and used my powers, I would upset the universal order of Maat and stand to be stripped of them. Is that what you want of me? Are you asking me to diminish myself, to care like a woman? If I did, that is what I would risk becoming.'

'A woman — is that so bad?'

'You tell me. You have always yearned for more. Is that your peculiar folly, Bowman? A great irony. You yearn for a goddess in a normal woman — and now you want a normal woman in a goddess. It is not normal to want both, nor wise.'

'Well, you have shown what you are. No normal woman could have done what you did back there, killing with a single glance.'

'All women are capable of throwing a look that can kill. Mine act more swiftly.'

15

Renenutet, Lady of Serpents

THEY REACHED THE HOLY OF HOLIES of the Lady of Serpents to find the way blocked. A squad of snake-headed attackers armed with knives guarded the doorway.

Janet turned to Neith. 'Go ahead,' she said. 'Give them the look.'

'I cannot. I would need to anger myself and it is ill for humanity to see too much of my anger. It can singe, like the nearness of lightning bolts. Besides, I may not intervene except to defend myself. This is *your* quest. You must reach the hidden *uraeus* on your own. But hurry.'

There was a wall of them, guarding the shrine of Renenutet. Ryder guessed he could loose one arrow, maybe two. Benwese went forward to meet them, sword in hand. Snakeback crouched low, ready to attack. The snakemen hissed like a wave running up a beach as they fell on the group.

Ryder released one arrow and saw a snake-man fall. Then he thrust the bow into Janet's hand and took her burning torch to use as a weapon. She stole a couple of arrows from his quiver before he went forward, swinging a flame in the face of the nearest attacker. He saw Snakeback launch itself at the serpentine neck of another, taking him down. Snakeback shook its head violently, the way a hunting dog kills a snake, and there was a crack as the creature's head struck the floor slackly.

Benwese defended himself against the flash of a long dagger blade. Ryder snatched up a fallen blade and slashed at the next attacker. Benwese pierced another through the chest. The snake-man hissed like a burst tyre. Ryder swept a scar of flame across an attacker's eyes and brought the flash of his blade up behind it. Benwese took on the next. Ryder slipped. He looked up to see a snake-man raising his knife to strike when an arrow quivered in the demon's chest. It bent its snake-neck to examine the arrow in mild curiosity, its tongue flickering, then it fell forward onto the arrow. Benwese despatched the last and the entrance was clear.

'Thanks, Janet,' Ryder said to the young woman with a bow in her hand.

'I haven't watched you firing this thing all these years without learning a few tricks.'

'Not firing — shooting; but I'm not complaining.'

Benwese was resting, his hands on his knees.

'Are you all right, my friend?' he asked. Benwese nodded and straightened, his face grim but satisfied.

'And you, Bowman?'

'Fine.'

Neith had watched the struggle impassively. 'Well fought.' Neith's way of killing was a lot cleaner, Ryder thought enviously, his lungs heaving for breath. It was a pity she did not use it. The stare he directed at her was accusing and saddened. She tossed her head and went on to the shrine.

They held out their torches to throw light into the chamber. 'Disgusting!' Janet said, shuddering. It was like looking into a graveyard for tyres, Ryder thought; shiny tyres, as if wet from the rain, except that these tyres, massed on the floor of the narrow shrine, were of different sizes, markings and patterns — and they moved. Hisses, like the sound of a thousand slow-leaks, came from the heap.

'There's the amulet,' Janet whispered. 'If only it were a bit closer.' At the centre of the shrine stood the bronze image of the goddess Renenutet, snake-headed, but with the body of a woman, and on her head a crown with a small, shining *uraeus*, spitting a lightning tongue of gold. Sapphires like buttons winked in her eyes.

'Just marvellous,' Ryder said in a dull voice. 'It couldn't be easy, could it?'

'Don't lose your enthusiasm, Wilson. You'll just have to shoo them.'

'You don't shoo a million snakes.'

'Well, you have to do something, unless you plan to run over the top of them. Do you think you could — if you made a dash?'

'No, I don't — and I wouldn't think of trying.'

'Then think of something else, quickly — before they decide to come out at us.'

Ryder wondered what it was that kept them inside the shrine — some magnetic attraction of the goddess figure? The pile of snakes was thickest and most excited around the base of the goddess, a squirming collar of reptile skins woven in patterns that constantly changed in front of their eyes, as if the cold-blooded creatures were fighting to get near some warmth.

How were they to reach it? He looked upwards, hoping to find a beam from which he could suspend a rope and then swing to the statue, but the polished, pink granite walls of the shrine rose smoothly to meet in a vaulted, triangular roof, decorated with a myriad of stars. The only irregularities in the granite were holes — snake holes constructed to allow the creatures entry and exit. They poured through these holes now, some fleeing, others coming closer with pink-flickering tongues to challenge the invaders.

Ryder scratched his chin. 'Any ideas?' he said.

'Can't you use a lasso?' Janet said, not to be beaten by the reptilian sentinels.

'Lasso the *uraeus*? It's only three centimetres high and it's not on top but in front, on the forehead. I'd like to see a cowhand toss a rope that accurately.'

'I don't mean lasso the snake. I mean lasso the statue, then use the rope to crawl above the snakes to the statue. We'll take one end of the rope and hold it taut, then you shimmy along and fetch the *uraeus*. Simple, right?' It wasn't a half-bad idea, Ryder thought, although it wasn't going to be as easy as she thought.

Ryder made a loop at the end of the *halfa* grass rope. The first cast fell over the head of a raised cobra and it hissed in protest as Ryder dragged the rope back for another throw. Janet chased the cobra back with a thrust of her torch flame. The next throw was nearer the mark, but missed.

There was no room to swing the noose around his head. He had to swing it at his side. He gave the noose a twirl and Janet cheered as it flew straight to the head, but the noose did not open. The rope bounced off the head of the goddess and slid limply to the floor where a large banded cobra at once befriended it, amorously entwining itself in its length.

Neith stamped her foot impatiently. 'You are taking too long, Bowman. Seth's confederates are everywhere and may have followed us. I should not do this — help you — but I see I must.'

I shouldn't be helping a goddess, either, Ryder thought. 'What do you suggest?'

'Give me the rope.'

He handed it to her without argument. If Neith believed that she possessed superior skill with a lasso, let her try. He made room for her to twirl the rope. She did attempt it however, merely holding the rope for a moment in both hands and closing her eyes. When she opened her eyes, they were brimming with light.

'Here.' She handed the rope back to him, holding it out. He took it. It was rigid as a staff.

Pharaoh's magicians threw down rods and turned them into snakes. Then they took the snakes and turned them back into rods. 'You could turn the snakes into ropes, I suppose,' he said hopefully.

'Hurry, Bowman!'

'It was worth a try.' Ryder ran out the stiffened length of rope between his hands, holding it above the wetly shining heap of tyres. It rasped through his hands with the coarse texture of *halfa* grass, but it was iron hard within. Soon the noose was suspended over the head of the snake-head of the goddess. He dropped it around the statue's neck and gave the faintest tug. Immediately the rope went slack and he drew it in.

'Very clever,' he congratulated Neith.

'It is an old magician's trick,' Benwese assured him. 'Many magicians can do it.'

'You hold onto the rope,' he told Benwese and Janet, 'and don't let me down, literally.' Benwese wrapped the end around his waist like an anchorman in a tug-of-war, braced the rope and Janet joined him, throwing her willowy yet strong body against it. Ryder put his weight on the rope and tried to climb along its length, but for all their tugging, the rope bowed and his weight dragged them further into the shrine. They were going to lower him into the snakes. Ryder gave up. He looked hopefully at Neith.

'We need your help, Neith,' he said. He had never used her name before.

'You ask help of me, even knowing that to give to you, I must take from myself?'

Snakeback growled as a snake slid off the pile and came over the floor to investigate them. It stopped and raised its head to stare at them, its body forming a question mark, its tongue flickering. The snake of fur on the dog's back rose to challenge it. The snake saw the white gleam of the ridgeback's teeth and lost its curiosity. It turned and dived back, stretching its body like an exclamation mark to reach the pile.

'We're stuck,' Ryder said.

Neith gave a sigh that was more troubled than impatient and took the rope in one hand, again shutting her eyes. The rope snapped straight with a twang like a bowstring.

'Go,' she commanded him. Ryder scrambled along the length of rope, going upside down like a sloth but at far greater speed. He looked down and his stomach squirmed at the moving scenery beneath him. 'Keep the rope tight,' he whispered to Neith. He was only a few bodylengths away. He twisted his head to look at the statue and now his hopes took a dip. A cobra had slithered up the statue and draped itself on the rope. Ryder shook the rope and swayed his body vigorously to shake it loose.

'What are you trying to do, Wilson, rip it out of our hands?'

'There's a snake on the rope. I'm trying to shake it off.' He shook the rope again. Then he felt the floor of snakes rush up towards him.

What was happening? He was going down. The snakes looked like stretching sinews. 'Don't let me down!'

'We're not letting you down,' Janet said impatiently. 'Look at the statue. Look at what you're doing to it.' Ryder, sweat stinging his eyes, looked along the rope to the statue. It wasn't standing straight any more, but had bowed on its pedestal.

Oh, no, would it come right off? If it did. . .

That didn't bear thinking about. He'd better go back. 'Don't you dare come back now!' Janet said. 'You're nearly there.'

The snake's nearly here, too, he thought. 'Shoo!'

It was nearly at his fingers. He froze. The rope dropped even lower. The metal base of the goddess gave a mournful metal sigh like a creaky hinge. Renenutet was going to throw him to the snakes.

The snake almost felt warm as it slid over Ryder's frozen fingers, then it came sinuously around the rope towards his face. The eyes in the diamond head, catching the flare of their torch flames, interrogated him with the unadorned stare of light bulbs. He felt like shutting his eyes. No, sudden movement could precipitate an attack. Maybe he could let go with one hand and swipe it aside.

Before he could try, the snake decided to leave the rope for the broad expanse of Ryder's chest. It dropped with a soft slap on his stomach, chillingly cool and heavy on his shirt. It saw a gap in the shirt between the buttons and streamed into it.

Ryder thought of many things at that moment, including letting go, not just of the rope, but of all hope. 'Hang in there, Wilson. He's only being inquisitive.'

It moved with a hideously sensual thrill under his shirt and only the bumps on his skin rose to stop it. He imagined the tiny nip of its fangs and the electric pain of its venom shooting through his body.

'Do not take too long, Bowman.'

'We're getting tired holding this thing.'

The snake emerged from his collar, curled past Ryder's neck and decided to swing down towards the soft living net of reptiles beneath it. It swung unhurriedly, not letting go. Would it change its mind and come back up? No — relief — it was gone. Ryder felt as if a fire had swept through his body and left him in ashes. If I move a muscle, I might crumble away.

'Go on — before the statue breaks!'

One snake had been bad enough. The thought of falling into a sea of them was enough to give him back the will to move. He took in a gasp of breath like a man who had been submerged overlong and had just come up for air. How long had he stopped breathing? He spoke silently to his fingers, persuading them to unlock their damp, rigid grip and allow him to move on.

The *uraeus* amulet was in reach now. Its eyes glittered. Ryder reached out with one hand, wrapped his fingers around the golden snake head and tugged. It was the final encouragement the idol needed to fall and it went down like a chopped tree.

'Don't drop the amulet!' Ryder instinctively clutched more tightly to the stiffened rope, even though it was taking him down. It was probably this that saved him for, as his back hit the bed of snakes, the rope in his hands was given a mighty haul and his body travelled over the backs of the snakes as smoothly as a boat keel going over rollers on a slipway. Benwese and Janet, grabbing Snakeback's collar, had fallen back as snakes, disturbed by Ryder's descent, streamed in all directions, hissing as though under the force of compressed air.

Only Neith stood in the doorway, the rope held in one hand.

Snakes slithered over her sandalled feet, but she cared nothing about it. Ryder jumped over an adder and was clear of them. Neith gave the rope a snap of her wrist and dragged it out. It was slack rope again and ran over the backs of the snakes.

'Hurry Bowman, we must go on to the next challenge.'

Janet was waiting outside the doorway. 'I'll take the *uraeus*,' she said, snatching the amulet from him.

16

The scorpion goddess

NEITH LED THEM OUT into the desert.

'Thankyou for helping me,' Ryder said, falling in beside her.

'I should not have helped. I regret it already. It is not my destiny. The more I lower myself to help you, the more my powers will weaken. I cannot mix my destiny with yours. I am putting myself at risk — a risk you cannot imagine.'

'Where is the next amulet? What do we face next?'

'Horrible danger,' she said.

Ryder shook his head in weary disbelief. They had all been horrible dangers. 'What could be worse than the things we've already faced?'

'A goddess under a rock.'

Another goddess. 'What's so bad about a goddess under a rock?'

'It is Selkhet.'

'The scorpion goddess.'

'Yes.'

'And I suppose she's surrounded with millions of scorpions?'

'No, there is only one scorpion.'

One scorpion? Neith had not been perturbed by a chamber full of snakes. Yet she described one scorpion under a rock as 'horrible danger'. Perhaps it was her weak spot and she had a horror of scorpions for some religious reasons. It was wishful thinking, he discovered, as she went on to describe the scorpion they would have to face.

'Selkhet is a scorpion the size of a warship and the scales on her body are as broad as planks. Your arrows will bounce off her armour. Your swordsman will no more than dent her limbs unless he strikes at the joints. But you have to overcome her, for she guards the sacred adze which must be used to open the mouth of Osiris.'

Was it his imagination, or were the tasks on this quest becoming more and more unnerving?

Neith then led them across the desert on a wearying trek. She changed her mind on several occasions and once, Ryder was sure, they had doubled back on the way they had been. Was it possible that the Opener of Ways was losing her way?

'We're supposed to be going towards the south-east and you keep bringing us back towards the river,' Janet said critically. How did Janet know what they were seeking? Ryder wondered. Was his archaeological colleague consulting the notes she had recorded in the tomb? He checked. No sign of a map — the only thing she carried was a bag containing the amulets that they had collected so far. Maybe she had committed the notes to memory. Neith stopped, her fingertips held to her forehead as if she were trying to draw on some guiding instinct in her brain.

'This way,' Janet said, breaking away impatiently and setting off in a new direction. 'I know the way.' Neith, to Ryder's surprise, gave a shrug and followed.

Benwese smiled at him. 'Your lady is growing in strength and confidence,' he noted.

'She's never lacked confidence,' he said. 'I'd never accuse Janet of that.' Something was changing in the group and Ryder felt a twinge of unease. What was happening to Neith?

Janet led them to a mountain in the desert. It was topped with a monolithic slab of limestone like a table top. The shadow beneath the slab revealed the deeper shadow of an entrance at the centre of it. 'This is the next stronghold,' Janet said, looking at Neith with a glint of triumph. 'The secret hiding place of Selkhet; am I correct?'

'The rock of Selkhet, the scorpion goddess,' Neith said, nodding. She looked afraid and vulnerable.

'How are we going to tackle it?' Ryder said. 'Any ideas?'

By way of reply, the taciturn Benwese drew his sword. 'We'd have more chance against it in the open,' Ryder said. 'Maybe we should try to draw it out.'

'She will not come out,' Neith said. 'She prefers the damp, dark secrecy of her place under the rock. We must go in. It is the only way to recover the next amulet.'

'The sacred adze amulet,' Janet said, almost licking her lips. 'Well, don't stand there, Wilson — get your bow ready.'

'My bow will be next to useless — unless I can shoot out its eyes.'

'You may hit one, but she will not give you time to hit two,' Neith informed him soberly. 'Besides, it would do no good. She can sense where you are. You must watch out for her tail which will strike at you over her back. It will descend like a dart of death on your neck from high above for she can arch it high above herself in the darkness of the ceiling.'

'We must try to immobilise her tail,' Ryder said. 'I'll make a noose.'

'I hope your lassoing is better than it was last time,' Janet said, without a great deal of confidence.

They lit the torches again and the two women carried them, leaving Benwese and Ryder free to defend them. Snakeback whined anxiously as they went inside, warning them of the danger and reluctant to go in. 'Come on, boy,' he said to the dog. 'Stick by me.'

A breeze of decay swirled out of the darkness to greet them, brushing itself against them. Janet shivered. 'Just keep thinking of the amulet,' she muttered, more to herself than to the others.

Ryder fiddled with the length of rope, checking the noose that was still at one end. 'Can you change the rope as you did before?' he asked Neith.

'You are asking my help again, Bowman. I warned you of the risk. Already you have asked too much.'

'Just a thought.'

The group went deeper under the rock into the lair of Selkhet. The entrance widened into a vault of rock, the ceiling rising to lose itself in darkness. Good, Ryder thought; it gave him room to swing the noose.

He remembered Neith's warning: *'You must watch her tail which will strike at you over her back. It will descend like a dart of death on your neck for she can arch it high above herself in the darkness of the ceiling.'* He pictured the barb poised above their heads, ready to lash. He felt a cold draft find its way down the collar of his shirt.

'Where will we find the sacred adze?' he whispered to Neith.

'In a shrine. On a pedestal.'

'That's right. We'll find it on a statue of a scorpion,' Janet said with certainty. 'There's a small platform on top of the tail and that's where it lies.'

'You're very well informed all of a sudden,' he whispered. 'Was that in your notes, too?'

'No, it just sprang into my mind like a snapshot. The scorpion isn't here yet, either. I'll tell you when she comes.'

'What makes you think you'll see her first?'

'I won't need to see her. I'll *feel* her.'

'Feeling a scorpion is not advisable.'

'With my senses.'

'Oh yes,' he said sceptically. He remembered the reason Janet had given for her planned sojourn in the tomb: '*I want to spend an extended period alone in the tomb. I've studied the surfaces of the tomb,*' she said, '*and now I want to explore its inner life — if the word "life" can rightfully be attached to tombs, and I believe it can, especially this tomb. I want to soak up its vibrations and observe its secrets with the inner eye.*' It had sounded like New Age nonsense to Wilson Ryder.

Janet had always had a well-developed faith in her feelings and intuitions and what she called her psychic ability, but this was a new confidence. He wondered if they could trust their survival to it.

'You're still too black-and-white, even after what's happened. But a new realm of feeling and perception has opened up inside me, a transcendence. . . I feel strangely removed from here.' He wished he felt removed from this place. He wished he were removed from it physically.

The vault narrowed and choked down to become a large tunnel. They followed it and it opened up into a cavern. 'Beware,' Benwese called, ducking as a sharp spine thrust down into their light.

Janet was walking right into its path. Ryder dived at her to knock her aside and grunted as his shoulder struck not the softness of a woman, but a firmness like a column.

'What are you doing, Wilson? It's only a stalactite, can't you see?' He drew back, rubbing his shoulder. She was right.

The calming disclosure almost distracted him from the shock of what had just happened. But his shoulder felt bruised. It was not only Janet's will that had turned tensile as steel, but her entire body. It was like diving against a statue.

'Look, there are hundreds of them,' she said. They held up their lights and saw the gleaming spears of an inverted army — giant calcite formations that lanced down at their heads.

This didn't help. The point of the scorpion's tail would be one more spike among the cluster. The stalactites would also make using the lasso more difficult.

A spear with a droplet of venom beading on its point appeared to shift in the flickering light. He shrank back. It was only a stalactite with a droplet of moisture at its end. A draught made the droplet quiver.

'Relax,' Janet said. 'She's not here yet. You can jump when I say so.'

'Just like normal,' he said, bitterly. 'Well, pardon me, Janet, but I'll jump out of my skin when I feel like it.'

'Sh — sh! She's here. Oh dear. She's bigger than I thought. Much bigger. I feel the entire darkness moving. Yes. It's her. She's coming fast.'

Ryder didn't ask for permission to jump. He leapt back and so did the others. Snakeback's hair had risen and it gave a seething growl. They took cover behind a rock. Neith and Janet held up their lamps. Benwese held the blade of the sword erect, ready to strike with it. Ryder softly swung the noose, keeping an eye on the ceiling for the first sight of the tail. They heard a scraping sound like metal on rock. There.

He saw the glint of light on shiny black metal and two eyes opened up like lights. There was a crack and whistling sound and a black wind rushed at his head. Neith grabbed his arm and dragged him aside with a force that almost pulled his arm from its socket. The scorpion's lashing barb, splattering venom, struck the rocky floor and split it open.

Now the creature slithered forward making a mechanical rumble like the sound of an armoured tank on steel tracks. He saw the scorpion's pincers sweep in at them from either side of the chamber. Their spread was stupefying. They ducked as the pincers met above their heads with a crash like a couple of converging earthmover shovels.

'Pay heed to the tail!' Neith cried out. The creature was trying to distract them with the pincers, for while they were trying to avoid them it was starting to draw its tail back, loading its muscles for another attack. Ryder swung the rope and threw. The practice in the shrine of Renenutet had helped. The noose behaved perfectly, opening gracefully in the air and dropping neatly over the tail. He did not even have to pull it tight. The rearing tail of the creature did that for him. It also ripped him off his feet and swept him head first towards the burning lights of her eyes.

'Bowman!' Neith called in alarm. Benwese ran at the creature and his sword flashed as he struck between the joints of a leg. He missed, striking the armour and there was a clanging ring like the sound of metal hitting metal.

Ryder tried to slow his careering slide across the floor. He brought up his legs and dug in his heels. The sweating limestone floor was as smooth as ice. He slid like a skater, his heels searching for a spur, ridge or crack — anything that could give him purchase. He crossed a patch of floor that was ulcered with rimstone pools. His boots went into one, splashing up water, and his heels hit the calcareous lip on the other side of it, slamming him to a halt. The rope seared his hands, but he held on.

He teetered, almost losing his balance and toppling forward. He felt the rope tremble and stretch in his hands. The tail had slowed. He'd checked its backward arc. He pulled harder. The tail thrashed. He held with all his strength, struggling against it. He looked for a rock so that he could lash the rope to it, saw a stalagmite and whipped a coil around the slippery surface. The scorpion took up the slack and tugged at the stalagmite. But now Ryder had a pulley and he drew in the rope. It was working. Maybe we won't have to kill it, he thought. Maybe I can keep it tied down while the others recover the amulet.

'Look out, Wilson!' The scorpion had swung with its pincer. But it made no attempt to attack Ryder. It merely opened the jaws of the pincer and closed them around the rope, snipping it like a thread of cotton. Ryder snapped to the stony floor, holding a useless section of rope. The scorpion's tail craned back into the height of the ceiling, preparing to strike. Snakeback flew at the grinding planes of the creature's mouth, snapping and barking.

Ryder saw a blur from the corner of his eye. It was

Neith. She raced to the scorpion's side and ran up one of its legs. She scrambled up the bulge of its back to stand on the top of it. The scorpion went into a grotesque dance to shake her off.

The girl stayed on its back, maintaining her balance as nimbly as a dancer, then went closer to the head. The stalky eyes tried to look up at the invisible assailant, lunging with a pincered arm. Neith jumped and it whistled harmlessly underneath her feet. She landed and ducked. It came back higher and went over her head. Maddened, Selkhet decided to use its tail. There was a crack like a whip and a whistling sound as the poisoned barb descended. Neith dived off its back. The lashing barb of the scorpion struck. It hit the shell of its own back with a crack and sank through it, injecting a gush of venom.

It was as if it had pressed a lever that threw a million volts through its own body. Blue lightning flashed from its skin. Its legs and pincers flailed and it danced in ecstatic agony, snapping off stalactites and propelling them around the chamber like spears.

The creature shrieked. It was the sound of tortured metal as it contorted and ground every plate of its body. Then it gave off a brilliant flash of light and fell with a crash. Selkhet lay still. Neith had tricked it into stinging itself to death.

'The amulet,' Janet said. 'I'll get it.' She ran past the scorpion. The smouldering heap of armour made a ticking sound like hot metal cooling.

'You've saved me again,' he said to Neith. 'If you hadn't tackled the scorpion, it would have been my body Selkhet's sting found and not its own.'

'Yes, but who will save me now? I have not only interfered to help you, but have destroyed a kindred goddess, evil though she was. The repercussions are universal. I have mixed my fate with yours and in so doing have diminished myself. I feel weak, Bowman.'

'I'm not surprised after what you just did. That was extraordinarily brave to jump onto her back,' he said in admiration. 'I've never seen a braver thing.'

'Or a more reckless one.'

'But we have the amulet of the sacred adze.'

'No. *She* has the amulet. The Lost One. She is finding new energies from the field of force she is carrying.'

'Don't worry about Janet,' he said. 'She's a collector who enjoys the hunt. She'll look after them for us.'

'I hope you are right. I have deep misgivings about her.'

17

The hazards of Hathor

IT STOOD LIKE A MASSIVE FOREST OF STONE, a thicket of ruined columns, each one surmounted with a carved head of the goddess Hathor in her bovine form, a broad-cheeked woman with large eyes and cow's ears. 'We must penetrate to the shrine at the heart of these columns,' Neith said, leading them in among the structures into deeper shadow. 'At the heart of the columns, in a shrine, is the image of Hathor who guards the *menat* amulet.'

'What's waiting for us this time?' Ryder said. 'What's the danger?'

Before she could answer, Janet said, 'Take a look all around you. These stone columns are the danger. Don't you feel it?'

'Feel what?'

'Their menace. They are leaning over us and want to topple.'

'Columns can create that impression,' Ryder said, turning his neck to look up at one of the carved Hathor heads that topped a bulging trunk of stone. 'It's a trick of perspective, meant to strike awe in the beholder.'

'These ones can do a lot more than strike awe,' Janet said. 'They can roll us flat like pastry.'

'The Lost One is correct,' Neith said. 'These are columns of destruction, set to fall on intruders and destroy them.'

'Naturally,' Ryder said. 'It seems everything in this world is invested with a peculiar lethality. Is nothing easy? Let's hope we'll be able to see them falling.'

'Only if you can see in the dark,' Janet said cheerfully.

'Then we'll hear them shift.'

'No, Bowman. Not until it is too late. Their fall is magically swift and silent. Yet they will hit the ground with considerable force that will shake the earth, making others even more unsteady so that they too threaten to topple on us.'

'Then how will we know when and where they're falling? How will we avoid them?'

'We'll use something you wouldn't understand,' Janet said.

'What's that?'

'Instinct. Something men have in short supply.'

'I have hunches, too, you know.'

'If you did, they'd be telling you to leave this to me. Trust them. There's only one male instinct you should count on here — the instinct to leave it to a woman. To me.'

'To you? Since when did you have infallible powers?' he said.

He remembered how she had found the way to the scorpion's nest and how she had detected the presence of the creature before they did: '. . .*a new realm of feeling and perception has opened up inside me, a transcendence. . .*

I feel strangely removed from here,' she had said.

A column of stone slid past him. It reminded him of the solidity of Janet's body when he had dived into her. Something was happening to Janet. Yet he wanted to deny it, even though he had seen the evidence and saw it now. A force greater than confidence flowed through her body and shone out of her eyes. 'I should also remind you that you're not the only woman here.'

'So the Mistress of the Bow and Ruler of Arrows is reduced to a woman, after all! I thought you said she was something more? We'll see. I have another instinct that tells me you are right and that your little friend is becoming something less. We'll see who has the greater powers of perception — the Opener of the Ways, or me. We'll see who it pays to trust.'

'Halt,' Neith said, stopping abruptly so that the others ran into her.

'No, keep moving,' Janet said urgently.

'I feel danger ahead.'

'No, it's behind. It's coming down right at us. Jump!' Janet gave Benwese a push and he staggered against Ryder who toppled against Neith. Something whistled through the air. The dog jumped. They dived. The column fell like a mountain collapsing, landing so hard that the ground shivered underneath them. They looked around. A giant column, in shattered sections, measured its length on the ground. Miraculously it had missed other columns and fallen cleanly between them. They picked themselves up.

'Everybody all right?' They were shaken, but unhurt.

'No thanks to the Opener of Ways,' Janet said, dusting her hands and glaring at Neith. 'We'd be rolled flat as pastry if we hadn't gone forward.'

'I was mistaken,' Neith said in a surprised tone. 'I

am sorry, Bowman, to have failed you.' The voice held a quiver of anguish. 'It has never happened before, but I — I have faltered. What use am I now, a Ruler of Arrows who has lost her way? I am a vessel without contents, a lamp without light, an arrow without its bow. Useless. Worthless.'

Like the scorpion, she was turning on herself. 'You'll be all right. At least you knew it was falling,' Ryder said, consolingly. 'I never heard or felt a thing.'

'So much for masculine instinct,' Janet said caustically. 'Whose instinct are you going to trust from now on?'

'Perhaps you were just lucky that time,' Ryder said.

'You think so? Perhaps you'll be lucky if I open my mouth again. Maybe I should let the next one fall on your head.'

'We're all in this together, remember.'

'Then don't stand around. Follow me,' she said, taking the lead.

'Don't you think Neith should lead us?' Ryder said. 'She probably knows this place.'

'No better than I do. Trust my feelings on this, Wilson, and you may survive. Hurry up.' They moved on through the stone forest, going deeper and deeper to where the dim light of the eclipse merely trickled down feebly.

'There is danger,' Neith whispered. 'Go forward, swiftly.'

'No, stop,' Janet commanded them.

'Run, Bowman!'

'Back,' Janet said. 'It's falling right in our path.'

'Here it comes!' Neith said. 'Leap away!'

'No, stay back.'

'Bowman, too late. . .'

'She'll kill you. Stop, Wilson. Stay back!'

Time slowed and the voices of the two women

tugged at his ears. Who did he obey? The goddess who ought to know — or the woman who seemed to know?

'*I have hunches, too, you know.*'

'*If you did, they'd be telling you to leave this to me. Trust them. There's only one male instinct you should count on here — the instinct to leave it to a woman. To me.*'

Ryder left it to her and grabbed Neith, pulling her back and, at the same time, grabbed Snakeback by the collar. He felt a shadow within the shadows descend and a gust hit him like a pressure wave. Then the column crashed with a ground-jarring force and blocked off their path. Dust rose up and settled on the cowering group.

'Forgive me, Bowman. I falter again. I am weakening and even you can tell it now. You did not listen to me.' There was reproach in her voice. 'You listened to her, instead.' She was desolate, as much it seemed about his lack of faith in her powers as in this new display of its diminution. A trickle of light fell on her face, but it found no answering gleam in the once clear-gazing eyes. The light was leaving Neith.

'Satisfied, Wilson?' The eyes shone in Janet's daring face. Janet's light was growing as Neith's faded.

'Do I lead — or don't I?'

'You lead, Lost One.'

'Don't call me the Lost One,' Janet said. 'You'd all be lost without me.'

The fallen column made a barrier too high to climb. They went around it.

'Stop!' Janet whispered. All obeyed without question. *Ker-boom.* Another silent tower of stone came down to measure its length in the thicket. The thicket trembled. Ryder spun around, expecting the reverberations to bring more columns down on top of them.

'Keep going!' Janet said, altering course to clear the column.

They reached a shrine hidden in the heart of the thicket of columns, and here they lit their torches before going inside.

Was it a funerary chapel? Somebody, or something, had prepared for them. They were surprised by the sight of two tables laden with food and wine. Behind the tables stood twin images of the goddess Hathor, not in the guise of a cow this time, but in the forms of two lissom, golden women. Their tight sheath dresses in electrum carried a fine, cartouche motif, like scales. They wore jewelled anklets and bracelets on their arms. Crowns with red sun disks set between spreading horns rested on their golden heads and sacred *menat* amulets drooped from their offering hands.

Hathor, goddess of love, music, food and wine. . . in duplicate.

'Which one has the true necklace?' Benwese said.

'Does it matter?' Ryder said. 'We'll take both necklaces, just to be safe.'

'That would not be safe,' Neith said. 'You must choose one.' She still looked chastened. Tears that she had wept secretly in the darkness beyond the shrine had stained her cheeks. 'We must take the true necklace or she will raise her arms and the whole complex will collapse, killing all and losing the amulet forever.'

'I might have known that would be too easy. So what do we do?'

'You must accept Hathor's feast. You must choose one of the tables and eat the food and drink the wine.'

'That's fine by me. I'm pretty hungry — and thirsty. How about you, Benwese?' The soldier gazed hungrily at the spread, but shook his head.

'I suppose it would be too simple to eat and drink from both tables? We could probably clean up the lot,' Ryder said.

'One of the tables holds poisoned food,' Janet warned him.

Neith confirmed her guess. 'The wine and the meal are laced with a poison that kills like the death strike of a cobra.'

'I'd expect nothing less. Ladies, after you,' he said, standing aside with exaggerated politeness. Neither was amused.

'Very funny,' Janet said.

'*You* must eat and drink,' Neith said to Ryder. 'The goddess has set out these tables for you.'

'A deadly welcoming feast,' he said. 'How thoughtful.'

'Go ahead, Wilson, stuff your face.' Janet said.

'Don't you care if I eat poison?'

'It would serve you right.'

'A mistake would mean death for all of us,' Neith said, warningly. 'The columns would collapse inwards on the shrine.'

'A pity,' Janet said. 'It really would serve him right.'

Ryder shrugged. 'Well, if you don't care, Janet, why should I? I think I'll just pick any table and try my luck. I could do with a drink.' He moved towards the table on the left.

Both women made a grab to stop him. 'Do not be hasty, Bowman,' Neith said. 'You may drink your doom.'

'Don't be idiotic, Wilson. You're not spoiling everything now,' Janet said.

'Just trying to get your attention. So which table is it?'

'Be quiet and let me think,' Janet said. She looked from one table of offerings to the other. A frown of concentration grew in her forehead.

'Well?'

'I'm trying to think.'

'Not so sure any longer, is that it?'

'Not with you hassling me.'

'This is the shrine of the Great Goddess,' Neith said as if it explained Janet's uncertainty. 'Although my star fades, I am still more accustomed to the radiance of Hathor than she. You must trust in me now, Bowman.'

'I wouldn't advise it,' Janet said. 'You know what would have happened if we'd trusted her. We'd be flatter than papyrus. She can't help now. She doesn't know any more than you do — if she ever did. How many more times do I have to prove that to you?'

Janet circled the tables of offerings. They held pottery jars of wine and golden goblets, plates of beaten gold filled with grapes, pomegranates and figs. Other plates held conical loaves and small roasted fowl covered in a honey glaze. The smell of the food made Ryder swallow hard. They all went nearer. He remembered Neith's warning and imagined his stomach feeling the sudden virulent grip of poison.

Janet stopped in front of one table. 'Yes, maybe. . .' She went to the other. 'On the other hand, I think I have a feeling about this one.'

'Shall I try it?'

'No, I'll trust my first feeling,' she said going back to the first one. 'I'll choose this one.'

'She's like this in restaurants,' he told Benwese.

'Yes, this is the good one,' she said confidently. 'That one's the poison.'

'I'll trust you,' Ryder said. He picked up the jug of

wine and poured the red liquid into a goblet.

'No!' Neith said. 'The other one!'

'Are you going to listen to her?'

Ryder lifted the goblet, sniffed the contents. If there's poison in this cup, it's well disguised, he thought. The tang of the grape was cool and inviting. Still, he was cautious. The poison could be odourless and tasteless. 'I don't usually go in for a lot of wine ritual,' he said, sniffing the wine again and swirling it in the goblet, 'except when the wine may be poisoned, which I must say doesn't appear to be the case.' He raised the goblet. 'Just a tasting — and maybe I'll be a purist and spit out.'

'It won't save you,' Neith said. 'Once the wine touches your tongue, you will begin your journey to the fields of Aaru.'

'Here goes.'

'Bowman — no!'

She made a dive to stop him, but Janet blocked her way. 'Wilson, trust me!' Janet exclaimed.

Neith struggled to get past her, but Janet was too strong. Benwese could not move. Snakeback barked. Neith's eyes, dark slashes of fear, turned in desperation to the dog. 'Hound with a Snake on its Back — hasten to save your lord!'

Snakeback ran at his master and jumped. The ridgeback weighed thirty-eight kilograms and it hit Ryder with the force of a football forward. The goblet went flying aside and so did Ryder.

Ryder fell flat on his cheek on the stone floor. A beetle ran past the startled wideness of his eyes. It scurried into the pool of wine, stopped, froze like a scarab carved in stone, then gave off wisps of smoke from under its wing cases. Ryder gulped.

'Well, you can't be right every time,' Janet said.

And that was all she had to say as the boat took them further upstream. Neith took no solace from her victory over Janet.

'You've lost none of your ability,' he told Neith while they rested in the deckhouse. Janet sat inspecting the latest addition to the collection, a miniature *menat* necklace, taken from the hand of the goddess. Benwese stood out on the deck. 'Without you I would be dead.'

'Don't forget Hound with a Snake on its Back and the role it played. It was the instrument of your salvation.'

Ryder patted the dog. 'I won't forget. But you detected the poison. You knew. You still have your power.'

She shook her head. 'You do not understand. I drew power from being in that place. But I have lost it again.'

'How can you be so sure it's lost?'

'Because of the new things I have gained.'

'What things?'

'Feelings.'

'Didn't you have feelings before?'

'Yes, but different feelings. They were feelings *about* things, not *for* things. These new feelings don't guide me or inform me; they rule me. They are for others and are very frightening.'

'Feelings for others are the best feelings in the universe. They come from the power that I — and all people who care for others — draw on.'

'What power is that?'

'God.'

'Who is your god?'

He told her then about his god and about the helpless baby king who was to be the salvation of people, about how he was hidden in a humble place from those who would kill him, about his tortuous dying and his resurrection that promised eternal salvation for all who believed in him and about his role in judging people for what they had done with their lives.

'But this is the story of the baby Horus — and the king Osiris who died, but must be resurrected. It is a story that is yet to happen. How can this be, Bowman?'

'A pre-echo,' he said.

He found the saturnine soldier leaning over a rail at the deck. He had a look of longing.

'Don't be homesick,' Ryder said. 'You'll soon be back with your lady Bint-Anath.'

'Perhaps. But this is only the beginning of an age of struggle against the dragon of darkness.'

'Dragon?'

'Apophis, the serpent of chaos — and Lord Seth is his instrument. Seth has condemned us all to a life lived like corpses beneath the earth but, if we can succeed in this quest, the spell will be broken and we will rise and surprise the demon and his confederates.'

'We must succeed.'

'I am puzzled,' Benwese said. 'Why is it that you of all men have been called to complete this quest? I have spoken to the Lady Neith and she has told me that you are a bowman from the future. Your bow, a magnificent weapon, the like of which I have never seen, seems to confirm what she has said.'

'It's true that I come from a world and an age away,' Ryder confessed. 'But I don't understand why I've been called. I'm not any wiser than you, nor any more virtuous. I have no special quality, except determination, that fits me to the task. I don't even have more courage. This place fills me with the powerless terror of a nightmare.'

'But there must be a reason why the Universal Lord has chosen you. You must possess some quality.'

'A good eye and a better bow. A dog with a snake on its back.' Ryder shrugged.

'Special beliefs perhaps?'

'Even those are unremarkable. Plain and simple. Black-and-white. It's a puzzle to me. Why don't you ask Neith the same question? Maybe she knows.'

'I have already asked her. She said that of all bows she has guided and all arrows she has ruled, yours are the truest. She also told me that not only has she been searching for you down the passages of time, but that you have always been searching for her.'

Had he?

18

The pursuit of the elusive jackal

THE BOAT BROUGHT THEM TO a necropolis on the western side of the river.

'This next challenge you must face alone. You must recover the *ankh*, symbol of life. I do not know where you will find the *ankh* and neither does she,' Neith said, throwing a glance at Janet. 'You will have to hunt for it — in the true sense of the word, with your bow and arrows.'

'How do I hunt it?'

'You must hunt its owner, the jackal god Anubis, the guardian of the necropolis. You will find the *ankh* attached to his sacred collar.'

'Anubis, the god of the dead?'

'A demon creature in one of his aspects. This wily guardian takes the form of 'Jackal, Ruler of the Bows'. He can appear in two forms, as both a bowman and a mighty black jackal.'

'But where do I look?'

'Anywhere and everywhere in the necropolis. You

must hunt him down, while at every step he will be hunting you down.'

'Can he be killed?'

'*They* can be killed. Remember he has two forms — a jackal and a jackal-headed bowman — and he may switch between them at any time. The two manifestations of the guardian must be vanquished one at a time, the dog and the bowman. But here is the difficulty — *only the same arrow can kill them.*'

'If there are two of them, a man and a jackal, will you face them alone? Shall I not come?' Benwese said.

'A sword is of no use against Anubis,' Neith assured him. 'Only the bow can defeat him.'

'It's better that I go alone. We can't hunt well in a group,' Ryder said. 'Snakeback and I will go alone. We'll be faster.'

'Beware of unseen necropolis guards and chariot patrols,' Neith warned him. 'And take only nine arrows with you.'

'Why nine?'

'It is a magical number that will give you some power against him. One of his epithets is Jackal of the Nine Bows.'

Ryder and Snakeback slipped through the reeds and entered a belt of palms and sycamores. The green of the fertile strip gave way abruptly to the stony desert of the west. The necropolis lay in a valley watched over by high cliffs. A falcon sailed over the whitewashed mortuary chapels and hidden tombs of the seekers of eternity. The place looked as white as bones in the dim light of the eclipse. The big black dog of death was in there, one more shadow in a valley of shades, slinking between the tombs and the shrines.

'Where is he, Snakeback?' he whispered to the dog.

'Find him, boy.'

The ridgeback's eyes flashed excitedly. This was what it was bred for. The hunt. This was what it loved. It put its nose to the ground and sniffed, its tail flicking stiffly. Could it smell the dog of death?

Ryder swept the rock-strewn plain that separated them from the valley. No sign of a chariot patrol. The darkness gave him useful cover, but it also gave cover to the jackal. He looked up at the blackened sun with its rim of flashing chromosphere and corona and wondered how an eclipse could last so long. Theoretically it was impossible. No eclipse could last for days. A lunar eclipse could last for three hours and forty minutes, but the longest possible duration of a total solar eclipse was eight minutes — and its track of totality never spread beyond 268 kilometres. Yet it seemed as if the whole universe had crept into darkness to hide and to wait for the outcome of their struggle, aching for the successful completion of the quest. Had time itself stood still?

The rocks on the plain looked like crouched figures. Could the jackal be lying in wait behind one of them?

He took an arrow from the quiver and prepared. The weight of the bow and the glint of the arrowtip were comforting as was the confident stride of the dog at his side. He could think of no more reassuring ally at that moment than the steadying presence of the African Lion Dog.

In what form would this Anubis first appear? As the man hunter with a bow? Or as the black dog? How was he going to kill both man and jackal with one arrow? One at a time.

That raised a question in his mind, an important question he had forgotten to ask Neith. Could the jackal and the bowman appear at the same time? That presented fresh difficulties. Don't worry about that now. Concentrate.

Wilson Ryder's sharpened hunter's sense swept the rocky plain for signs of a presence that he hoped to detect like incoming pressure waves. He glanced at Snakeback. Its head was turning, too, the round amber eyes alert.

One arrow. Two enemies. A black jackal-dog and a man. Did the guardian of the necropolis combine the senses of both? The eyes of the hunter and the nose and hearing of the dog? That would make him doubly dangerous. But then Snakeback and I are also one, he reminded himself. We hunt as one.

They reached the fringes of the necropolis, a city of walled funerary chapels, some with pyramids of whitewashed mud brick surmounted with limestone caps on their roofs, others with sealed doorways in entrances that slanted into the stony ground. Ryder and Snakeback moved along the outer wall of a tomb, staying close to the wall. Snakeback sniffed. Could it smell the spoor of the jackal or the odour of death of this place?

Hunting the jackal among these buildings would be next to impossible. They needed to tackle it on more open ground. Perhaps they should allow themselves to be hunted for a while and lead the jackal to open ground beyond the necropolis, an area hemmed in by an amphitheatre of cliffs. He reached the end of the wall and cautiously peered around it. 'Come on, boy.'

They slipped like shadows to the next walled tomb. They passed a gateway in the wall and saw a small courtyard and a porticoed forecourt. Here relatives of the dead would meet on feast days to enjoy food and drink in the company of the dead and to leave offerings for the nourishment of the soul.

The jackal could be lying in wait inside — in any one of these walled structures. But it would be more likely to be running free, loping around the edges of the cemetery. Ryder needed a better view. Did he dare go higher? What if the jackal were watching? Maybe the guardian of the necropolis was ranging in the desert or the cliffs beyond.

'Stay, Snakeboy,' he whispered. The dog seemed uneasy, but sat. Slipping the bow over his shoulder he grabbed the top of the wall and hauled himself up, gaining a foothold on the top. Straightening but keeping himself low, he went along the wall to the roof of the porticoed chapel and then along the roof to a whitewashed mud pyramid. It had a limestone pyramidion on top. Inset in the pyramid was a recess containing a stela with a carving and prayer for the tomb owner.

Ryder leaned against the pyramid and stole a view of the necropolis. From his raised position he could see that the chapels were arranged haphazardly. There were no streets between them. They ran back for about a kilometre. The whitewashed pyramids looked ghostly in the pallor of the eclipse.

Was the guardian watching him now? It was doing more than watch him, he discovered. The guardian had been drawing careful aim on him. An arrow flashed past his ear and struck a spark off the granite pyramidion at his shoulder. Ryder dropped, crawling around the other side of the pyramid.

He slipped the bow off his shoulder and readied to shoot. A black head with pricked ears like a mask, but raised to the height of a man's head, turned around the corner to look for him. It was the barest glimpse of his quarry, but Ryder let fly.

His metal alloy arrow sped like a bullet and took a chunk of whitewashed plaster off the wall. The jackal drew back swiftly, bits of plaster showering into its face. Maybe that would teach him some caution.

He saw Snakeback move down below. The dog rose, stiffened, then took off, a growl rumbling in its throat. Ryder climbed off the roof of the chapel on the blind side, went quickly along the top of the wall, keeping low, and dropped lightly to the ground.

He edged cautiously around the wall. Be careful, the attacker could be circling you. That arrow on the rooftop had been close — but the disturbing thing was that it had missed. That bothered a marksman like Ryder. I wouldn't have missed the target of a man standing on a rooftop, he thought.

He could draw only two conclusions from it. The jackal guardian was fallible — or, more likely, betraying an unnerving confidence. There was every likelihood that it had been a warning shot. The jackal was playing with him. Ryder tasted the beginning of a long fight. This was going to be a battle and the jackal had scored the first hit — against his confidence. Snakeback came back looking baffled and guilty. The dog had lost the quarry.

This graveyard will kill us, Ryder thought. The jackal knows it better than we do and there are too many places to hide. He had to draw the guardian into more open country, where the superior distance afforded by his modern composite bow would give him an advantage.

With Snakeback at his side, Ryder picked his way between the tomb buildings, running fast and low between open spaces and flattening himself against the whitewashed walls to check before making the next dart to cover.

Had the jackal fled? The buildings were thinning out now and he saw glimpses of desert and the cliffs beyond. He spotted a gully at the end of the necropolis. That would give them some cover.

He ran for it in a weaving line and dived, keeping flat. Sand jumped into his mouth and he spat it out. Did he dare lift his head and check for the jackal? It might be the last thing he did.

Ryder's nerve endings told him they were being watched. He felt that minute convergence of attention that he usually brought to bear on a target being trained in his direction. Just how good is this jackal? he wondered. As a marksman, Ryder wanted to know. He looked around the gully. He wished he was wearing a hat so that he could lift it above the edge of the gully and see if it drew the jackal's arrow. I dare you to show a finger, that convergence of attention beamed to him — just a finger.

Perhaps I'll test the air with something finer, he thought. He took one of the wooden shafted arrows of the Mesniu and raised the fletching above the rim of the gully. A wind whipped over his head. The arrow kicked in his hands and suddenly he was looking at a piece of cleanly-cut shaft. The fletching had gone, snapped away by a speeding arrow.

And now he grunted and slid down into the gully, looking forlornly at the piece of arrow in his hand. The dog crawled over and sniffed at the piece.

'So that's how it is.' I'm not sure I could have done that, Ryder thought, tossing the piece away. Maybe. But I wouldn't like to live or die on the certainty. The guardian was more than a marksman of the target-shooting variety. This was a sniper. The display unnerved him, but also sharpened and excited him. I'm going to have to shoot better than I've ever done in my life and then a bit better.

'We're in for a fight, Snakeback.' Snakeback wagged its tail slowly. The round eyes flashed, daring him to fight on. The animal looked confident. Snakeback believes in me and is trusting me to win. And so are the others on the boat.

He was glad now that he had come alone, even though his nerves felt stretched to cracking point. He was going to have enough trouble keeping himself out of the line of fire without worrying about others.

What would they do if he never came back? He hoped they wouldn't make the mistake of coming after the jackal. It would be the last quest they embarked on.

Range. That's my only advantage. 'Come, Snake, let's crawl,' he muttered to the dog.

Keeping low, they worked their way along the gully towards the desert. The gully deepened after a time and they were able to straighten. He lost sight of the gleaming pyramids of the necropolis.

They continued along it for a long time before the gully shallowed, coming to an end. A cluster of boulders at the edge offered cover when they emerged. They left the gully and crawled around the boulders. Ryder allowed himself a look back. They had come several hundred metres, well out of the range of an Egyptian bow. Ryder looked up at the cliffs. The cliff face was in heavy shadow. Take the high ground, his hunter's instinct told him. Let's see how the sniper enjoys being sniped at.

Ryder and the dog crawled into the shadow of the cliffs. They looked for a way up and found a cliff path. No, the guardian would expect that.

There was another way up, going from rock to rock.

He chose that way instead. They climbed. Snakeback came up behind him, nimble as a mountain goat. We're vulnerable, Ryder thought, feeling his back exposed. It spurred him to increase his effort. He grabbed a loose stone and it clattered down the surface. He saw a good vantage point halfway up the cliff face. That would do. They climbed on until they reached it.

It was a ledge with a cover of a chunk of rock. He hid with Snakeback behind the chunk of rock and nocked an arrow to his bow.

The valley was spread out like a blanket underneath them. A rabbit couldn't move down there without my seeing it, he thought. He relaxed, caught his breath and settled back to wait and watch. Would the guardian come after him? Or simply wait for him to come down? Ryder hoped that the Ruler of the Bows liked a good fight.

19

Snakeback

WITH EVERY PASSING MINUTE that the guardian did not appear, Ryder felt tension coil more tightly in his stomach. Perhaps their quarry would not be coming. Perhaps the enemy was already up here with them. Was it possible that the jackal bowman had raced here ahead of them?

Maybe he was on the cliff face already and working his way into a position from where he could strike.

Ryder saw a large black animal break from the cover of a tomb building and run at speed towards the gully. *Remember he has two forms — a jackal and a jackal-headed bowman and he may switch between them at any time, Neith said.* He had changed into a jackal. He reached the gully and sped along it. At the rate he was running he would be with them in moments.

He was still almost two hundred and eighty metres away, but Ryder knelt and took aim. He bent the powerful composite bow, lined up with the black running streak, then led his target, making adjustments for trajectory. He released.

The arrow streamed like a thin beam to the plain

below and kicked into the sand in front of the animal. The shaft caught the running foreleg, sent the animal tumbling. Ryder whipped another arrow from his quiver.

The jackal stood up, raised its black snout to gaze up into the cliffs in disbelief. Now it knows it has a fight, Ryder thought with grim satisfaction. Well, that could be your last thought. Ryder snapped another arrow from the bow.

But just as the arrow blurred from the bow so did the image of his target. The black jackal dissolved as swiftly as a shadow hit by light. The arrow struck empty sand. It landed where the jackal had been standing in the gully an instant before. It was a true shot, but it had missed because the jackal had vanished. Ryder lowered his bow and his shoulders slackened.

Where has he gone? Into thin air? Ryder had forgotten. The jackal was a demon, not a man. What now? How did he fight an invisible enemy? He should have waited until the animal was closer and made sure of ending it properly.

I've wasted an opportunity, he thought, and my enemy may not give me another one.

Did they still have the high ground? Ryder wondered. He couldn't be sure. He now felt exposed and restricted on the shelf of rock. Go higher while there's still time, a warning voice urged him. He followed the urge, looking for a way up. The cliff path was in sight. They could reach it by following the ledge and then climbing for a time. No, keep away from the path.

They climbed and went along. It was a wise decision, he discovered an instant later.

The jackal bowman had chosen a position that gave him a view of the path. Ryder saw him waiting on a narrow shelf. The attacker heard him coming, but couldn't shoot without making an awkward movement on a narrow shelf of rock. He spun around to loose an arrow, but bumped his shoulder on a wall of rock. Ryder flattened himself. The arrow snapped into a crack in the cliff face, centimetres from his shoulder. Ryder stepped out, bow at the ready. Now the jackal bowman flattened himself against the rock, hiding himself. But it wasn't enough. Ryder punched a metal alloy arrow into the demon's calf.

The strike produced a howl of rage and pain; not a man's howl, but the howl of a hit animal. The leg vanished. Ryder and Snakeback went after him. He saw the jackal-headed man emerge on the other side of the shelf and run, limping towards the top of the cliff.

Ryder took another shot, but the shelf was too narrow and the rock hampering and the arrow whizzed harmlessly across the cliff.

'Follow him, boy.' Snakeback ran yelping ahead.

Let's see if the demon can hide a blood spoor, Ryder thought. He saw him appear again, still running and limping, and Ryder shot another arrow, but the jackal-man was too quick. They had reached the top of the cliffs, a stony surface tortured by the wind into rounded, sculptured shapes.

Where had it gone? Snakeback took off for an outcrop of rock shaped like a sphinx and disappeared from view. A giant black jackal ran into view from the other side, taking Ryder by surprise. He snapped off a quick shot, but the arrow missed by a good metre or two. The jackal was climbing up on the sphinx to ambush the dog below. Ryder shot again. Missed.

The dog was in danger. Ryder reached into his

quiver. One arrow rattled loosely inside. The last arrow. He had brought only nine arrows.

He remembered the words of Neith: *'You must hunt him down, while at every step he will be hunting you down.'*

'Can he be killed?'

'They can be killed. Remember he has two forms — a jackal and a jackal-headed bowman — and he may switch between them at any time. The two manifestations of the guardian must be vanquished one at a time, the dog and the bowman. But here is the difficulty: only the same arrow can kill them.'

Snakeback ran around the outcrop again and now the black jackal was on top of the rock and crouching to spring. It would land on the ridgeback's neck. One bite and twist of its massive jaws would finish its pursuer.

And now Ryder saw another movement.

A man limped from cover, hurrying to hide behind another rock, a rock that sheltered him, but allowed him a shot at Ryder. Ryder did not hesitate. He bent the bow and went for a neck shot on the jackal.

The broadhead arrow snapped home with a sound like one going into a sandbag.

Thwack. The jackal quivered and gave a howl, but did not drop. It slunk back across the rock and went down, running along the cliff path. My last arrow, Ryder thought. Snakeback saw it go.

'Fetch!' Ryder called. Then he dropped to the ground as an arrow from the jackal-man's bow smashed into the rock near his face.

Ryder crawled around the rock to gain a view. He saw Snakeback overhauling the wounded monster. It swung around, saw him coming and turned to attack. The black jackal towered over Snakeback, big as a lion. But Snakeback had been built to hunt lions and it did not shrink from this wounded enemy. Snakeback dived at the animal's throat. The two animals, locked together, rolled in a spinning, snarling buzz-saw of teeth and claws.

The jackal was taken aback by the ridgeback's ferocity, but it knew its strength, though ebbing, to be superior. Snakeback couldn't hold it. The jackal broke free, rolling to its feet. It shook itself, the arrow still stuck in its neck, and went back at the dog.

The limping bowman came around the rock. Ryder had no more arrows. He was defenceless.

He rolled down the hillside, grazing his elbows, to reach a shelf of rock and ran along it, keeping low. It rounded a curve in the cliff towards the path.

But the shelf never reached the cliff path. It ended just short of the path and dropped into a dizzying gap. The gap was too wide for a man to jump.

The jackal-headed bowman gave a snarl of victory and came down to the shelf to claim his prize.

Two choices rolled into Ryder's mind like a pair of dice in a losing throw. Both choices meant defeat. He could wait for his own execution or deny the bowman his victory and take a jump off the cliff to extinction.

He thought of home, not his real home, but the canvas tent on a plain in a place and a time far away. Can I die here, when I lived then? He saw the faces of Neith, Janet and Benwese crowd anxiously around him. What can I do? Nothing can help me. No power on earth or above it.

The bowman passed out of view. He was working his way unhurriedly down the cliff to reach the shelf and would meet it on the blind side of the curve.

'Help me,' Ryder said to the sky.

There was a third choice. It came blood-smeared and

limping along the cliff path, looking as if it had been shot through the muzzle, with the shaft of an arrow on one side and the fletching of the arrow on the other and its eyes flashing both a warning and a light of victory.

'Snakeback!'

The animal broke into a run and leapt off the cliff path, the arrow still in its jaws. It sailed across the gap and landed safely on the shelf beside Ryder. The arrow was back. This arrow had not got away from it. This arrow he had taken from the dead body of a defeated enemy. The dog dropped the arrow proudly at Ryder's feet and wagged its tail in weary satisfaction. Ryder remembered. *'The two manifestations of the guardian must be vanquished one at a time, the dog and the bowman. But here is the difficulty, only the same arrow can kill them.'* Snakeback had brought it back. The same arrow. Ryder snatched it up.

The guardian, broad-shouldered but with a wily jackal's head, came lightly along the ledge, an arrow nocked to his bowstring, so confident that he had not bent the bow. The ears were flattened for attack, though, and there was cool intent in the eyes. They quickly turned to surprise. The ears straightened and jagged teeth in the pointy face unsheathed themselves in fright. He dropped, bending his bow to loose the arrow, but Ryder's arrow was deep in his heart before he hit the ground.

'I'll fetch this one,' he said to the dog. He bent over the dead creature and removed the gold *ankh* that was attached to an ornamental collar at his throat. Then he retrieved his arrow, the same arrow that Snakeback had retrieved from the neck of the dead jackal.

'Well fetched, Snakeback. Good boy.' Snakeback had brought back more than an arrow. He had brought his master from death. He examined the dog. It was gashed in a few places and stained with blood, but most of the blood had come from the jackal. The blood had a peculiar odour of decay mixed with the tang of embalming spices.

The dog of death was dead.

Ryder and Snakeback washed themselves at the river's edge. He washed the blood off the dog's coat and it shook itself vigorously, covering him in fine spray. Ryder laughed and picked up the big dog, wet as it was, and carried it back to the bank and the smell of its wet fur somehow gave him a pang for home and for the world he remembered. They returned to the boat.

Neith was waiting on the river bank. Her eyes looked dark and distraught, but the darkness fled at the sight of the bowman and his dog returning through the reeds. Ryder held up the amulet that had been attached to the animal's collar.

'Bowman, you are back. I was mortally afraid for you. Yet I see you have done the impossible and defeated the mighty jackal of the bow!' Neith knelt as the dog ran happily to greet her and she gave it a welcoming rub on its back. She noticed the cuts and injuries with concern.

'It was a fight and Snakeback had the worst of it, didn't you, boy? He took on the wounded black jackal and fought him to death,' said Ryder.

'Poor brave hound. Truly, you are an enchanted animal.'

Janet and Benwese ran down the gangplank. 'You did it!' said Janet. 'Well done, Wilson. You didn't let us down. Show me the amulet.' She took the amulet from his hand and ferried it on board to examine more closely. Benwese thumped him heartily on the shoulders and demanded Ryder relate the entire story of his battle.

'I would know this, too,' Neith said, 'in every detail.'

They sat in the deckhouse, Janet turning over the amulet in the light of a lamp, while he told them the story, pausing to chew on a conical loaf of bread and to sip from a jar of Egyptian beer. Neith and Benwese grew very still as he told how the battle suddenly turned badly and how it seemed to be over and he was stranded, arrowless on a ledge, with the jackal bowman advancing to kill him, when Snakeback came bloodied and limping up the path, an arrow held in its jaws as if it had been shot through the muzzle. Tears sprang into Neith's eyes.

'Truly, I love Hound with a Snake on its Back,' she whispered, not trusting herself to speak aloud. 'I think I always have.' Neith's emotions washed over them like a tingling wave. Neith certainly had feelings.

Then he told how he had taken that final arrow brought back to him by the dog and used it to shoot the surprised bowman through the heart and Benwese whooped and cheered as if the scene were happening in front of his eyes and Neith clapped her hands in delight. To Benwese and Neith, the words were vivid and magical and stood for real things. They were as real as the events they described and they produced real reactions. Words still had their full coinage and had not been devalued by time and usage. Their minds vibrated to his words like instruments to a musician's fingers.

Were they unsophisticated? He did not think so. In a modern age when scientists could create the marvel of electronic images on a screen, people had lost the power to create pictures in their own minds the way these two were so clearly doing. By an irony, was technology making the mind less sophisticated than it had been at the dawn of history? he wondered.

20

Death tomb

LATER RYDER FOUND A QUIET MOMENT at the rail of the deck, watching the papyrus-fringed banks slide by as their wind took them southwards.

Neith came out onto the deck to join him. 'I'm glad that you prevailed over the jackal. And not just because you recovered the amulet. My thoughts were with you every step, even though I could not be beside you as I once would have been.'

'Thankyou,' he said.

Neith turned her face away from him. 'Why did you have to come to this realm, Bowman?'

'How can you ask? You brought me here.'

'Yes, but why did it have to be *you*?' She turned and he saw that there were tears in her eyes, not tears of flashing light as he had seen before, but the tears of a woman. He touched her. The marble coldness had gone. Her skin was softened, warm.

'Why are you upset?'

'Did you come to destroy me? For that is what you are doing. I told you before, I cannot mix my destiny with yours — only at the risk of losing my powers.

I am losing them, Bowman,' she said in a voice that shook with despair. 'They are fading, moment by moment.'

'You have lost none of your power over me, Neith,' he heard himself say.

'But that is not the power I should have. It is ill that I should care for your safety and commit myself to your protection.'

'Is that what divinity means?' he said. 'Is a Divine One a being who has risen above feeling, transcended love for others? If losing your powers makes you love, then you are not losing powers, but gaining power.'

'I am gaining a power to suffer.'

'I think a part of me flew to you in every arrow that I ever shot into the sky,' he confessed.

'You were seeking the divine.'

'Was I? My longing for the divine is already filled,' he said. 'Or so I thought. I believe in another one, a higher god.'

'The creator god above all, whose son came to save humanity.'

'Do we believe in the same god, Neith?'

'Can there be more than one higher god, above all?'

Semantically, no, there could not be, he reasoned. But could an ancient, pagan entity like Neith truly be on the same path as he was?

Janet came out of the deckhouse, still holding the bag with the amulets. She frowned at the sight of Neith in earnest conversation with Ryder. 'Ryder, I want to talk to you,' she said. 'Please leave us alone,' she said to Neith in a peremptory tone.

Neith stiffened and her eyes locked with Janet. Yet the flashes came not from Neith's eyes, but from Janet's. Neith lowered her glance, giving up her place beside

Ryder and leaving. 'Remember what I told you. She's a heartless pagan,' Janet said.

'She has more feelings than some. What's happening to you, Janet?'

'I feel a new power. Look at me. What do you see?'

'I see a woman with a steely purpose and a determination to achieve her goal at all costs, regardless of anybody else. I can't see the Janet I used to know.'

'That's because I am so much more than before. Isn't that what you want, Wilson? You've always longed to find that elusive mystery in woman, that divinity that was missing. You wanted more than an earthly woman and now you have it — in me. Don't you see it? The power is rising in me. I can give you what you always wanted, but you must be with me.'

Janet had never looked so beautiful. Something had taken her beauty and refracted it through a lens into unearthly radiance. She touched his arm with fingers that were cool and firm as marble. He had always loved Janet, for all her faults — when she was less than now; this extra light of mystery that shone from her eyes only bound him to her more.

'Of course I'm with you,' he said. 'And I'm staying with you until I can take you back.'

'Good,' she said, relaxing. 'Your future's with me, not with her. Just as she once had the power to bring you here across time and space, so I now have the power to transport you to a state of ecstasy that you could never have dreamed of.' This was a new Janet, one with a power that both excited him and frightened him.

He felt despair. I love them both, he thought. Was it the pagan pitilessness in woman that he was captive to?

The boat set them down in the west. 'The next stronghold is the death tomb,' Neith informed them.

'The tomb of a king of the Crocodile Nome.'

'Death tomb? What does death tomb mean? All tombs are for the dead.'

'This tomb *kills*. It is a deep, cliff tomb filled with deadly obstacles. In the burial chamber are the last of the amulets we need — except for the stolen eye of Horus. The mummy itself holds a tiny crook and a flail. Then, within the mummy wrappings are two amulets we seek — the Amulet of the Heart and the *was*-sceptre amulet. We must take these as well as the Crook and the Flail. But first we must survive the deadly passages.'

'What sort of obstacles will we face?'

She shrugged. 'I am unsure. I cannot see, Bowman. There is a mist in my eyes.' The mist was mortality. Once, Neith would have known.

'Why do you ask her?' Janet said, overhearing her reply. 'You should ask me.'

'Go ahead,' he said. 'What do we have to face?'

'You can sweat, Wilson. I'm not going to tell you now. You should have asked me first.'

'Don't be cross-grained, Janet. If you know, tell me.'

'No.'

'Why put us at needless risk? Do you care if we die?'

'I'm not sure I can die.'

'Be sensible, Janet.'

'You went to her.'

'She's our guide.'

'Not any more.' She pushed past them and went ahead.

The swordsman Benwese smiled at Ryder. 'We have a new guide,' he said.

They followed a path high into the cliffs. 'This is it,' Janet said, stopping at a doorway sealed with plaster and bearing the seal of necropolis priests. 'We must break the door down.'

'If we'd known — if you'd told us — we could have brought picks.'

'We don't need them,' Janet said, putting the palms of her hands flat against the surface. She pushed. The plaster squeaked, cracked and pieces fell through with a hollow dumping sound. It gave way as easily as icing. It must have been thinner than it seemed, Ryder thought.

He grabbed a jagged edge in his hands and pushed. His fingers whitened, but he couldn't shift it. The plaster resisted him, just as he resisted the conclusion he was compelled to draw. Janet had developed a hideous strength.

'Stand aside,' she said tiredly. She raised a boot and rammed it against the door and more of the doorway fell with a crash into the passage behind. She pulled away some more chunks with her hands, making enough room for them to pass through. 'There,' she said, dusting her hands, a smile of superiority on her face.

'Lucky break,' he said, raising an eyebrow at Benwese. His archaeological partner Janet was changing in a bewildering way.

They lit fresh torches and Ryder went in first. They found themselves in a forecourt with dumpy columns carved out of the solid rock. A frieze of painted bas reliefs ran around the walls. It showed a procession to the grave, a line of servants carrying a dead man's funerary furniture, ornamental chests, beds, chairs, pots and jars, gameboards — even his writing palette and his sandals.

A black square doorway led beyond. They bent to go through it and found themselves on a sharply descending ramp that ran down into the cliff. They struck along it. Dense columns of hieroglyphs marched along the walls. Janet was the expert on hieroglyphics, but she did not give them a glance, pushing on with a determined jut to her chin. A seated low-relief image of the god of the dead, Anubis, with a black, jackal head, erect ears and a sharp snout dominated this section of passage. Ryder looked down at Snakeback. The dog seemed easy, panting rhythmically after the climb up the cliff face.

He remembered how the dog had run at the jackal to attack it, ignoring the risk to itself, and he felt a bond of affection with the tall dog that the animal seemed to feel. It rolled its head to turn up and look at him and something passed between man and dog that did not need words.

'We've come a long way from home, old boy,' he thought. 'Who could ever guess that the arrow you chased on that morning could have brought us so far?'

Janet quickened her pace and fell in beside him. Neith and Benwese brought up the rear.

They had nine amulets now and this tomb held another four. What more could face them? His mind went over the challenges he had faced: the charging black boar of Seth, the crumbling maze where he had met Janet and found the Djed column, the battle against the demon charioteers and the struggle against the marauding Sekhmet lioness, the giant crocodile and the Heqet frog, the infiltration of the harem to retrieve the buckle of Isis, the boulder-rolling beetles and the scarab amulet, the *uraeus* and the snake-headed attackers, the scorpion monster and the sacred adze, the jackal bowman with the *ankh*. Janet had them all, softly rubbing together, in the bag hanging from her shoulder.

With each struggle and the gathering of each amulet he had sensed more than the acquisition of another valuable object; he had felt a gathering of force around them, a heightened expectancy in the air as if the entire universe were stirring, sitting up and watching their progress. They were not only gaining momentum; they were gathering might. He could feel it rising up, buoying them like a wave of optimism. He felt his arm tingle like an electric shock and, turning, he saw that the bag on Janet's shoulder had brushed against him. He touched it again, on purpose. Energy crackled from it like static electricity.

The amulets. Was the concentration of power already mounting within the collection of nine objects? Maybe that explained the growing change in Janet. She was taking power from the amulets!

He looked at the short-haired young woman striding loosely beside him. It explained a lot of things: her assertiveness, her certainty of direction, the new strength she had revealed in knocking down the sealed doorway. He remembered diving against her in the scorpion's lair and the solidity of her body stopping him like a stone pillar. He recalled the way her eyes had flashed at Neith, the way her beauty had refracted into a radiance and the cold, almost repellant feeling of her touch — like stone.

It was the way Neith's touch had felt — before she had abandoned her detachment and come to his aid, first with the rope, then leaping onto the back of the scorpion. There is a bewildering phenomenon taking place in these two women, Ryder thought.

They were both changing. Neith was becoming a woman. And Janet was becoming — what? Superhuman? Could Janet Nancarrow, his long-time archaeological partner and sweetheart, be transforming into something divine?

Janet was right. I have always longed to find the divine in woman. But now that the fire of divinity is aglow in Janet, I long to find the woman again. I longed to find the woman in Neith but, now that she is less of a goddess and more of a woman, I miss the drowning depths of her divinity.

What did he want most? A divine Janet, or an earthly Neith? Ryder felt his head spin like the twisting shadows of their forms on the walls. They went down a long flight of steps. There were more columns of hieroglyphs and a few painted guardian figures, a crocodile-headed monster known as the Eater of Souls and then a dog-headed ape with two swords in his hand.

They entered a circular chamber and now they stopped and looked around in puzzlement. An ant's nest of passages ran off in every direction. 'Where to now?' Ryder said.

'Look,' Neith said, pointing to the centre of the chamber. The chamber was some kind of shrine, for a crocodile lay on a dais of stone. It did not move. Ryder reached for his bow.

'It cannot harm us,' Neith said, staying his hand. 'It is long dead — a holy relic.'

'A stuffed crocodile,' Janet said thoughtfully. 'Interesting. Not mummified in the usual way — more like the kind of stuffed crocodile we're used to seeing in a museum. The Egyptians sometimes did the same thing. They stuffed the hide with scraps of linen and papyrus.'

The crocodile lay like a rippled, grey-green log, its head lifted, jaws slightly apart, and its inlaid eyes shining in the flickering light of their lamps.

'Well, if a stuffed guardian is the only guardian, we're

in luck,' Ryder said.

'He is not the guardian,' Neith informed him. 'Listen. The guardian comes.'

They fell still. It came from afar. It was a dragging sound of something heavy being hauled along one of the passages. They looked around at the ring of passage doorways. Where was the sound coming from? The dragging sound seemed to rush out of each doorway like a sigh.

'What is it?' Ryder said.

'The Soul Eater.'

'Ammit?' Janet said.

'You know his name.'

'What do we have to do?' Ryder said to Neith.

'Avoid Ammit at all costs. The creature will eat your heart. But to avoid it we must choose the right passage before it comes. Only one passage will lead to the tomb. That same passage is safe from Ammit. The others lead to death.'

'Do you know which one?' Ryder said.

Neith gave a helpless shrug. 'I — I do not know, Bowman. I cannot see any more.'

21

The swallower of secrets

'SO MUCH FOR YOUR OPENER OF WAYS,' Janet said.

Ryder turned to Janet. 'Presumably you can do better?'

'Not me.'

'Are you trying to be awkward?'

'Don't be ridiculous, Wilson. I simply don't know the answer. There's something about this place — a field like magnetism. I can't see the way either. We're going to have to use our heads.'

'We'd better be quick,' Ryder said, listening to the shuffling sounds that were emanating from the passages. 'By the sound of it, that thing's getting nearer. Maybe we can discover which of the passages it's coming along and try to stop it.' He went one way on a circuit of the doorways. Benwese went the other way. They stopped at each doorway, listening for the approach of the Soul Eater. There were deeply incised symbols above each doorway: a crocodile, a lion, a feather, a sword, a bee, a bird. . .

'You're wasting your time,' Janet said. 'It doesn't

matter which passage that thing's coming along. What matters is which passage leads to the burial chamber.'

Ryder and Benwese each stopped to listen at one of the square, black doorways. This is the one, Ryder thought. The dragging sound was magnified and distorted by echoes. It sounded like the shuffle of a steam locomotive. He went to the next one. No, this was louder. He shrugged. The next was even louder.

'I cannot tell!' Benwese said, experiencing the same difficulty on the other side of the chamber.

The sound was funnelling into each passage. 'I told you, you're wasting time.'

Janet had turned her attention to the stuffed crocodile. 'There's some writing carved on the stone base,' she said, holding a torch nearer.

'This is hardly the time for archaeology, Janet.'

'Oh shut up, Wilson. You've tried your way. Now I'm going to use some brainpower instead. Look at this. Interesting,' she murmured. 'It could be a clue.'

Ryder and Benwese continued circling the chamber and listening at the doorways.

'Let's see. . .' Janet could lift meaning out of a column of hieroglyphics like a magnet lifting pins off a table top. She was far more adept than Ryder and had pursued Egyptian philology with her usual intensity, making it her specialty. Ryder could work his way through Egyptian texts with the best of them, but it was a labour of the brow and it took him twice as long. She had often said teasingly that he deciphered hieroglyphics at about the speed of a child at second-year reading level.

The dragging sound had turned into a rumble like that of a lion, but there was a new sound that made Ryder stop at the door to the next passage — a heavy rasping like a blowtorch. Was it the sound of the creature breathing?

He held his torch into the gloom, expecting to see — what? Ammit? A creature of wild improbability that was said to devour men's souls — a mutant that was part crocodile, part hippo and part lion.

'I am the swallower of mysteries. . . no, of secrets. . .' Janet said, running her fingers over the incised hieroglyphics as she translated the script.

'Why don't you let Neith read it?' Ryder said.

'She probably can't read. Very few ancient Egyptian women could.'

Benwese and Ryder met at the last doorway. Benwese shrugged, but he had his sword drawn, Ryder noted, and an inward look of fear in his dark eyes at the approach of the unseen Devourer of Souls. We all fear death, Ryder thought, but this man's fear is greater than mine because he fears the final death, the fate that every Egyptian dreaded, the destruction of the soul and the everlasting nothingness that followed.

'The way beyond this chamber I preserve in my heart, no other knowing, or seeing,' she read on. 'Now what does that tell us?'

'Not much,' Ryder said. 'I think it may be time we played our hunches. Pick a passage, any passage.'

'This is not a card trick, Wilson. There are swirling forces of confusion here. This place is built to deceive. Don't disturb me; I'm trying to think.'

The dragging sound was interrupted by a bellow that made them all jump, except Janet who gazed unblinking at the incised hieroglyphic figures as if she were trying to look beyond them to penetrate their secrets.

'He is close,' Neith said, shivering as a cold breeze wrapped itself around them. 'Very close.'

Ryder nocked an arrow to his bowstring.

'Give me your sword,' Janet commanded Benwese.

'What for?' Ryder said. 'Do you plan to tackle Ammit yourself?'

'Don't be silly. Force isn't the answer to everything. Do something useful and turn the crocodile on its back. I want to take a look inside him.'

'We're wasting time.'

'Do it, Wilson. Didn't you hear what the text said? *"I am the swallower of secrets. . . the way beyond this chamber I preserve in my heart, no other knowing, or seeing. . ."* This crocodile is stuffed with scraps of papyrus. If you'd taken more interest in hieroglyphics you'd know that the scraps of papyrus used in stuffing animals often contained fragments of texts that have turned up unexpected information about Egypt, like the lost endings to unfinished stories. . .'

'I get it. The swallower of secrets has the secret inside him.'

'Very good,' she said. 'Now, will you get moving?'

Ryder spun the crocodile onto its back. It was dry and light and made a sound like a hollow log. Janet gave her torch to Benwese and used both hands to plunge the sword into the pale underside of the reptile. She sawed vigorously, slitting it open from tail to neck. She allowed the sword to clatter to the floor and dug her hands up to her elbows in the fibrous entrails, hauling out handfuls of stained-looking linen and papyrus. A smell of fishy decay, masked with aromatic spices, rose to assault their noses.

The creature approaching their chamber let out another bellow that beat through the passages. The noise attacked their cowering eardrums from all directions.

'Here,' Janet said, grabbing a strip of papyrus with

fingers that shook, more with delight at her discovery than in fear of the approaching menace. 'Bring me light,' she whispered urgently. Benwese brought the torch nearer.

'No clues, only drawings,' Janet said disappointed, looking at a faded sketch made on the surface with a reed pen.

'Wait, it's a map!' Ryder said, peering over her shoulder. 'It's a plan of this chamber.'

'Do you think so?'

'Yes, look.' Ryder pointed to the map. 'This square here in the middle is the dais and those lintels represent the doorways. Does it tell us which doorway leads to the burial chamber? Let's see. It should be marked. Yes, here.' He stabbed at the yellowed strip of papyrus in her hands. 'This doorway is marked with red ink — the lintel with a feather symbol on top.'

'It's the feather of truth — run!'

As they reached the doorway, a black wind-force howled into the chamber. They ran and ran along an endless gullet of time.

They saw another open, darkened doorway. Ryder went to run through, but pulled up without warning as a figure swung into the doorway as if on hinges, blocking the way. The others collided against him, gasping in surprise.

It was a giant squatting ape and it filled the doorway. It had a sky-blue gown draped over its knees, a sword brandished in one hand and a bow and fistful of arrows in the other, and deep-set eyes beneath an overhanging brow. Ryder was about to pass his torch to Neith and reach for his bow but stopped. Would a bow be effective against this apparition?

It was not a real ape, but a spectral creature. Was it

a demon? Its eyes, burning in their deep sockets, held them in a narrow gaze.

'The great ape!' Neith said. They drew back. It did not follow, but merely held its ground, clutching the weapons in front of itself. Its arms poked through the gown that covered its squatting legs. Its long muzzled face emerged from a blue wig that descended to below its shoulders. The ape's face pointed at them like a gun barrel.

'I wonder which ape it is,' Ryder murmured. 'Is it Thoth? Maybe we can reason with it.' He took a step nearer the creature.

'Who are you?'

'Who are you?' it boomed back.

'I don't think this is the time for introductions,' Janet whispered. 'We've got to get past it. Use your bow.'

'I'm not sure it will have any effect, but I'll try.' He gave his torch to Janet and unslung the bow from his shoulder, fluidly nocking an arrow to the string.

'Hurry!' Janet said. 'The ape's getting ready to fire!'

It was true. In an action just as smooth as his, the ape had put down the sword and nocked an arrow to its bow. But it had not raised the bow to aim or bent it — and neither had Ryder. It seemed to be waiting.

A duel.

Who could loose an arrow first? Bowman or ape?

'Do not shoot, Bowman,' Neith warned him. 'He will match you.'

'I think I can do a bit better than an ape.'

'Not this ape.'

Ryder raised the bow and drew. The ape mirrored his action. Ryder felt himself facing the point of a barbed arrow.

'Stand aside,' Ryder said.

'Stand aside,' the ape threw back.

'Fire!' Janet commanded Ryder.

'Fire!' the ape echoed in an equally commanding voice, startling Ryder so that he almost released the arrow.

Ryder felt the world converge on his own arrow tip. A heart shot would be cleanest. He altered his aim minutely. The ape did the same. Ryder saw the ape's arrowhead train on his own heart. It all came down to the twitch of the fingers. Who could do it first? But after shooting, would he have time to avoid the arrow that would almost certainly come back at him?

He looked into the ape's eyes. It looked into his. What was it thinking? It's thinking what I am thinking, Ryder guessed.

'Have you two hypnotised each other?' Janet whispered. 'Fire your bow, Wilson, and stop wasting time.'

'Release the arrow and you kill yourself,' Neith warned him anxiously.

Ryder felt beads of moisture migrate under his shirt. Who would blink first? This was like one of those gunfights in the wild west. Just one twitch of the finger muscles. He felt his fingers tremble on the bowstring.

Maybe he should aim for the hairy hand on the bow-handle and hope to deflect the arrow. He shifted his aim again and the ape, seeing his intention, did the same.

The great ape. That was it. This creature was a mimic. It apes everything I do. How could you defeat a creature that matched your every move?

Ryder lowered the bow and the ape did the same.

'Oh very good, Wilson. That scared him!' Janet said caustically.

'It does everything I do. It's like a mirror image,' he said.

'Yes, I see the resemblance. Give the bow to me.' Janet grabbed the bow, drawing it out of his hands as easily as if he had been a child. The arrow fell to the floor.

There was a clatter at the doorway. The ape had also dropped his arrow. Janet bent and the ape mirrored her action. They both swept up their arrows. Janet fiddled with the arrow, trying hastily to put it to the string. The adept ape now also fumbled. She drew and swung. The ape did likewise. It was suicide. Janet's sense of her own powers had risen like strong brew to her brain.

'No, Janet.'

He threw himself at her. It was like hitting a field of force. The bow did not waver, but was held in an iron grip. The arrow. He swept at it with the heel of his hand, just as it slipped from the bow.

An arrow tore through the side of Janet's khaki field jacket, narrowly missing her. He spun to look at the ape. Janet's arrow had torn into the ape's blue gown, passing to one side, again a narrow miss.

'Wilson, you lunatic. You're making me so angry. Look where you made me fire the bow.'

'Are you feeling particularly indestructible or can't you see that the ape is mimicking everything we do? The ape is doing what apes do — aping every move we make. Don't you see? You just narrowly missed him and so he's just narrowly missed you. It's a brainless mimic.'

'I don't believe you.'

'Well, say something to the ape.'

'Like what?'

'Anything.'

'All right.' She turned to the ape. 'Wilson is an idiot.'

'Wilson is an idiot,' the ape said.

'I thought you said it was brainless, Wilson? I think you're an idiot, too, after what you just did.'

'The ape is saying the same thing.'

'Well, it's right. It was a very stupid thing you did.'

'The ape is saying the same thing,' he said again.

'And so are you. It's very annoying.'

'Don't you see?'

'I see that the ape and I agree on something. Maybe we *can* reason with him.'

'Janet, you don't understand. Say something else and it'll copy you.'

Janet thought about it. 'I think you and I can reason with each other.'

The ape thought about it. 'I think you and I can reason with each other,' it concurred.

'See,' she whispered, turning. 'He's prepared to be reasonable. Now leave it to me.'

'I don't believe this.'

'You don't believe in simple negotiation and agreement. No, you wouldn't. You think everything's got to be solved with violence.'

'You were the one who shot an arrow at him. The ape will match anything we throw against it with similar force.'

'Then why use force? I'll use diplomacy.' She handed him back his bow. Then smiling engagingly, she walked towards it. It bared its teeth. She went nearer and drew back suddenly as it snatched up the sword from the floor and lunged at her.

'Now look. You've angered it. The door of opportunity was open, but you slammed it shut,' Janet said.

'You advanced against him, so he advanced against you — in the only way he could. He's copying your actions,' Ryder said.

'He has a sword. Let me test him,' Benwese said, stepping forward, sickle-shaped sword in hand. 'A squatting ape should be no match for a trained swordsman.'

Benwese held a flaming torch in one hand and brandished his sword in the other. The ape raised his sword to mirror the same angle. Benwese swung the torch flame at the ape to distract it. In return, the ape swung its empty hand, fingertips extended and a burst of flame crackled from its finger tips. Benwese swung his sword. The ape swung, too. Their blades met with a clash of bronze. Benwese swung again. The ape swung. Sparks exclaimed at the impact. Benwese tried a lunge and nicked the ape's blue gown. The ape's sword nicked Benwese's loincloth.

Benwese threw a wild arcing sweep at the ape's head. An arcing blade matched his and struck his sword with a force that jarred his arm and made him drop the sword. The ape saw the sword fall and dropped his own. Benwese dived and tried to grab both swords. The ape extended its long arms in a mirror movement to do the same. Benwese changed his mind and grabbed his own sword. The ape picked up its own sword. Benwese withdrew.

'We'll have to attack it together,' Ryder said, nocking an arrow to his bow. 'Let's see how he goes against two attackers. You engage him on one side and I'll try to get in a shot.'

The great ape had an answer for this, too. With two attackers facing him, he matched them by dividing himself into two. His skin stretched and swelled and then he flashed brightly and suddenly there was not one, but two blue-gowned squatting apes facing them, one with a sword and the other with a bow.

They withdrew. A flash of light surrounded the ape and the two halves joined and shrank back to one.

'What are we going to do?' Janet said.

'It is impossible to defeat the ape,' Neith said. 'No other creature can defeat it.'

'Then we can't get the amulets. Are we going to let it end here?'

22

Neith's solution

'THERE IS ONE WAY,' Neith said. She held out her hand to Benwese. 'Give me your sword.' She was helping them again, risking further loss of her powers.

Benwese turned his sword around and held it out to her by the blade. She took it by the handle. Did she think she could do better with a blade than the soldier? Could she defeat the ape guardian where they had failed? What did she hope to accomplish? It would emulate every action of hers, just as it had done with the others. Ryder was puzzled.

Neith held the sickle-shaped sword in two hands, above her head, the blade pointing down and went to confront the ape.

The ape grabbed his sword in both hands and dangled the blade in front of himself in an identical attitude. Neith's back was to him now and Ryder could not see what she was doing. But he did not have to watch her to know what she was doing — he had only to watch the ape.

A cry tore out of his throat. The ape had turned the blade to his own heart.

'None can kill me except myself!' Neith cried.
'None can kill me except myself!' the ape echoed.
'No!' Ryder shouted. 'Stop!'
'Leave her!' Janet said, blocking his way. 'Don't you see? It's the only way.'

The ape gave a mighty tug on the handle. The blade sank deep into its chest.

Neith gave a chilling scream. The ape screamed. Light flashed from the falling body of Neith. Light flashed from the tumbling form of the ape. Then all was still.

Ryder ran to her and dropped to his knees. 'Neith!'

'I did not fail you in the end!' she said. 'Now swear that you will go on from here and recover the other amulets, including the eye of Horus that lies in the power of Seth. Only when they are all gathered in one place will they have the power to raise the Helpless One from the dead. They must be given to Isis and Horus. They will take them to Osiris in the land of Amenti. Swear it.'

'Neith — '

'Swear it!'

'I swear it,' he heard himself say.

'Then it is done. Farewell, Bowman, to you and to Hound with a Snake on its Back.' Neith's head fell slackly back. Snakeback came to her side and whined forlornly.

Ryder looked accusingly at Janet. 'I tried to reach her.'

'Don't glare at me. It was her own idea.'

'You stopped me.'

'I had to.'

'You let her do it.'

'It was the only way. She said so. She wanted to do it for the cause.'

'It wasn't worth this. Nothing is worth this.'

'She thought it was. Respect that. You think you can overcome every situation, Wilson, but you can't. Some things are out of your power.' His mind went back. *The girl shook her great mane sadly. 'For too long you have been a loose arrow, happy merely to watch its flight and to share its freedom in the air. But you must learn that the true meaning and joy of life is to commit yourself to a great cause, a cause for others — worth dying for. You must have a target, Bowman, not clouds.'* Ryder put Neith to rest on the floor.

'Neith,' he whispered. 'You were worth more than any cause.'

The chamber closed in, suffocatingly hot around him. His determination to go on had gone with the life of Neith. Without Neith, it all seemed pointless.

Janet saw his shoulders slacken. 'We must go on, Wilson. She made you promise. We can't give up. I know this is a ghastly shock. But don't make what she has done a waste. And don't forget why you came here,' she said. 'You came here to find me, not her.'

'Did I?' Then he remembered the time, long ago it seemed, when he sat beside Neith in the boat:

'This Lost One that you wish to recover, is she beautiful, Bowman?' Nothing he had ever seen was as beautiful as the woman sitting in the deckhouse beside him. He felt dizzy in the scented pool of her presence.

'Janet is beautiful to me in many ways. She was worth crossing the great divide to try to get back.'

'Are you sure you crossed for her and not another?'

'Who?'

'Never mind, Bowman.'

But he was intrigued. 'Who else could you mean?'

The radiance of ancient Egypt and this woman on the floor were one and the same. Bright tears stung his eyes and a cold hand settled on his spirit. Neith had done this for others, for them and for Osiris so that they could deliver the amulets to his kingdom and restore him to life and so overcome the evil of his brother Seth.

But wait, he thought, hooked by an idea and spun in a new direction: if the combined power of the amulets could restore Osiris — could they also restore Neith? His fight came flooding back like a tide. 'We'll go on,' he said.

The chamber was hot, but Ryder was coldly determined.

'You came across the divide for me, Neith,' he said to the dead girl. 'Now I'll come to lead you back, too — or die trying. I swear it by my God and, who knows, maybe yours.'

They stepped cautiously around the toppled hulk of the ape and went deeper into the tomb. Ryder pressed ahead of the others, careless of danger to himself. Janet hurried to catch him. 'I hope you don't blame me for what's happened. You're wrong to hold me responsible. I didn't make her do it.'

'But you're not particularly sorry that it's happened, are you?'

'You'd rather it was me lying back there, I suppose. Why did you ever come for me, when you always wanted something other than me?'

'Get out of my sight,' he said. *'I'll come back to lead you back, too. . . or die trying. I swear it by my God. . . and, who knows, maybe yours. . . The words reverberated in his head.*

He remembered another vow he had made in another time, when Janet had vanished from the tomb and he'd stumbled down the cliff path to their empty tent. Something had tried to stop him from making the vow, a book with soft black covers that had once told him:

'You should never swear, either by heaven or earth or with any other oath.'

'I'll try, Janet, I swear by heaven and earth and hell — if I can get to you, I will. Hang on. I'm coming.'

Now he was making new oaths to save a pagan entity from a pagan death and vowing it not only in the name of his own god. . . but hers. But was hers a different god? Were there two great gods? There can only be one higher God, above all, Neith had said.

Things were not clear now to Ryder. The comfortable clarity of light and shadow had blurred and he saw now that it was not the black-and-white of beliefs spelt out with precision that were uncomfortable, but the shades of grey, the mystery, the uncertainty, the parts he did not know, the uncharted wilderness of faith.

Will I lose everything in this place, he thought despairingly, even my comfortable certitude? He thought of Neith lying on the stone floor behind him, the stone even now cooling her body. He'd risk his certitude to get her back. He'd risk everything. Everything? His faith included? Don't ask that of me, he prayed silently. Don't put me to the ultimate test. I am only a man.

They entered a decorated passage. Scenes from the Book of the Dead brought the walls vividly to life. The soul of a dead man stood under a canopy aboard a boat and his boat was being dragged through a section of the underworld Nile by a row of lean-hipped goddesses.

Their slender forms tore at Ryder. The lovely, painted eye of a goddess ambushed his gaze. It held a pleading look. The loss of Neith stung his eyes.

It almost blinded him to the danger that came up

suddenly at the end of a passage. Benwese grabbed his arm in strong fingers as he teetered, finding himself staring wild-eyed over the edge of a pit. It was a trap, cleverly placed, for the floor dropped away without warning and attention was diverted by carved stone statues flanking the wall, while behind them a painted frieze continued across the gap, giving the illusion that the floor continued uninterrupted and that the darkness of the pit was merely the fall of shadows.

They hunted for a way across. There was none, they discovered — no foot or handhold at the edge, no planks to run out across the gap — and it was too far to jump. He could shoot an arrow and rope across, but there was nothing to attach it to.

'The statues,' Benwese said. 'Let us use them to make a bridge.'

'It just might work,' Ryder said.

The statues, identical, were of a king, muscles rippling in veiny black diorite, and wearing a nemes headcloth, but they bore no cartouches to identify them. The two men put their shoulders to the back of one and heaved towards the pit. It was solid, on a heavy base and would not budge.

Janet shook her head at them. 'Let me help.' As soon as she added her weight, the statue grated and moved.

'Let it rock, then fall across the gap,' Janet said. They pushed it and let it come back, grinding the stone floor.

'Don't let it come too far. It'll fall on us.'

'It won't fall on top of us. I'm holding it,' she said. They heaved. The stony king leaned, paused for a moment, then toppled like a tree. He hit the tip of his headcloth on the other side and the whole head sheared off. The torso, legs and base followed it into the pit.

Seconds elapsed before the far-off crash of its impact drifted up the shaft.

Ryder seethed with disappointment.

'We must try the other one,' Benwese said.

'Yes, but this time push it nearer the edge,' Janet told them.

Easily said, Ryder thought. It was one thing to rock a statue of this size and then allow it to topple. It was another to shift a monolith weighing tonnes.

They tried, pressing their shoulders to the statue. Sweat ran down their necks. Benwese stopped and wiped his forehead.

'You want my help again?' Janet said. She put her hands to the statue and at once it began to rumble across the stone.

'Not too far!' The king's great sandalled feet stuck over the edge of the pit. Would it reach across the gap this time? Ryder glanced up at the serene face of the king. The head should reach the other side. But what if the neck broke? They would have to take the risk. There was no way to cushion its fall.

'Here goes,' he said. 'Push!' They pushed as one. The king rocked on his base, the giant toes in the carved sandals leaning out over the void.

The king came back. One more shove. They heaved. The king leaned, hesitated, then slipped away from their grasp, but it did not fall straight, twisting and going at an angle.

Ryder groaned. Was it going to slip into the void without touching the other side? The king hit the far side of the pit with a bang like a falling building and his head broke off with a crack like lightning and rolled into the passage beyond. But the point of one shoulder, al-though cracked, held. Amazingly, he had spanned the gap.

They froze and dared not breathe for fear that the slightest movement would send it on into the pit. But it held.

'We'll have to try it,' Janet said.

'I will go first,' Benwese said. 'It was my plan.' He stepped onto the king's ankles and, balancing himself with the torch held out on one side and with his outstretched arm on the other, went out nimbly along the king's body. The statue shifted, gave a crack and the king's right arm fell away, slipping into the blackness. Benwese turned into a statue himself, fright jumping into his face.

But the bridge held. He went all the way across. Ryder let Janet go next and then he picked up Snakeback, fearing the animal might lose its footing on the polished diorite surface. He went after the others, choosing not to look down into the void. He reached the other side and put the dog down. They were across.

The passage ahead opened into the burial chamber. It was a golden vault, covered with painted scenes of creatures from the underworld and it was dominated by an oblong, rose-pink alabaster sarcophagus, not anthropoid in shape but in the older style, designed with sides like the facades of a palace with deeply carved columns, buttresses and false doorways.

The lid would weigh tonnes.

'Give me a hand,' Janet said. They pushed and the lid scraped and rumbled; a dry breath of pungent, sweet-smelling air escaped like a soundless sigh from the eternity seeker who lay revealed within the darkness of the sarcophagus.

They raised their torches over the sarcophagus and looked inside. The mummy, wearing the mask of a vulture, held a miniature crook and a flail, which emerged between blackened mummy wrappings.

Janet snatched them unceremoniously from the dead king's grasp and there was a dry snap as his wrists broke. She shoved the crook and the flail into the bag at her side.

'Let's get him out of this,' she said, grabbing the head while Ryder grabbed the feet. They lifted him out and placed him on the floor of the chamber.

Ryder had attended many unwrappings of mummies and had even watched Janet supervise such a procedure in the days before it became the practice to use less invasive methods of exploration such as X-rays and ultrasound. It was normally conducted with the care and dexterity of an open heart operation, but Janet now went at the dead king's body with the clawed fingers of any tomb robber. Bandages were ripped, dust rose and amulets flew from the layers of wrapping. Near the neck she located the faience *was*-sceptre amulet and finally, in the mummy's chest cavity, the amulet of the heart, made of lapis lazuli.

'We have them all now — all except the eye of Horus. When we have that, Wilson, we have the power to raise the very dead! Osiris himself.' Or Neith, he thought.

'But don't think I care about Osiris. I haven't gone to all this trouble for his benefit. Oh no, these will not be wasted on giving him power. The power is for me and for those who have aligned themselves with me. Thankyou for helping me. I know where the eye of Horus rests and I will not even have to fight for it. It will be given to me.'

'The amulets aren't yours, Janet. You can't have them. Give them to me.'

'Don't you wish it. No, I know what you're thinking. You're thinking they have the power to raise that girl.

But you see where she has got you? Nowhere! The divine woman of your dreams was just a phantom. I am the closest you will ever get to divinity and you can't see it. Or can you? Can you forget about her and be with me? I'm still prepared, even at this late stage, to forgive you and let you share in the radiance. What will it be?'

She was mad, Ryder thought. Was it the loneliness and privation of her sojourn underground that had done this to her — or had she always been a little crazy?

'Give them to me, Janet. You've had some mad ideas, but this is the craziest. They don't belong to you. They don't belong to me, even though I fought for them. You were only along for the journey.'

'No, it was you who was only along for the journey, I now see. I came to this place before you, remember. I would have got them all — you just made it quicker and easier. I'm going now, Wilson. You and Benwese can find your own way out and maybe you can find your way back to the world you can't seem to let go of. Goodbye.'

Ryder stepped in front of her. 'You're not going.'

'What are you going to do — fire your bow at me?'

'Shoot.'

'I wouldn't try either. I can feel the power growing in me and your arrows won't harm me.' She moved to go around him.

'I mean it.' He blocked her way.

'Don't provoke me.'

'Give me the bag.'

'Don't make me hurt you.'

'I won't let you go.'

He took a step closer and she stiffened. Janet Nancarrow was a tall woman, but she seemed to rear even higher like a snake and light rimmed her eyes like tears, then spat blazes of anger at him. Ryder was struck by a force that snapped him to the ground.

'Stay out of my way!' she said in a voice that ground like a stone lid sliding over a sarcophagus. Then she left him lying on the floor. What had she become? Snakeback gave a solitary whine.

23

Shadow of despair

THE DARKNESS SEEMED TO THICKEN like a barrier as the two men and the dog ran calling after Janet. Empty passage after empty passage stretched to hopeless lengths in their torchlight. The dense darkness was not only there in the tomb, but inside Ryder. *I have lost them both now, Neith and Janet. Why go on? Why did I come here?*

Neith's words returned to him:

'Who are you?' Ryder said.

'I am Neith,' the girl said lightly as if he should have known, 'The Opener of Ways, Mistress of the Bow and Ruler of Arrows. I will come with you and open the ways on your quest although I may not help you in your struggles,' she said. 'It is your destiny to advance the struggle of Osiris. Hurry. We must begin the search. I can help you reach your Lost One, but only after you have completed your quest.'

'Quest? I'm not here on any quest.'

'Ah, Bowman. For too long you have been a lost arrow, happy to watch its flight, enjoying its freedom through the air. But you must learn that the true meaning and joy of life is to commit yourself to a great cause, a cause for others worth

dying for. You must have a target, Bowman, not clouds.'

Neith. How could this young woman be Neith? *'Am I dead?'*

But where was the great cause, a cause for others worth dying for? What did he care about a pagan entity named Osiris, his wife Isis and his son Horus? What did he care about the struggle of a race in such distant days?

They crossed the pit along the fallen body of a king.

But he did care. He cared about Neith and her loss was more than a darkness inside him; it was an aching void that pulled him down to nameless despair. And this dark soldier who ran with a light footfall beside him — Ryder cared about him, too. He cared about him and his young love Bint-Anath and about the others he had never met who were forced to live like the dead in tunnels and caverns beneath the earth because of an evil that was abroad.

But most of all he cared about Neith.

They reached the doorway with the hulk of the ape. They stopped running. There, where they had left her, lay the still, pale form of Neith, her linen dress stained with blood. He knelt and held her wrist, hoping. It was colder than marble. He closed the lids of the lovely eyes that had once gazed so clearly. The dog with the snake on its back drew close.

It all stops with her. My desire to go on is as dead as she is. How could Neith, who was divine, die like any woman?

Because she had become like any woman. Vulnerable. This was not a goddess who had given her life, but a feeling, fearing woman. Did she die for Osiris alone, or for us, too? But what could he do? The dog licked the cold cheek, then gave a long, low, morose howl. *'I love Hound with a Snake on Its Back,'* she had said. *'I think I always have.'*

I can fight on, Ryder thought, fight on even against hopelessness and the shadow of despair. I can hunt Janet down, wherever she has gone and get the amulets back, then go on to find the last remaining amulet, the Eye Of Horus and see just what power resided in the relics. Could they bring Neith back?

Osiris could wait for his turn.

Ryder picked up the girl in his arms and carried her out of the tomb and back to the boat. The crew looked afraid to have a dead body brought on board and they raised their arms in the Egyptian way to ward off evil. Ryder put Neith to rest on a grass mat in the deckhouse.

'Watch over her, Benwese,' he said to the Egyptian soldier. 'We'll see if Snakeback and I can track down Janet.' He took the dog and went back towards the tomb, hoping that Snakeback could pick up her trail.

'Where's Janet, boy?' he said. 'Find her.' The dog looked up at him with a questioning light in its amber eyes, but it wagged its tail in understanding and took off. It led him back towards the river, to a place where the dense mystery of the papyrus thicket thinned and the long-stemmed plants merely gathered in secretive clumps that seemed to watch him and conspire together. But there was no Janet.

Ryder heard a *plish plish plish* sound coming through the papyrus clumps. His hand went to the bow, his fingers curving around the handle. He took an arrow and put it to the bowstring.

It was a wading bird, or at least the head of it was; the lower section was that of a man with scrawny arms, chest and shanks that were grey-white with age. The fur on Snakeback's spine sat up and it growled, but the hair flattened again and its tail wagged slowly.

Ryder blinked at the creature. *Plish. Plish. Plish.* It came slowly towards them, picking its way through the shallows with an air of deliberation, lifting its feet high and carefully placing them in the water so that it stood for moments at a time with one leg suspended in the air, giving it a comical air. The feet were long and thin, the toes spaced widely. The bird's head, framed by a triangular wig like a pharaoh's *nemes* headdress, was bent, the long, curved black beak lowered as if it were searching for small fish in the water.

Ryder lowered the bow.

'I'm edified that you do not plan to turn your bow against the Lord of Magic, Scribe of the Gods, Reckoner of Time, He Who Sees into All Hearts, Possessor of Every Kind of Knowledge, Great in Power of Charms, Master of Wonderworking Formula,' the stranger said in a voice that seemed awed by its own utterances.

Ryder smiled at the wordy introduction from the stranger. 'Let me guess — Thoth.'

'Thoth some say, but I prefer Tehuti. And I suppose you are the Bowman from the Future, and this is the Hound with a Snake on its Back,' the bird-man said, turning his head on a snake-thin neck, so that the long, black surgical beak was flung out in profile and a single eye regarded the man and the dog with scepticism.

'Seeing you know so much, sir,' Ryder said to the venerable bird, 'perhaps you'll tell me what's become of my ladyfriend.'

'Oh, I can tell you that, but first you must agree that you will accept the help of the Lord of Divine Words.'

'I've already asked your help.'

'No, you haven't. You have merely asked me a question.'

'That's the same thing.'

'Not at all.'

'Aren't you splitting words?'

The bird winced. 'Do you expect any less from the creator of words and the inventor of script? Words are finely fashioned instruments and they have power. Careless people do not know the chaos they cause with them.'

'Will you answer my question?'

'Will you accept my help? In myth there is always a Wise One who comes to help the hero in his quest and sets him on the path to victory, but only if that hero is wise enough to accept the help.'

'Why wouldn't I accept your help?'

'Because I am Tehuti, Lord of Magic, and I know the secrets of men's hearts and I also know that you believe in another.'

'Yes, I do,' Ryder confessed.

'And that you cannot accept magic.'

'Well, that depends what you mean by accept. And what you mean by magic.'

'Now who is splitting words?'

'I wouldn't refuse help just because it came by way of magic, if that's what you mean. Help often looks quite magical.'

'That's not what I mean. What I mean is what I say. Do you accept magic?'

'I don't accept it has a reality.'

'There, you see,' the bird said, gratified. 'You don't accept magic.' His mind was as sharp as his beak. 'I have a hero who cannot accept. And if he cannot accept, then he cannot succeed. What am I to do with him?'

'You could answer his question.'

'Three truths you must learn, Bowman from the Future. They are these. First, the One You Believe In *can* work in and through any realm he chooses — even through myth and what you call magic. Next, you have a simple faith in the One You Believe In and that is good, but simplifying the One You Believe In is not good. Finally, a truth about your secret yearnings. No. . . ' The bird broke off and shook his beaked head. 'This last truth you must perceive for yourself. It is about your hopeless search for the divine in other than the divine itself and about where you should be content to find happiness.'

'I don't understand. What are you saying? Why are you telling me these things?'

'Because I know every truth. Now, will you accept?'

'I'll accept your help.'

'But will you accept magic? Will you not accept that magic is reality in the realm of myth and magic? Why, it is miraculous that you are here at all — and, even more so, that you have survived so many fearsome trials,' he prompted Ryder. 'Do you not agree?'

'I suppose it is miraculous. I've stopped questioning a lot of things,' Ryder said, 'and started to believe many others. So, yes, I'll suspend my disbelief if you'll help me.'

'I need more than suspension. That is mere postponement of doubt. I need faith.'

'Faith in a man with the head of a bird? If you know all things, you'll know I can't give it to you.'

'Faith in faith. And hope in hope. That is all you need. You must use your faith like hands to accept what help I give. The hardest thing of all is to receive, not give.'

'I'll accept that. And I'll try to have faith that is big enough to receive.'

The bird sighed. 'I suppose that is as much as I can expect. Before I help you, though, you must accept a mission. Among my titles is He Who Restores the Eye of Horus. I must take the eye of Horus back to the child in the nest of reeds at the Delta where he waits with his mother Isis. Through this amulet, Isis, by means of her great magic, will restore the eye of her son. It will bring light to the land.' He cast an eye up at the sun. 'It will take away the blindness of the eye of the sun that has plunged the world into darkness. After that, the amulet must go with Isis to Amenti to revivify the limbs of Osiris.'

'Knowing as much as you do, you'll know that finding the amulet is my next task. But where do I look?'

The bird pointed a withered finger into the water. 'I can show you. Bend over the water and look into it and I will show you sights that have been and have still to be for I have the power to look into the past and the future and perceive them as the present.'

Ryder bent his head. He saw three small fish dart away and tear streaks in the surface of the water. The surface calmed and now a haziness moved over the water and tiny lights dazzled his eyes. Then a picture emerged.

He saw Janet. She was coming out of the tomb passage onto the river bank and waiting for her was a figure of a man with square-topped ears, a long droopy snout and burning eyes. Ryder knew him. It was the evil Lord Seth, murderer of Osiris and the usurper of the Mummy King's Realm that the prince Horus should have inherited. He had a bow over his shoulder and a quiver of arrows. He raised his hand and pointed a finger and Janet fell to her knees.

Now the scene changed. Ryder saw a plain before a fortified palace and on the plain was gathered a throng at some kind of feast day. Again he saw the man with a snout-head. This time he was aboard a golden chariot and again he had a bow in his hands. A throng of animal-headed onlookers roared their delight as the man in the chariot raced across the plain, passing four poles on which were tied prisoners. He raced past the poles and fired an arrow into each prisoner as he passed.

The scene turned to mist and now another appeared. Ryder saw a throng gathered under the wall of a palace. The cheering throng looked up at a 'window of audiences'. There were figures in the window and their image drew nearer. In the window he saw the square-eared one — and beside him, her neck looped with a gold chain of amulets, stood Janet, his Janet, hand-in-hand with the beast.

'That's enough,' Ryder said angrily. 'This isn't magic. It's crude trickery and it's a lie. Janet couldn't do that. Not with that creature.'

'You think so? That is a mask he wears. Seth does not have a demon head like his evil legions. Beneath the mask is the face of the most handsome man in creation, a face that shames his evil nature and is despised by him. Who do you think took her to the first tomb, began her on the quest and worked his evil influence on her all along?'

'I don't accept that.'

'You don't accept that. Then accept this. She has all fourteen amulets. Look at the chain around her neck. See, even the golden eye of Horus is there. He has given it to her. Why? To reward her for her collaboration. You must go to her and you must get them back.'

Small fish darted back, just under the surface of the

water and dragged a curtain of ripples across the scene. When the ripples went, the images went with them. The water was blank

Ryder looked up. 'What do I have to do?'

'Get them back and give them to me so that I can fly with them first to the child Horus and then to Osiris in order that his glorious revivification may occur so that this benighted land will prosper again and the armies under the banner of the sun eagle shall march against Seth.'

'If I do regain the eye and the other amulets — and I've no idea how — then you must use them to help me. I have a special need for the amulets of power. There is another who is in need of revivification.'

'The divine one.'

'Neith.'

'Do you go on searching for her, even beyond the doorway of death?'

'Beyond the gates of hell if I must.'

'You would delay the revivification of Osiris in order to save this Neith?'

'Osiris can wait.'

The old man shuddered and clapped hands to his ears. 'I hear the groans of the universe! Don't you know that the whole universe yearns for his revival?'

'My mind is made up.'

'I can see the last truth will be the hardest for you to accept. Gaze one more time into the water and I will show you what you must do.'

Ryder bent his head again. The three fish returned, spreading calm in their wake. Haze grew upon the water and then a luminescence and in it a scene.

The Lord Seth appeared. Once more he was racing in his chariot and this time there were targets surmounting the four poles, each one shaped like a cowhide, but made of burnished copper. The creature-man with erect, square-tipped ears was aiming a bow as he rode at speed in his chariot. It was a mighty bow that he bent and it sent an arrow deep into the copper. Then Ryder saw the cheering audience. Set away from the crowd in the shade of a small tent pavilion sat Janet, a gold cup in her hand, a smile on her lips and the circle of amulets around her neck.

The little fish came back, dragging the scene away and bringing back an empty patch of water. Ryder continued to stare in bewilderment. It was like discovering that Janet Nancarrow was in league with the devil. Was it possible? Not anywhere else in the universe. . . but here? He broke away.

As ghastly as this evidence was, and as much as he wanted to resist it, it did answer a number of questions. But was Janet evil? He had never thought it. And yet he had thought it of Neith, the first time he had met her. . .

Her beauty was almost repellent, he felt, swallowing. Yet there was something purely natural about her, like one of the lotus blossoms growing at the edge of the river.

'If you think you are dead, then you must think I, too, am dead. Do I look like a corpse?' She made an amused face at the strong, dark bowman.

She didn't look dead. There was a humid gleam in her eyes.

'No, perhaps not,' Ryder said. 'But perhaps I am dead.'

'You do not feel dead, Bowman,' Neith said, touching his arm with fingers as cool as marble. What was he in the presence of? Evil? Was this breathing creature with the cold touch a pagan divinity; was she malignant?

It was possible to think it of Neith, but Janet? Could he have lived and worked with somebody in the close fellowship of archaeology, through years of patient searching, disappointment and achievement, without knowing her essential nature? Ryder and Janet had known the camaraderie of the campsite, the patient, brush-and-sieve tedium of the dig; they had crawled through numberless passages and tombs together, combining their focus, like torchbeams, on the clues that would lead them to new discoveries in their shared passion for Egypt's past. Had he been living that close to evil all along — if evil it was?

'Tell me, what do I have to do? How do I get the amulets back? She was strong before. Now that she has all fourteen amulets, she'll be like a giant.'

'You must break the spell that lies over her,' the wise old bird told him. 'Two things must be done. First, you must upset the cosmic order. There is a feast day tomorrow and Lord Seth will again display his archery skills in an exhibition. He will fire arrows at copper targets a hand in thickness, using a bow that none can bend, and his arrows shall fly deep into the copper and even appear a hand's breadth on the other side. This is a feat that no man in the land can match. It is his custom, however, in order to make his glorious skill shine all the brighter, to invite challengers to attempt to match his feat. It is impossible, of course. The pharaoh must win. To lose would be unthinkable. It would upset the cosmic order of Maat, so that the sky would blacken still more and rage and the Dragon of Chaos, Apophis, would be set free.'

The concept of preserving Maat was more than an Egyptian reverence for convention, Ryder recalled. The goddess Maat, a lady wearing an ostrich feather in her hair, was the symbol of truth and cosmic harmony. She embodied the laws of the universe and gave a pharaoh his authority to govern. It was a principle of Maat that held that the pharaoh be invincible, irresistible to his enemies, always victorious. To challenge that principle was to risk the stability of the cosmos, the sequence of time, seasons and celestial movement, even harmony between people, inviting catastrophe. It was no more than royal propaganda, Ryder had always believed, but the bird-man believed it.

'To break the spell, you must accept the Lord Seth's challenge and equal his feat of bowmanship. But, of course, it is quite impossible. Not only would it upset Maat, but you would need to overcome the circle of power of the amulets.'

'So it's impossible.'

The old bird-man winced. 'Do not say that.'

'Why not? You said it.'

'It is impossible to me and to every Egyptian. But it must not be impossible to you. You mustn't even think it. By doing so you are offending your own concept of order, your illusion that you cannot be defeated in contests of the bow. You are giving words and power to an idea you do not accept. Have a care for what you are saying. *I* believe it is impossible for you to succeed, because Maat requires this belief of me but, going further, I believe that it is impossible for you to succeed — *on your own.*' Here the bird paused and turned his beak-face up to check on the sky as if he feared it would fall on them. He lowered his voice. 'These are dangerous intimations and are threatening to the equilibrium of the universe. Come closer, Bowman.' Ryder moved nearer. 'You can only succeed,' Tehuti whispered, 'with the help of the One You Believe In.'

'You, a pagan divinity, are counting on the intervention of the one I believe in?'

'No, *you* are. But if the impossible can be made possible, if you can succeed, shocking as that may be to the order of things — ' and here he raised his arms before his face in the Egyptian way in order to ward off evil, 'there will be heard such a wailing and raging and a gnashing of teeth from the forces of chaos that for a moment the universe will be thrown off balance. Then you will have a chance to snatch away the amulets. . . '

'Janet will never let go of them.'

'I will give you the added protection of an amulet. It will neutralise her power, but you must act as soon as the spell is broken and while the wailing fills the air. I will provide you with everything, even a chariot of shining electrum and two chargers, but I cannot guide your arrow. Only One can.'

The old man handed him an amulet, shaped like an ibis bird. It was attached to a cord.

'Wear it around your neck. Although your Lost One is under a spell, remember that in me is found the source of all magical power that is contained in charms and spells. This magic will protect you — along with the magic of faith that you and your Trusted One will use.'

The old man left and waded back through the shallows. *Plish. Plish. Plish.* He passed out of sight behind papyrus clumps and then Ryder heard a whistling of wings and a beautiful white ibis bird took off into the sky.

Help had come from the most unexpected quarter, Ryder thought, yet he felt he had turned a corner in accepting it. In the realm of myth and magic, he was learning to accept the strange and the wonderful. He watched the bird climb higher and his hopes climbed with it. Was the soul of Neith up there? Or watching him? He would go on. He could not give up.

24

The watching universe

THE BOAT'S TIMBERS CREAKED AND ACHED like his heart as the wind took them upstream. Rider sat in the deckhouse in a vigil beside the still, stretched-out form of Neith. The twisting light of a lamp seemed to accentuate the circle of hovering shadow that lay around him.

Neith, Opener of Ways, Mistress of the Bow and Ruler of Arrows. She was now as unattainable as a beauty in a tomb painting or an Egyptian statue. Was that emptied, stretched-out form the unattainable he had always looked for in woman? If it was, he did not want it now. He wanted the living woman, to feel again her clear-gazing eyes.

Perhaps the death of Neith was just a phase in a divine cycle, a magical death and she would awaken. But he knew it was a vain hope and that she would not.

Can I pray for her soul? he wondered. Can prayers help the soul of a divine entity? But if she truly were divine, how could she have died in the first place? Divine beings weren't supposed to die.

But one had.

That event had happened in history. That divine one

had died because he had become man. And Neith had died because she had become woman. He bent his head and tried to get in touch with the one he believed in. The words of the ibis-man came back to him:

'*Three truths you must learn, Bowman from the Future. They are these. First, the One You Believe In can work in and through any realm he chooses — even through myth and what you call magic. Next, you have a simple faith in the One You Believe In and that is good, but simplifying the One You Believe In is not good. Finally, a truth about your secret yearnings. No. . .*' The bird broke off and shook his beaked head. '*This last truth you must perceive for yourself. It is about your hopeless search for the divine in other than the divine itself and about where you should be content to find happiness.*'

What do I ask for her soul? Ryder thought. I ask for it back, that's what I ask. Just as I crossed a boundary of time and reason to try to bring Janet back, I want to bring Neith back. Help me to triumph even if my triumph is beyond reason. Am I asking for and accepting magic? In a realm of myth and magic, was there any other way by which things could happen? I must accept the reality of this world even if that reality is unreality. Help me, he thought, even here in this distant realm. Help my courage, my arm and my unbelief.

His mind turned to Janet. He remembered the day that she disappeared in the tomb and he had stumbled down the cliff path to their empty tent. A photograph of Janet had caught his eye. He had put it up to comfort himself in her absence, hanging it on the tent pole. The slender, daring face smiled fearlessly out at him. He took the photograph out now and turned it so that it caught a sheen of light from the lamp.

She had come under the spell of an evil influence, the

bird-man had told him. Willingly? You're alive, Janet, yet you're as far away from me as the dead girl on the floor, he thought, staring at her photograph. Those daring eyes of hers were looking into hell. Yet he felt a pang for a softer Janet and for the times when her voice had filled his ear, loving times, when there had been the warmth and humid mist of life behind the murmurs: *'If I don't come back, forget about me and don't even think about trying to come after me. . . I'll be all right.'* Where are you now, Janet? Was there evil in Janet? Or just an openness to evil?

There were two mentalities that put the spirit most at risk: the one that feared any collision with its own beliefs and the one that borrowed too freely from all beliefs. Perhaps a mind that was too open could not hold a faith inside itself. And a faith that was prepared to let anything into its abode must also expect to admit evil.

He reflected on the changes in Janet — her steely resolve, the flight of softness, a heartless determination to achieve her goal.

It was a warning to him to keep the sentry to his mind alert. Many new ideas were crowding into his thoughts, but he must take care not to let them in unchecked. Challenge them. Receive them no less critically than he had received the old ones. Test them. Make sure where they came from and who brought them and be careful of what they might do once they were inside him. Many could come in pleasant disguise, in radiant beauty — like Neith.

Was Neith an evil he had let into his life, unchallenged? She did not look evil lying there in the pallor of death. And yet, and yet. . . Everything was a mixture. Everything had a potential to harm — and to bless.

He thought of the Evil One, Seth. It was easy to conjure him in that cabin of shadows. Seth, the vile, was said to have torn himself savagely from his mother Nut at birth and was forever after linked with storms and violence and was the personification of the arid desert and the destructive heat of summer. Like Satan, he was doomed to be banished for his overweening pride.

Benwese came into the cabin and set a consoling hand on his shoulder. 'It is not good to dwell in the shadow of loss. You mourn for both the dead and the living woman?'

He nodded.

The soldier sighed. 'I do not know which would be the hardest to regain. The girl who lies in the grip of death — or the one who lies in the grasp of Seth.'

Ryder had told him about the appearance of the wise bird and of Janet being in league with Seth — and of his determination to go on.

'How I wish I could smuggle this one from the Mansion of Death, just as you helped smuggle Bint-Anath from the House of the Secluded.'

'Thankyou, Benwese.'

'You are brave to go on.'

'No,' he confessed. 'Not brave at all. I am afraid to stop.'

His eyelids grew heavy and he slept in a corner of the deckhouse on the floor, with Snakeback at his feet. Neith ran through his dreams, holding his arrow, and Snakeback ran alongside her. She turned her head to look at him and there was a look of helpless pleading in her eyes. He awoke thinking that he was listening to the sounds of his heart aching, but it was only the timbers of the boat.

Before the borders of the Nome of Seth, the boat

232/The watching universe

stopped and set him ashore. He left Snakeback and Benwese on board and pressed his way alone through the papyrus thicket.

'You are late,' said Tehuti, the Reckoner of Time. He stood in a clearing on the bank beside a chariot of burnished electrum which was harnessed to a pair of shivering, pawing horses that looked eager to run. 'As you can see, I have been generous in my help. Two fleet horses and a chariot so light and cunningly engineered that it flies like a swallow. But this is all I can do, Bowman from Tomorrow. The rest is up to you and the One You Believe In. Your arm must be strong, your aim straight. I shall be watching, circling high above, but I cannot help you succeed.'

Tehuti shivered. 'It is a dangerous day when a man attempts to upset the cosmic balance. To break the spell and upset the universe, you must do more than equal Seth's feat; you must surpass it. And remember you have little time once the spell breaks. You must be swift.'

'Thankyou, Wise One,' Ryder said, accepting his help.

'You will need these, or your Lost One will recognise you and betray you.' He handed Ryder a kilt of linen and the mask-head of a falcon. 'You will strike a blow for Horus, the falcon-headed one, by wearing his mask.'

Ahead of Ryder, a throng lay spread like an army on a plain outside the walls of a mud brick palace with towers, battlements and crenellations like a medieval castle, but with massive pylons at the entrance.

He saw the clearing, marked out with fluttering pennants, the target poles spaced twenty metres apart, with copper targets shaped like cowhides on top and wretched prisoners tethered to their bases; not animal-headed creatures like the crowd, but followers of Osiris, three men and an old woman. He also saw the small, gaily-coloured pavilion, like a tent, where a figure sat in deep shadow.

Up above, a big white bird circled watchfully.

Ryder reined in his chariot among others in a line as heralds appeared and blew a fanfare of brazen blasts on straight-stemmed trumpets that flared at the end like lotus blossoms.

He came, shining in his armour of a leather tunic with scales of bronze. The blue war crown was on his head, set between the pricked, square-tipped ears, the evil donkey snout raised in an attitude of lofty assurance, a dark-skinned being with immensely broad shoulders. Standard-bearers and fan-bearers ran beside his chariot and there was a huge animal which Ryder took at first to be a dog since it was obscured by the chariot. Then it ran ahead and Ryder saw that it was a deep-chested lion.

Seth reined in his two black chargers before the target run. The crowd of beast-headed ones fell silent. A standard-bearer called out in a bellowing cry like a bull in a slaughtering yard: 'His Majesty, Lord Seth, Mighty of Arm, Great in Strength, Lord of the Two Lands. Life! Health! Strength!'

'Life! Health! Strength!' the crowd roared back.

'During a single passage of the chariot, the mighty Lord Seth will shoot four arrows, symbolising his dominion over north and south, east and west, at four targets from the Asian land of copper. Each target is an ingot of hammered copper three fingers thick and the targets are spaced forty ells apart. No man's arrows can penetrate these plates, but would bounce off like flies, but His Majesty's arrows will transfix them. An impossible feat, for all but our heroic Lord Seth, radiant and mighty!'

The heralds then blew another enfilade of piercing notes. It was the signal for the exhibition to commence.

Seth cracked the reins over the horses' backs and the chariot lurched forward as if propelled by a catapult. Seth lashed the reins around his waist and drew four arrows from his quiver. He ran in a straight line at a distance of about twenty metres from the targets. The horses bent their necks and the skeletal chariot flew across the sand, throwing up plumes of dust.

Seth clipped an arrow to the string of his bow, a powerful composite weapon, made from both hard and soft wood and strengthened with animal sinew and lime, and the prisoner on the first pole, an old woman, cowered. He drew smoothly and released. The arrow hit the copper target with a clang like a gong of doom and the arrow pierced it through, showing a hand's breadth on the other side.

Fluidly, he aimed another. This next one hit the target even harder. *Clang*. It snapped through the hammered copper, revealing a quarter of the arrow shaft on the other side.

Now he was racing parallel to the third target. Again he nocked an arrow to the bowstring and bent the powerful bow. The arrow seemed to smack as soon as it left the bow. It hit the copper with a clangour of a blacksmith's blow, striking so hard that the arrow pierced the target, half of its length revealed on the other side. The crowd gasped in wonder.

He had left the last target a little late and moved quickly to draw the bow and aim. The arrow struck with a blow like thunder and went deep, almost to the fletching. The crowd howled like hounds with delight.

Seth had penetrated all four targets, shooting four arrows, and he made a victory circuit of the archery field, waving his bow above his head and accepting the adulation of the demon-headed ones. The trumpets blasted. The standard-bearer bellowed. 'This is a deed never done before, whose report has never been heard, done in view of you all so that all might see the strength of his arms in bravery and dread him. Great is Lord Seth, mighty in valour, strong in arm, with power that none can match. Who in the land will try? Is there a challenger who will attempt to match this glorious feat?'

Ryder looked along the line of chariots. None made a move to accept. He flicked the reins over the horses' backs and ran towards the target line. Seth turned in his chariot to direct a look of surprise at the falcon-headed challenger in the shining electrum chariot. A low rumble of excitement grew out of the throats of the onlookers.

'A challenge!' the herald boomed. 'Know this then — if you dare to challenge and fail, you forfeit your life!'

The crowd cheered in delight. This was news, Ryder thought, feeling a growing humidity under the falcon's mask. If I fail, I forfeit my life. It was one tiny detail the old bird had neglected to mention. But if he failed, the end would probably be the same anyway, he thought, giving a small shrug.

The eyes of Seth hardened as he saw the shrug, which he took to be dismissive.

The heralds blew blasts on their trumpets. Ryder sent his horses running, going not in a straight line as Seth had done, but moving wider before approaching the targets, giving himself an even longer shot — another twenty metres. Some words he had heard earlier were imprinted on his mind: *'To break the spell and upset the universe, you must do more than equal Seth's feat; you must surpass it.'*

He stopped to await the signal for his run, glancing back over his shoulder. Seth had thrown back his head and was laughing at his challenger's audacity — or foolishness.

The heralds blew their trumpets. Ryder took four metal alloy arrows from his quiver and then cracked the reins. Thoth had warned him that the horses were swift, but the first target rushed up too quickly and he still had the reins in his hands. No time to wrap them around his waist. He lashed them around one arm and swiftly nocked an arrow to the bowstring. He bent the twenty-two kilogram draw-weight bow, taking the arrow all the way back to the anchor point at his chin.

He saw the first target. The world converged on it. His brain sent the message to his fingers to release. Then disaster. The horses veered and the reins pulled on his bow arm as he released, throwing the arrow off course. He saw the old woman, tied to the post, duck and the arrow flick across the gap.

Bang! The metal alloy arrow struck low down on the target and to the left of Seth's, but deeper, only half the shaft remaining visible.

Ryder couldn't risk the same mistake. He peeled the reins off his arm and lashed them around his waist. But he had lost time. The second target was almost level. He snapped an arrow to the string and shot. *Clang.* Close to the middle this time, but hammered through, almost to the fletching. A low sigh of wonder, like wind, came from the crowd.

Ryder took time to prepare his next shot. He bent the bow, released smoothly. He knew it was good even before the arrow left the bow. *Crash!* The arrow struck dead centre in the copper target, running right up to the fletching. There were howls of dismay.

Now the last target raced up to challenge him. Make no mistake with this one, Ryder thought. He drew the arrow to the anchor point, his focus converging on the target so that he felt the world retreat and melt and blur and he felt that the only solid thing in the universe was that target of hammered Asian copper.

Then the left wheel of the chariot hit a mound and threw him off his feet. Cheers broke from the crowd. He staggered to his feet. The target had slipped past the direct line of fire. The cowhide outline of copper was shrinking, closing, leaving only an oblique angle. He had an arrow ready, but even if he hit the narrowing plane, his arrow would glance off the hardened surface.

There was only one chance. He would have to aim his arrow at the minute point of convergence between Seth's arrow shaft and the target. It was the only thing that could give his arrow tip purchase. Ryder felt for that fine meeting point, willing the tip of his arrow into the entry point.

The arrow whistled from his bow. Ryder went with it, guiding it, feeling its stretching flight. *Clang*. The arrow hit, snapped off Seth's arrow at the shaft, but bit, going clean through the target and dropping to the ground on the other side. A low moan shook out of the throats of the crowd and grew to become a wail.

He turned the horses. A wind rose with the wailing, howling off the sand and buffeting him, stinging his face and eyes with sand. Ryder slipped the bow over his shoulders, wheeled the chariot and sent the twin chargers hurtling towards the pavilion that fluttered in the wind. Was it the crowd or the wind that now shrieked around him? He saw a figure emerge in panic from the pavilion and try to jump clear of the chariot and he drew on the reins, running the horses into the pavilion. They reared as they hit the pavilion, slowing the chariot long enough for Ryder to reach out.

Janet had stumbled and fallen and was trying to get up. The chain of amulets swung around her neck. He reached out to grasp them and, as he did so, the roar of the gale thinned and time itself stretched like the lengthened flight of an arrow. He was back in the empty tent. He remembered his thoughts then: *If there was a breath of chance — a swallow's breath of chance — that he could reach her, or understand what it was that had taken her, he was going to try — in the face of all he knew and all he believed, at whatever risk it meant, even crossing the boundaries of time and reason and maybe sanity. He wanted to know what had happened in there.*

'You should never swear, either by heaven or earth or with any other oath,' a book with soft black covers had once told him. *It didn't stop him now.*

'I'll try, Janet, I swear by heaven and earth and hell — if I can get to you, I will. Hang on.'

But Janet was evil. It was black-and-white. He crossed one of those sharp boundaries between shadow and light and found himself in a mist of grey uncertainty.

Things weren't so clear any more, seeing Janet there, down on her knees, the nape of her long, slender neck exposed. He did not grab the chain of amulets of power. Instead, he grabbed the woman, hauling her up into the chariot beside him.

He turned and raced away. An arrow flicked past his head. The eclipse-dimmed sky darkened as black clouds rolled in like boulders. Lightning split jagged cracks in the sky. Thunder banged like boulders, colliding above their heads.

Janet was hanging on white-faced and white-fingered to the rail of the flying vehicle. Ryder snatched the chain of amulets from around her neck and stuffed them into a pocket. She did not struggle or fight to get it back. He tore the mask from his face and it whipped away in the wind.

'You!' she said.

'Yes, me.'

'Do you never stop coming back for me? Why did you do it? Do you know what you've done?'

'Yes. *I* knew what I was doing,' he yelled above the beat of the horses' hooves. 'But did you?'

She shook her head as if trying to struggle from a dream. There was a haze in her eyes. 'I don't. . . know. . . what happened. I've been to the edge of something, Wilson. . . and you've snatched me back. . . but I'm still shaking from it. I turned against you, yet you came back for me.'

'Not just for you.'

'Only the amulets? You did all this for Horus and Osiris?'

'Not just them.'

'For that girl. Is that it? For *Neith!*' The haze cleared from her eyes and a bright blaze broke through. 'Why didn't you just snatch the necklace? Why did you take me, too?'

'It was a promise I made to myself. I couldn't let you go to hell. Not yet, anyway. I'll take you back, then you can go there.'

'You go to hell, Wilson!'

They were lost in a howling dust storm that spun around them. He looked back to see if they were being pursued, but the dust had drawn a curtain.

25

The night of the Thing of the Night

THE CURRENT AND A BUFFETING WIND carried their boat swiftly downstream. The sky grew darker still.

The old bird-man Tehuti had come on board to receive the amulets of power and to carry out his promise to revive Neith, but he showed no inclination to begin his work. He stood outside the deckhouse looking up into the sky with an anxious eye, his curved bird-beak raised like a question mark.

Lightning threw glittering serpent tongues across the sky. 'It is the monster Apophis, primal serpent of chaos, who hid these amulets, who rages,' he informed them. Thunder growled like an angry belly. 'We shall come under his attack this night and he will surely attempt to devour us. With the eye of Horus in our hold, we have the sun with us and Apophis is the eternal, sworn enemy of the sun and of light. Just as he attempts to swallow the sun in the underworld, so he will attempt to swallow us now.'

'Then we are doomed,' Benwese, the soldier, said in

a dead voice.

'Not in the company of the Lord of Magic, and with some efficacious use of magic, we are not,' Tehuti said with a dry cackle. 'I must prepare.' He withdrew into the deckhouse where the body of Neith still lay. Janet followed him inside.

Ryder, standing at a deckrail, shivered. There was evil on the river, a black wind that cowed the thickets of papyrus reeds on the banks and threw up scaly waves on the water. He felt a fear that he had not felt since the time he had stepped out of the tomb passage to find himself in a primal marshworld, in another place and time and reality. It was not a fear of personal danger that tingled around him, but a spiritual fear. It was a fear for his *soul*.

Apophis. It was a creature of terror, a serpent of evil and a black hole that devoured souls forever, the Great Enemy of the human soul in the Egyptian underworld.

Another serpent's tongue of lightning flashed jaggedly ahead of the boat and Benwese groaned. The flash came from black clouds that lay like an open mouth on the horizon. 'The worm that never sleeps opens his maw to receive us,' Benwese said. He grabbed Ryder's arm and drew him into the deckhouse.

Lamps burned on the floor and Ryder's eyes were drawn to the form of Neith, lying in stillness. Tehuti had drawn a ring on the deckhouse floor. This ring included the lifeless form of Neith, three lamps and a bowl of fire. 'Sit inside the ring,' he said. 'We must stay inside the ring, for the symbol of the outer darkness is a great serpent, the tail of which is in its mouth, forming a divine circle. Do not leave this ring until the storm abates.'

The two men, the woman and the dog went into the

ring and sat around the kneeling man.

Tehuti had produced a box from which he withdrew various items, first of which was a piece of new papyrus and a pen and palette. He squatted on the floor like a scribe, his kilt drawn tightly across his legs to form a writing surface and then, using green ink, he wrote the name 'Apophis' in hieroglyphs. This he put down and next produced a lump of wax. He rolled the wax on the floor, like a child with modelling clay, making a cylinder that swiftly thinned into the length of a snake. He made a pointy tail on one end and a head on the other. He made the jaws wide and thrust the tail inside the jaws.

Lightning flashed overhead, very close, so that a tingle ran through the room and thunder cracked with a nearness that made their eardrums cower. A hissing sound grew around them. Was it the wind blowing sand against the grass mats of the deckhouse, or the approach of the serpent of terror? Were its jaws already opened wide to swallow their boat?

Benwese and Janet looked uneasily around, but Ryder's eyes remained on Tehuti who, unmoved by the threat of the serpent, attached the scrap of papyrus to the snake, rolling it around the body and tying it fast with what appeared to be strands of black hair.

Now he took a knife from the box. He put the snake on the floor and climbed to his feet as if fearing the waxen snake might strike. He raised the knife above his head and struck at the wax snake. Did it writhe or merely twist with the blow?

'Apophis, Fiend, Betet!' he shouted. 'Serpent of twilight, darkness, night, gloom, the blackness of eclipse, fog, mist, vapour, rain, cloud, storm, wind, tempest.' He spat on it four times, stamping it with his foot.

He picked it up with a stick. Ryder blinked as it twisted in the air. Tehuti shook the stick distastefully, allowing the serpent to drop. It fell into the bowl of flame. The snake, or the wax, spat angrily in the flames and the bowl rocked as if the snake were writhing.

Lightning turned the basketwork cabin around them into a glowing cage. Thunder beat down with a force like a hammer blow.

'Apophis has fallen into the flame,' Tehuti chanted gleefully. 'A knife is stuck into his flesh. His name no longer exists upon this earth. It is decreed for me to inflict blows upon him, to drive darts into his bones, to destroy his soul. He is given over to the fire which obtains the mastery over him in its name of "Sekhet" and it has power over him in its name of "Eye Burning the Enemy". Tehuti, mighty of strength, decrees that he shall come in front of the boat; his fetter of steel ties him up and makes his limbs so they cannot move. Tehuti repulses his moment of luck during his eclipse and makes him to vomit that which is inside him. . . '

The flames rose up tall in the bowl and hissed, then the lamps went out and the darkness rushed in.

'Do you hear?' Janet said.

'I do not hear anything,' Benwese said in a shaken voice.

'Exactly. The storm has gone.'

'We have prevailed. Did you expect anything else from the Lord of Wonderworking Formulae?' the old bird-man said modestly. They went out and the wind had gone. The water had calmed and the papyrus reeds were straightening their heads. The ripples on the waves sank like scales.

The danger had passed.

26

Revivification

THE VENERABLE BIRD-MAN, DRESSED NOW in a panther skin, placed the chain of amulets around the neck of Neith.

The deckhouse was filled with blue, sweet-smelling smoke that issued from an incense jar. Ryder and Snakeback were alone with the Lord of Magic. They watched the proceedings from a corner, Snakeback panting softly, a lolling tongue hanging from its mouth, its amber eyes fixed on the Wise One.

Tehuti held a small metal adze in his hand. He bent, his surgical beak nearing the ear of the dead girl and he whispered into it: 'Your mouth was closed, but I have set in order for you your mouth and your teeth.' He placed the blade of the adze on her lips and began a chant: 'I open for you your mouth, I open for you your two eyes, I have opened for you your mouth with the *Seb-ur*, divine instrument of Anubis, the iron tool with which the mouths of the gods were opened. Open the mouth, open the mouth!' he commanded in a rousing voice. 'Obey me for I am Tehuti, Lord of Magic, with power of magic words. The dead shall walk and shall speak. I have ordered your mouth and your teeth for you in their true order. You have opened your mouth. You have opened your mouth!'

Ryder swallowed nervously.

What I am wanting to happen in this deckhouse could not happen in the real world, he told himself — only in dream and in myth. It would not even be attempted in real life; but that was not to say that it would not be longed for in real life and he was longing for it now with a reality as tangible as physical pain. It was no shadow-self of Ryder that hoped against hope for a miracle, but the real man, who asked for it with every fibre of his body.

He wanted Neith back. Remote and divine, human and vulnerable. He didn't care, he just wanted her back, to feel again her gaze.

But if such an event could not be expected to happen, *was* it happening? Or was this only a dream within a dream? Was the only difference between myth and reality the unlikelihood of events? How unlikely that God should allow his Son to be born a helpless child? How unlikely that a man should die on a cross and then rise again? Unlikelihood did not prove anything; unlikelihood was the realm where myth and miracle lived side by side.

It was not much of a faith that only believed in the likely. It was not much of a fable that did not spring from truth. As G.K. Chesterton wrote: 'Fable is more historical than fact, because fact tells us about one man and fable tells us about a million men.'

He had read once, without understanding or believing, the words of the English scholar, C.S. Lewis: 'We pass from an Osiris dying nobody knows where, to a historical person. We must not be nervous about "parallels" and

"Pagan Christs": they ought to be there — it would be a stumbling block if they weren't.'

So I will cling to my hope in hopelessness, he thought. Live, Neith. He bent his head and prayed: 'If you could intervene in history, Father, with the incarnation of your Son, then intervene now in myth — if this be myth — with Neith. Breathe life back into her lungs. Reverse the stream that carries her body to dissolution, revive the cells thrown into steep decline, the heart grown cold, skin dry, summon the humid mist of generation that rose on the first dawn. Breathe back the spirit that once shone from her clear-glazing eyes.'

Neith's lips trembled, they parted and a soft, rustling sigh like a breeze stroking reeds escaped from her. Outside, a wind came up suddenly and swirled around the deckhouse, plucking at the walls of grass matting.

'Hail, Neith, open thy two eyes and thy mouth!'

Snakeback whined, its tail slapping against the floor.

The bird-man now put down the sacred adze and produced a jar in his left hand, smearing the mouth and the closed eyes of the girl with his forefinger. 'I have anointed your face with ointment, I have anointed your eyes. I have painted your eyes with *uatch* and with *mestchem*. Breathe, see, hear, arise, Mistress of the Bow and Ruler of Arrows. I, Tehuti command it!'

Neith sat up. Ryder tried to hold the dog, but it could contain itself no longer and reached the girl in a bound, yelping delightedly and licking her cheek. 'Hound with a Snake on His Back,' she whispered, enfolding the animal in her arms. 'I can think of no more joyous welcome!'

She saw Ryder and he felt again the power of her clear-gazing eyes. Neith was back. Ryder joined the dog and took her arm. The arm was cold like marble and the eyes were filled with power.

It was not only Neith returned; it was the divine Neith returned in all her strength. 'You succeeded in your quest, Bowman from the Future. I knew it even in my rest. You have done what you have come to do and now you must return.'

'Return?' he said. 'But I have just got you back. . .'

'You have completed your task. Now the young prince Horus must grow and prepare for the conflict to come.'

'And I must take the amulets of power, including the eye of Horus, and fly to the nest in the Delta to restore the prince's eye,' the ibis-man said. 'And then I will journey with Isis and Horus to the mountains of Amenti where Osiris sleeps, so that the good king will be restored and his son may rise to avenge him.'

*   *   *

The shadow of death left the sun and golden light shone down, sparkling on the river. It was like the first golden dawn again as the boat set them down on the river bank. The papyrus plants lifted their heavy umbels to greet the light after the days of darkness.

'Tehuti has restored the eye of Horus,' Neith murmured. 'You have been victorious, Bowman.'

'I want you to come back,' he whispered.

'You want wrongly.'

'I want you. Come back with us.'

'I shall miss you — and Hound with a Snake on his Back — but I shall be there in the flight of the arrow.'

'Will we never see each other again?'

'Perhaps. Look out for me in the flight of your arrows. When your arrow is lost, that time may have come again. I see a day when a king and his lion will face a bowman and his dog on the field of battle. But go now into the passage of the tomb. It will take you back.'

The soldier Benwese clenched Ryder's arm and shook it firmly. 'Farewell, Bowman from the Future. You gave me back my lady, Bint-Anath, and we will never forget you.'

'Come on, Wilson, don't drag it out,' Janet said irritably. 'If we're going, let's go.'

Neith bent and patted Snakeback. She bent and whispered in its ear, 'I shall run with you in the arrow's flight, Hound. Farewell.' She made it easier by walking away and going into the reeds. His last glimpse of her was the slender vase-like form vanishing among tall reeds, then she was gone. It was as if the sun had gone into eclipse again.

Ryder tore his glance away and went with Janet and the dog into the darkness of the tomb entrance.

27

The boundaries of existence

THE THREE WALKED SILENTLY ALONG deep-cut passages that were lit faintly by a source from above, not by enough to make it light, nor by so little that it made it dark. The passages were grey, like the stone surfaces of the walls that slid past them. There *were* shades of grey, he thought — between myth and truth, between life and death, between doubt and belief.

Nothing was black-and-white, not even faith. The real gaining of wisdom was not a discovery of the blinding light of goodness nor of the deepest blackness of evil, but of the frontiers of grey between them, frontiers where the mind and spirit were challenged before they could move on. There was a fear that hung around all frontiers, somebody once said. He had been afraid of those frontiers. He risked the safety of his soul in crossing them.

In that sense Janet had been right all along, he thought. He glanced at her walking beside him, pursuing her own thoughts with an intent, closed look on her face. She had always accused him of being black-and-white in his ideas and resisting new ones. But that state had fled.

His ideas had moved across a gulf of space and time so that this was not only a journey back from a place, but from a new realm of ideas and possibilities, many that he could never leave behind. He had feared the collision of new ideas, feared a meeting that might shake his faith to its foundations, believing that a good faith was an untroubled faith — fixed as a star, undisturbed by questions and doubts and, most of all, by disturbing parallels.

But every living thing had growth and change or it died. Every living thing had potentiality, tendency and movement. Even our bodies, he reflected. We were not mere matter filling space, but highways of meetings, synapses, joints, branches and connections. Nothing inside us sat inertly filling space, not even the cells. Every cell was changing in itself and exchanging with others.

Somewhere there is a dream dreaming us, the Bushmen of Africa believed. What dream had dreamt him on this journey — dreamt the nightmares he had faced, dreamt the losses and the blessed reunions? Was it Neith, Mistress of the Bow and Ruler of Arrows? Or the Dream that Dreamt Us All?

Everything began with a dream, even the creation. *Mere dreams.* He would never dismiss them again.

They went deeper into the grey and somewhere, under the steady, hypnotic bump of their footfalls, there was a point where their knowledge of where they were and how long they had walked and even what they were thinking became grey, like the memories of a waker after a dream whose dreams swirl like colours mixing in a palette, only to emerge a nondescript grey.

He remembered thinking before he disappeared into it that it was only through greyness, through neutrality, that anything could pass from one state to another. How fitting, he thought, that we turned grey before we died... The man, the woman and the dog melted into the grey, like vapours within mist.

* * *

Was it a dream or a long awakening? Ryder was lying on cold stone with a shaken feeling in his bones as if he had landed hard. He lay in thick darkness. He felt in his pocket for his torch and snapped on a beam. He saw above him the broad, painted eyes of a goddess, like Neith, on the ceiling.

'Wilson.' It was Janet. He sat up and turned his beam onto the camp bed. She lay half across it as if a giant hand had flung her down like a doll.

Snakeback lifted its head into the beam. Its eyes were sleepy and dull.

'Have I slept?' Janet said. 'I don't remember getting here.'

'Neither do I. But do you remember going?'

'Yes.'

'So do I.' A silence, like the tomb, only more intense came between them.

'So where do we go from here? Back to where we started?'

'I'm not sure we can ever do that, Janet.'

She nodded, blinking in his light. 'No, I suppose you're right.'

28

The final truth

WHAT WAS IT THAT DREW Ryder back to the edge of the desert with his bow and a quiverful of arrows and Snakeback at his heels? Habit, a search for the healing power of activity to heal the sickness of loss? Or a futile hope in hope?

Janet had packed up at the campsite and left. He had lost her and he had lost Neith. He had recovered fourteen amulets of power and run across space and time to get them, but he had come back with empty hands.

He nocked an arrow to the string. Snakeback growled, its amber eyes flashing a challenge, daring him to shoot. Wilson Ryder bent the bow, aiming into the shimmering plain.

'Fetch!' he whispered to Snakeback and let the arrow fly. The dog flew after it. Ryder's heart went with the swiftly shrinking arrow that flew through the sky and he knew where he wanted it to land.

The dog took off across the sand, its powerful legs kicking up dust.

'Look out for me in the flight of your arrow,' she had said to him.

And to the dog she had whispered, '*I shall run with you in the arrow's flight, Hound. Farewell.*'

He lost sight of its fall, but Snakeback was on its path. He saw a blur of movement out on the glare of the plain. His heart trembled like the arrows in his quiver as he gave a start and straightened, shielding his eyes. Somebody was out there. Yes, moving. They stopped, bent and picked up his arrow and then walked back, going out of sight behind a rock.

Ryder ran. She had come. I shouldn't have wanted this. I shouldn't want it now, but she's come.

He reached the spot where the arrow should have landed and a girl stepped out into view from behind a rock. She held the arrow behind her back. 'Look where you fire that thing; you could hurt somebody,' she said.

'Shoot,' he said. 'Not fire.'

'I'm only a woman, Wilson, but you shouldn't want more. I don't have any powers and I don't want any powers. I just want you and that spiky-backed friend of yours. . . and the way things used to be before this happened to us.'

Snakeback ran to her and jumped up, tail wagging happily. And then Ryder knew what that last truth was: about his hopeless search for the divine in other than the divine itself and about where he should be content to find happiness — the truth the bird-man had said he must perceive for himself.

It was one more piece of advice he must accept and it was the best.

She gave him back his arrow.

'Let's go home,' he said.

The bowman, the woman and the dog walked back to the campsite in brilliant sunlight.